To Dane:

My first Upfield, and
arguably one of his best.

One I can read again
every few years. Without
the initial surprise but
with the enjoyment still.

Love
John

The Widows of Broome

DETECTIVE Inspector Napoleon Bonaparte has never been better than in this baffling case of a killer who seemed to be picking off the town widows one by one.

Bony arrived in Broome just after two well-to-do widows had been brutally strangled. The local police were short of help and completely stymied by a murderer who carefully left no clues. Bony pressed into service a Mr. Dickenson who combined the qualities of a gentleman, a scholar, and the town drunk.

Then another widow was killed. But this time the murderer was just a little bit careless. Bony added two footprints, a beer bottle that hid petrol, a sound made by clicking teeth, three bundles of silk rags, and a passion for tidiness, and came up with a composite picture of the murderer.

Then Bony staged a trap with the fourth widow as bait— and the stage was set to nab a vicious killer!

Scene: Northwestern Australia.

This novel has not appeared in any form prior to book publication.

The
Widows of Broome

ARTHUR W. UPFIELD

Doubleday & Company, Inc., Garden City, N. Y.

All of the characters in this book are fictitious, and any resemblance to actual persons, living or dead, is purely coincidental.

Contents

The Widows of Broome

Chapter One: THE MAGNET AND THE FILING

Situated on the barren, inhospitable coast of the northwest of Australia, Broome's only excuse for existence is pearl shell. Before Japanese aircraft put a stop to the industry some ten million pounds' worth of the finest quality shell had been raised from a thousand miles of shell beds, pearls of exquisite lustre and size being the plums which attracted adventurers from all parts of the world. Following the drastic restrictions imposed by war and its resultant economic conditions, millions upon millions of dollars' worth of shell is now maturing and just waiting to be picked up and despatched to hungry markets.

Prior to the events which attracted Detective Inspector Napoleon Bonaparte to Broome, the majority of the people walked with somnambulistic tread and daydreamed of the glorious past when booze was cheap, when money was as plentiful as the dust, and when ribs were tickled with knives and craniums caressed with sandbags . . . over the rape of pearls.

The first of two murders having several points of similarity mildly stirred the people of Broome. The second crime, however, inoculated them with an energy serum. They waited expectantly for the police to produce the murderer, but nothing happened. They stared at the homicide squad flown up from Perth, and became really annoyed when still nothing happened. Actually, the people of Broome should have been proud that one among them was alert enough, and clever enough, to commit two murders without leaving a clue indicating either himself or the motive.

The senior police officer stationed at Broome was an administrator, not a detective. His job was keeping general law and order over a land area of about a third of a million square miles, not tracking down an intelligent murderer. He was assisted by juniors—one of whom was an expert in the bush and the handling of trackers—and when they failed to uncover the murderer of the first victim, and met with no quick success following the murder of the second, he washed his hands and called for the C.I.B.

A detective sergeant accompanied by a photographer and a fingerprint expert arrived from Perth. They remained two weeks. Thereafter, Sub-Inspector Walters continued with his administrative duties, and the murderer continued to stroll about Broome in the cool of the evening.

At four o'clock on the afternoon of June twenty-fifth, Inspector Walters sat before a typewriter in the station office, grimly determined to write a private letter in official time. He was two inches under six feet, lean and tough. His greying hair was stiff, and authority gleamed in his dark eyes and was stamped on his thin-lipped mouth.

The envelope he rolled into the machine was addressed to: "Mr. Sylvester Rose, Headmaster, Cave Hill College, Broome." The letter which followed the envelope ran thus:

DEAR SIR:

Reference my son Keith Walters. I have regretfully to draw your attention to what appears to be a conspiracy among a section of your boys to which my son belongs. I am aware that in these modern times handwriting is considered of small importance and that spelling is an art no longer necessary to be cultivated. You will, I am sure, agree with me that sound pronunciation of our language must be, with force if necessary, inculcated in the rising generation, that English shall not deteriorate to the gibberings of baboons.

I have repeatedly heard my son pronounce the word "just" as "jist"; for "I am going to" or "he is going to," he persists in saying "I'm gunner" or "he's gunner." Vocal reprimand being unavailing to correct this fault, I have administered corporal punishment . . . still without result. Cross-examination has elicited the fact that a number of your boys in collaboration deliberately invent these horrible distortions which, when practised, become permanent in their speech.

2

Knowing how much you have the boys' welfare at heart, I am confident that you will bring your very wide experience to bear on this problem, the solution of which appears to be the detection of the ringleaders of this conspiracy.

I remain as always, my dear Mr. Rose,

Yours very sincerely,

HENRY WALTERS. *Inspector of Police.*

Having signed his name in calligraphy appearing much like helmets on the heads of tin soldiers, Inspector Walters sealed the letter, stamped it, and tossed it into his "outward" basket.

The police office was, save for himself, deserted. Sergeant Sawtell had gone to the airport to meet the inward plane from Perth. Constable Pedersen was out in the barren McLarty Hills with one of his trackers, seeking a wild aborigine who was wanted for wife maiming, and Constable Clifford was making enquiries concerning the indentures of a Malay shell diver.

The month being June, and midwinter, the temperature of the office was moderately low, and now the shadows of the palm trees were long across the open space between the large bungalow-styled station house and the roadway which it fronted. The storm shutters were raised high, and the entire front wall was open and fly-netted. When a flashing new car swept in through the open gateway and drew to a stop before the steps leading to his office, Inspector Walters almost snarled. He was pretending to read a report when through the swinging fly-netted doors came a woman. Under forty, and wearing honey-coloured slacks and a peasant blouse, she was still vivid and markedly self-possessed.

"Good afternoon, Inspector," she said, her voice brittle. Her bold brown eyes were hard as she faced Walters, who had risen to his feet. "I've called to give you a piece of my mind. Have you any objection?"

"This Department is always at the service of the public."

"Well, then, it's my considered opinion that when two defenceless women are murdered and no one is arrested for it,

3

it's a shocking disgrace to the Police Force. I don't understand it. No one in Broome understands it. What kind of policemen are you people? Tell me that, instead of standing there like a dumb-cluck. You can catch a poor Chinese for smoking opium, but you can't catch this person who strangled two women. Two women, mind you, not one. You can tell that gang of ruffians who came up from Perth that I'll make their thick ears burn if they don't produce results."

A second car drew up outside the station, and Inspector Walters attempted to assure the lady that the Perth homicide men would make an arrest when they were ready, that another detective was coming north to continue their investigation.

"Well, we people of Broome want results," went on the woman. "You policemen think you're the bosses of Broome, and you are going to learn your mistake—all of you—from the Chief Commissioner downward. I'm the boss of Broome, and don't you forget it. Mind you, I'm talking officially. Privately, I consider both your wife and you as my friends. What was the name of that fool from Perth?"

"You are referring to the senior detective?"

"You know I am." The woman turned to glare at two men who entered the office: one wearing official uniform, the other in smartly cut civilian clothes. "Well, it doesn't matter. You tell him from me that if he doesn't stop these murders I'll expose his fool doodling in the *West Coast News,* and in case you don't know it, Mr. Walters, I own that newspaper . . . and the *Perth Saturday Record* . . . and about half of the *Perth Daily Reporter.* Is Esther at home?"

"Yes. She's somewhere in the house."

"No, no! Don't bother. I'll find her." The woman turned from the still rigid Inspector Walters. She nodded to the second policeman, who sat down at a desk and was taking up a pen. The civilian had his back to them. He was studying a wall map of Broome and the surrounding district, and as though conscious of being examined, he turned to meet the angry brown eyes with eyes as blue and as bland as the Indian Ocean that day.

4

"Who are you?" demanded the lady.

"My name is Nap."

"Spell it, please."

"K . . . n . . . a . . . p . . . p."

"Are you a policeman?"

"Er . . . a kind of policeman. I am a psychiatrist."

"What's that?"

"I heal, or try to heal, sick minds."

The woman frowned. This stranger was distinctly dark. Colour in him somewhere. She was glad she had taken the stand with him that she had done. Then she didn't feel glad at all when he smiled.

"By whom am I addressed, madam?"

"Me? Oh, I'm Mrs. Sayers. A healer of sick minds, you say." She almost giggled. "You've come to the right place. They've all got sick minds around here. Someone killed two defenceless women and they can't catch him." She swept towards the house door and there turned to survey the stranger with eyes no longer furious. "What kind of medicine do you give sick minds, Mr. Knapp?"

The stranger bowed slightly, and smiled.

"Hemp," he murmured. Mrs. Sayers did giggle. They listened to her high-heeled shoes impacting the linoleum within the house, and then Inspector Walters advanced with proffered hand.

"Bit of a tartar when she's roused," he explained, "otherwise nice enough. Women! They always beat me. Glad to meet you, Inspector Bonaparte."

"And I to meet you. Permit me to present my credentials."

Sub-Inspector Walters read the order from Perth to give Detective Inspector Napoleon Bonaparte every assistance in the investigation of the murder of Mrs. Elsie Cotton on the night of April twelfth, and the murder of Mrs. Jean Eltham on the night of May fifth. There was more of it, and when done, Walters looked up to observe the stranger in Broome seated at the opposite side of his desk, rolling a cigarette.

"Well, Inspector, all of us here will be glad to co-operate," he said.

"Thank you." Bony lit his cigarette. "I like that word, co-operate. True doctors co-operate when the G.P. calls in a specialist for consultation on a difficult case. Regard yourself as the general practitioner, and me as the specialist. A specialist I am. I specialise in homicide. I know little of general police procedure or administration. So it's every man to his profession. By the way, I'd like to be known as Mr. Knapp. All my friends call me Bony. Might I be honoured by including Sergeant Sawtell and yourself among my friends?"

Faint warmth spread over the iron-hard face of the inspector, and Sergeant Sawtell, who had met Bony at the airport, expressed his pleasure.

"We're both very glad you are here," Walters said. "We have enough normal work on our hands without the addition of investigating murders which don't have any possible motive. Been a worrying time. One constable away in the bush after a blackfellow, and the other is just out of hospital with a knife wound received down in Chinatown. Have you made arrangements about accommodation?"

"No, not yet. I understand there are five hotels here."

"There are, but perhaps you'd consent to put up here. The wife and I would be glad to have you."

"That's kind of you. I would like that. And I'd try not to put Mrs. Walters to great inconvenience." Bony smiled his thanks in addition to the words. "We could then go into conference at any time suitable to yourself and Sawtell. I know enough about these police-administered districts to understand the thousand and one calls on your time. Yes, that would be an excellent arrangement. I could be a civilian friend staying with you."

A car engine burst into restrained power, and the inspector raised himself to look beyond the fly-netted veranda front.

"That's Mrs. Sayers leaving. Ought to get a cup of tea now she's gone." He stood up and Bony also rose. "Fine woman, but volcanic."

"A local power?"

"The local power. Owns one of the stores, two of the hotels,

6

six of the luggers, and fifty per cent of the houses in Broome. Her father was a pearl dealer. Her husband was a store owner, shell dealer, and lugger owner. She has more money than the King . . . and spends it faster than Rockefeller did."

Bony was conducted from the office to a tastefully and sensibly furnished lounge, was left there a moment, and then was being presented to Mrs. Walters. She was slight and dark, and he liked her at first sight.

"So you're Inspector Bonaparte!" she exclaimed. "Well, I am glad you have come up from Perth. I've a sister, you know, in Brisbane—married to Detective Sergeant Knowles—and we've heard much about you from her. I'm so glad my husband suggested you stay with us."

"It's really delightful of you both."

"Not a bit. Why, we've been terribly anxious about these murders. People are asking who will be murdered next. It's been dreadful for everyone. And not a clue—not a single clue pointing to who committed them and why. Seems that he just killed for the pleasure of it. You will have a cup of tea?"

"That is a question I never answer in the negative," replied Bony, and Walters offered cigarettes.

It was plain that these two people had been suffering strain, for their pleasure at his arrival was unmistakable. Walters was in the unenviable position of being the senior police officer in a small town where everyone knows everyone else, a frontier town where people must associate or mentally perish, a town in which the senior police officer is the most important personage and one whose power of protection against criminals is assumed to be unassailable. The success of a murderer in escaping detection was a slight both to their social and their official standing.

Mrs. Walters brought afternoon tea, and Bony said:

"I must make one small condition to accepting your hospitality, Mrs. Walters. I insist on being treated exactly as any member of your family . . . and I understand you have two children to look after in addition to your husband. You see, I know what guests mean—the extra housework, the extra washing up. D'you like washing up, Walters?"

7

"Damned if I do," exploded the inspector.

"Damned if I do, either, but when at home I'm damned if I don't. Hullo!"

In the doorway appeared a schoolboy, his case in one hand, a cap of black and white rings in the other. His eyes sparkled with excitement, and when his father asked sharply what he wanted, he answered in the gruff tones of early adolescence:

"Abie's taking the petrol cure, Dad. He's down behind the gum tree in the compound."

The inspector jerked to his feet and made for the door. The "petrol cure" being a new one to Bony, he excused himself with Mrs. Walters and hurried after the inspector and the boy, who led the way through the kitchen and out across the rear veranda. Ahead was a space of some several acres, bordered on one side by stables and outhouses, and on the other by a row of ten or a dozen cells. A hundred yards from the house grew a solitary gum, and as they approached the tree so did the boy and his father walk stealthily. Silently, the three moved round the trunk.

With his back to it and reclining at ease was a booted and overcoated figure, identifiable only by the hands as an aborigine. The head was enveloped by an exceedingly dirty dress shirt from which arose the smell of petrol.

With swift action the inspector whisked away the shirt. Gripping the man by the coat collar, he stood him up as though he were a straw. The round face was vacant. The dark eyes rolled in their sockets. With his left hand the inspector slapped the black face and shouted:

"Where did you get the petrol, Abie? Come on now . . . tell!"

"Bin milk-um jeep. Lemme lo."

"Coo! All right, my lad. I'll attend to you after you come round." Walters lowered the almost insensible man to the ground, and his son knelt and made Abie's head comfortable on the battered felt hat. "He'll be all right in an hour. Can you beat the blacks for finding out new ways of getting drunk."

"One of your trackers?" inquired Bony.

8

"Yes. Not enough work for two, and this one's a lazy devil. Always in mischief when Pedersen's not here to keep his eyes on 'em."

"Not as bad, though, as Mr. Dickenson, is he?" said the boy, and his father snapped out:

"Worse. Old Dickenson only drinks the acid out of car batteries."

Chapter Two: THE WOODPILE

Broome has no Main Street. It has no shopping centre, no shops fronted with plate-glass display windows. There are no trams, and no railway. Several air lines use the airport, but no one knows when a plane is due, or when one is about to depart. Sometimes a ship arrives to be moored to the long jetty at high tide. When the tide goes out the ship rests like a tired hog on the sand beside the jetty and the loading is languidly carried on while the tide comes in and refloats the vessel.

The town is situated behind coast sand dunes, sprawled on the flats north of the Dampier Creek. The streets are very wide, and all the houses sit down like old ladies wearing hoop skirts and being far too ladylike to take the slightest notice of their neighbours. Every house occupied by the white population is of the bungalow type, and every house is protected with storm shutters, some even wire-cabled to the ground, for when the summer willies blow they are apt to lift more than dust.

The Police Station was a large house squatting in about four acres of straggly trees, dying grass, and bare earth. The floor rested on piles three feet above ground, and the rooms were many and airy.

At dinner on the day Bony arrived at Broome, there sat at table the inspector and his wife, their son Keith, aged fourteen, their daughter Nanette, aged thirteen, and Inspector Bonaparte, alias Mr. Knapp. Inspector Walters carved the roast. His back was straight. His hands dextrously employed the bone-handled carving knife and fork with the bright steel shield. His expression was severe. He said nothing, and, sensing the slight strain, Bony opened the conversation.

"You mentioned a gentleman named Dickenson who drinks the acid from car batteries," he remarked. "What happens?"

10

Young Keith opened his mouth to reply but remained silent at a warning glance from his mother.

"Hospital," replied Inspector Walters. "Old Dickenson is a queer character, but quite a decent old pot when sober. Receives a little money every quarter day, and that gives him about two weeks on the whisky. As he hasn't any credit at the pubs, after his benders he will, if given the opportunity, milk a car battery and drink the fluid. Naturally, when found, he has to be taken to hospital. Battery acid is bad to the stomach, so they say."

"Wonder he doesn't die," observed Bony.

"Too tough to pass out for keeps. He doesn't take it straight, mind you. Ten drops in a tumbler of water is the correct strength, I understand."

"Poor old thing," murmured Mrs. Walters. "They paint him blacker than he really is. Has been quite a gentleman. He was very rich at one time in his life. He owned an estate in Hampshire, England, and an ocean-going yacht."

"Been living in Broome long?"

"Fifty years. What finally broke him was the willie of March 1935. Twenty-one luggers and a hundred and forty lives were lost, and old Dickenson's remaining fortune went down with three of those luggers." Walters snorted. "I've been asked to move him out of town, but I won't do it. The only harm he does is to himself. You can't tell a man to move out of town when the nearest town is one hundred and thirty miles to the north, and the next nearest three hundred miles to the south."

"All the kids like him," edged in young Keith. "Tells us yarns about foreign places and his adventures among the Indians in South America."

"Oh!" murmured Bony. "That's interesting."

"Yes, and I don't see why Old Bilge should lecture us about him and tell us not to speak to him. Old Dick——"

"How many times have I told you not to call your headmaster Old Bilge?" irascibly demanded Walters. "I've a good mind to write and tell him what you call him. Here's your mother and I scraping and saving to give you a good education, and you go around saying 'jist' for 'just' and 'gunner' for 'going to.' Anyway, you'll have much to answer for tomorrow."

"I've heard something about this Cave Hill College," Bony remarked soothingly, and Mrs. Walters was not sure about his right eyelid when he glanced at her. "Quite a good school, isn't it?"

Walters explained that Cave Hill College was considered among the best in Australia, drawing boys from as far distant as Perth as well as from the vast hinterland.

"Must be about five hundred boys there now," he went on. "And only a few day boys, too. We couldn't afford the boarding fees."

"There is, of course, a state school?" pressed Bony.

"Yes. Quite a large school. Nan goes there. Doing very well, too."

"Good!" Bony smiled at the girl, who flushed and fidgeted. "Why, Keith, do you boys call your headmaster Old Bilge?"

The boy hesitated, and this time Bony's eyelid did flicker.

"His name's Rose."

"Ah! I see now the allusion. Rose . . . perfume . . . Bilge . . . evil smell. What form are you in?"

The subject of Cave Hill School and the rising education fees provided the subject of the remainder of the meal, and Bony was given word pictures of the seven or eight masters under Mr. Rose. It would seem that, in the opinion of his hosts, the only reason for Broome's continued existence was its college.

An hour later Bony was seated at ease with Walters and Sergeant Sawtell in the closed office, and Walters was voicing his assumption that Bony had read the Official Summary of the two murders and the more detailed statements gathered by the C.I.B. detectives.

"Yes, I did go through the Summary," Bony admitted. "I didn't go into the statements and reports because I like to keep my mind as free as possible from cluttering data. So, you see, I know next to nothing beyond that the medical report indicates that both victims were strangled by the same man. I would like you to tell me about it."

The two policemen looked at each other.

"You relate the facts, Sawtell," urged Walters. He turned to Bony. "Sawtell specialises with the Asians and the locals. Pedersen, who's away, is the bush expert. We're all a bit sore, you know, that this bird got away with two murders. It bashes our pride. I'd like to ask a question."

"Certainly. Go ahead."

"Is it true that you have never failed to finalise a case?"

"Quite true," replied Bony, and neither man could detect vanity in him. "It's true because so far I've never been pitted against a clever murderer. It's my great good fortune that there is no such person as a clever murderer."

Walters smiled frostily.

"This one is too clever for us, and for the Perth men, too," he confessed. "The fellow we're up against is as clever as the Devil."

Bony was engaged in rolling one of his dreadful cigarettes.

"If your murderer is as clever as the Devil, who according to the authorities is high above par——"

"This fellow's well above par, sir," interrupted Sawtell, whose light blue eyes held fire. "He's so far above par that he doesn't leave fingerprints, he doesn't murder for gain, he never makes the mistake of being seen immediately before and after his crimes, and he doesn't leave foot tracks for our boys to fasten on to."

"It promises more and more," Bony almost whispered. "Your boys in the top form?"

"Yes. Pedersen swears by two of 'em. He should know, for they accompany him on his routine patrols as well as on special jobs."

"Those two he swears by. Are they away with him now?"

"No. One is having a spell up the creek and the other is that fellow we found smoking himself with petrol."

Sawtell decided that never previously had he seen a cigarette rolled so badly. The middle was oversize and the ends were pointed like pencil tips. The black hair, the dark complexion, and the sharp features of the cigarette-murderer seated in the swivel chair comprised the pieces of a picture puzzle always presented to strangers, and the sergeant was yet to watch the pieces fall into position to portray this unusual product of two distinctly opposite races. Certainly unconscious of inferiority to anyone, Sawtell was now conscious of the power behind the broad forehead and the blue eyes again directed to him.

"Until men grow wings they must walk on their two feet," Bony said, and lit the alleged cigarette. "I see a problem I've often come across—the gulf existent between the mind of the white man and the mind of the Australian black man. As the mind of the Occidental differs widely from that of the Oriental, so differ as widely the minds of the Australian black tracker and the Australian white policeman. My birth and training fashion me into a bridge spanning the gulf between them. Your murderer left his tracks, without doubt."

"Then why——" began Walters.

"Your trackers did not understand exactly what they had to look for. You did not tell them what kind of man committed the murders?"

"Of course not. We don't know what kind of man he is."

"Well, then, you couldn't expect your trackers to find his tracks. Had they been sufficiently instructed they might have seen tracks about the scene of the second murder which they remembered having seen about the scene of the first, but, even had you done that, the trackers would have had to be abnormally intelligent." Bony waved the remainder of his cigarette in a short arc. "It's like this. You receive a report that a lubra away out in the desert has been murdered. Off go Pedersen and his tracker. The tracker knows all about the killing, and all about the victim. He even knows who killed the woman, although no one could possibly have told him in any spoken language. We know this is so, but we keep to ourselves our beliefs how such intelligence is broadcast because of fear of ridicule by educated fools. Your tracker, then, is familiar with the killer. He is taken to the scene of the crime, and then he is no more or less than a super bloodhound who has been allowed to smell something to which clings the scent of the hunted. In the case of a white killer you have to describe him to the tracker: the way he walks, his approximate age and weight, and his probable health."

"But, sir, we didn't know what this white killer is like," protested Sawtell.

"Conceded. It will be my job to create a facsimile of the murderer from tiny bits and pieces. I have to obtain a picture of him from the very dust of Broome, so that I'll see his mind, and I'll know his probable age, and his trade or profession. And then I'll look for his tracks, being myself independent of your black trackers. In me is enthroned the white man's power of reasoning and the black man's gifts of observation and patience. The only cause of failure in this case would be if your murderer has left the town. Would you both be kind enough to grant me a favour concerning a matter I've already mentioned?"

"Most certainly," Inspector Walters hastened to say. The personality of this man, in addition to his words, made him feel a junior in his own office.

"Please omit the 'sir.' My immediate chief, even my Chief Commissioner, invariably calls me Bony. My wife and my three sons name me Bony to my face. I'll wager you don't know what your children call you behind your back."

The stiffness fled from the inspector. He chuckled, and Bony warmed towards him.

"They call me—out of my hearing—Ramrod. I got that appellation years ago when I was a recruit instructor."

Bony's slim fingers again became employed making one of his amazing cigarettes.

"Well, now, let's get down to your two murders. If I interrupt, don't mind, and don't be thrown off the mental scent. Go right ahead."

Inspector Walters nodded to Sawtell, and the sergeant cleared his throat.

"Five miles out of town there's a permanent water hole on the Cuvier Creek, and on the bank of this water hole stands Dampier's Hotel. The place is a favourite picnic ground for people from Broome."

"Reputation?" asked Bony.

"Good. A man named George Cotton was licensee for fifteen years. He was a great footballer down South and did a bit of ring work in his time. There was never any trouble so far as we were concerned. He married after he gained the licence, and when he was killed his wife was a young woman, and their only child, a boy, was eight years old.

"Cotton was accidentally shot one afternoon when duck-shooting up the creek. There was nothing whatever suspicious about that. After he died, his wife took over the licence. That was three years ago. She boarded the boy at Cave Hill College and engaged a man, known all over the Northwest as Black Mark, as her barman and undermanager.

"Last April, on the night of the twelfth, the hotel had been very busy all afternoon as there were several picnic parties out from the town. The evening was busy, too, but Mrs. Cotton had early told Black Mark that she had a bad headache and would go to bed. The bedrooms for single men are built along one side of the yard, and a man making his way from the back door of the pub to his room fell over a body in the yard. It was a dark night, and he was partially drunk. He thought the person he fell over was also drunk.

"That would be about half-past eleven. The drunk managed to strike a match to see who had tripped him, and what he saw sobered him enough to make him rush back to the hotel bar and announce that Mrs. Cotton lay naked in the middle of the hotel yard.

"Naturally, neither Black Mark nor anyone else there believed it, but they trooped out to the yard with lamps and there was Mrs. Cotton, her body nude and her nightgown lying beside her. Pedersen and I, with Abie the tracker, got out there at ten minutes to one. The body hadn't been moved and was then covered with the nightgown. All about the body the ground had been tramped on by the boots of thirty-odd people.

"That Mrs. Cotton had been strangled was obvious. The doctor arrived a few minutes after we did. The woman was so manhandled that her neck was broken. We checked up on the man who found her body. The time he left the bar and the time he rushed in to tell what he had stumbled over, as well as other facts we gained from those thirty-odd people, let him out."

"Is the time known when she went to bed?" asked Bony.

"Yes. It was nine-twenty. The drunk found her in the yard at approximately eleven-thirty. Her injuries, according to the doctor——"

"The medical report later. What was the condition of Mrs. Cotton's bedroom?"

"Quite in order. She had gone to bed. A bottle of aspirin and a tumbler partially filled with water lay undisturbed on the bedside table. There was no evidence of a struggle in the bedroom."

"The weather that night?"

"Calm and dark. There was a slight haze masking the stars."

"Warm?"

"Not so warm that a woman would wander around in the yard in her nightgown only."

"Her moral reputation?"

"Excellent."

"The examination of the twenty men in the bar produced nothing of interest?"

"Nothing. And nothing was obtained from the staff and the guests who were not in the bar at the time."

"The nightgown . . . was it damaged in any way?"

"Yes," replied Sawtell. "It was ripped at the back from top to bottom. That was done deliberately because the neck seam was extremely hard to rip apart. I tried it."

"I was out at the hotel at daybreak," said Walters. "We think that Mrs. Cotton walked in her sleep as she had some-

17

times done, and that the murderer found her in the yard and killed her. We examined and cross-examined every man jack on the place, and every one had an alibi from one or more of the others."

"And we couldn't nail down any motive," supplemented the sergeant. "I've known Mrs. Cotton even longer than the inspector, and I'm sure she wasn't up to any hanky-panky with a man in one of the bedrooms off the yard. Besides, if she were, she wouldn't leave her room on an adventure of that kind wearing only a thin silk nightgown. Motive is what baffled us."

"H'm! And now it's June twenty-fifth . . . more than nine weeks since the night of the murder," murmured Bony. "Well, I have great distaste for easy cases. Tell me about the next murder."

Chapter Three: BACKGROUNDS

"A Mrs. Eltham was the second victim," Sawtell proceeded. "She came here to work at one of the hotels. That was in 1945, when there wasn't much doing in the pearl-shelling business. There's only twenty-two luggers operating even now, and there used to be more than three hundred before the war. Anyway, this woman arrived at Broome on an Air Force tender from Nooncanbah, and no one seems to know where she joined the tender. She came here to work, and she worked. Pretty girl about twenty-five. Could have married better than she did, and could have married worse, too. She married a lugger owner, and then there was plenty of money. During the fishing season from April to December, when her husband was at sea, Mrs. Eltham worked as a barmaid, and we became a little uneasy about her behaviour with her husband absent."

"Moral?" interrupted Bony.

"Not flagrant. Well, one morning at sea during the '47 season, Eltham himself went below. He had been down several times before but he wasn't an experienced diver. Something got him, and no one knows what, because neither of the regular divers were down with him. All they brought up of Eltham was what was left behind inside his helmet.

"That was brought in and there was the usual inquest and funeral. After the funeral Mrs. Eltham left her work at the hotel and stayed at home, setting up as a discreet entertainer of gentlemen. The local parson and the head of the college both asked us to move her on, but——"

"She didn't keep a disorderly house," interrupted the inspector. "She did permit me to glance at her bankbook, which showed a balance of well over four thousand pounds, and so she could not be charged with having no means of support.

19

Besides, she wasn't a bad little woman. In fact, she had more culture than the majority of the women here. If we booted out all the victims of gossip and spite, there would be no one left here at all. Go on, Sawtell."

The sergeant eased his slightly emphasised paunch, opened his shoulders, and lit a cigar.

"As the inspector says, the Eltham woman had character as well as good looks. She liked parties, and at the parties in her own house she always behaved well. Her gentlemen friends were carefully chosen. She dressed well, never flashily. When we went through her house we found pictures and paints and things, pictures signed with her initials, and books, dozens of the best books. It added up to what we learned about her afterwards."

"That she lived that way because she rebelled against Society following three years or four of freedom in one of the Services?"

"That's about the strength of it. She had no domestic living with her. A woman reported every morning at eight and left again at six. This woman usually found the kitchen door open on her arrival in the morning. If it was locked, she would go home and return again at midday.

"On the morning of May sixth, she found the kitchen door locked. When she returned at noon it was locked. She went away and came back again at four, and the door was still locked. The milk, delivered at seven in the morning, was on the doorstep. She came to us, and I went along. I broke in through the kitchen door. There was no key in the lock, and the key was never found. All the fly screens on the windows were fastened on the inside. The remains of Mrs. Eltham's supper was on the bench at the kitchen sink and the house was in perfect order. We don't know how the man got in."

"We think he crept into the house and hid himself before Mrs. Eltham closed it for the night, or he could have been admitted by Mrs. Eltham and when leaving, in his excitement, he took the key of the kitchen door after locking it," supplemented the inspector.

"One or other of those things happened," Sawtell agreed. "I found Mrs. Eltham lying on her bed. The clothes were pushed back as though she had either left the bed or found the clothes too warm and folded them back herself to sleep on top of them. The body was unclothed; the nightgown tossed beside the bed was ripped from top to bottom. The doctor said she had been strangled in the same way as had Mrs. Cotton. The neck, however, was not broken."

"Pedersen was here then and he took Abie along——"

"One moment, please. Do you think that the murderer tidied Mrs. Eltham's bedroom after he had killed her, or was there evidence that he held her down on the bed as he strangled her?"

"We think that he tidied the bedroom. We think he removed the nightgown from the body and for some reason or other ripped it and left it on the floor beside the bed. You'll remember that Mrs. Cotton's nightgown was found beside her body."

"You have photographs?"

"Yes."

"Pedersen being home, where was the tracker he had away with him when Mrs. Cotton was murdered?"

"On spell with his tribe," replied Sawtell. "Abie was on hand, and Pedersen is confident of Abie. Anyway, the boong didn't have much of a go because all around the house are cement paths, and a man could walk in from the street and amble around without once putting his feet on soft earth."

"Abie reported nothing?"

"Nothing. Pointed to the cement and laughed."

"Was he taken inside the house?" pressed Bony.

"No. Why?"

"With what are the floors covered?"

"Small mats here and there. The floors are linoleum-covered. There was one peculiarity, however. The electric power was turned off at the master switch, which is on the outside wall of the house . . . at the front."

"The house . . . has it been reoccupied?"

"No. Nothing much was touched in it by us or by the Perth men. We have the keys here."

"Good!" This item definitely pleased Bonaparte. "The doctor seems certain that the same man killed both these women. There appears to be no connection between them, nothing to unite them on any point save that they were both widows."

"Both still attractive widows."

"And both had money."

"Mrs. Cotton's estate hasn't yet been submitted for probate. It totals many thousands."

"Who benefits?"

"The boy. He gets the lot, save five hundred pounds left to Black Mark, who was made the boy's guardian."

"The barman sounds interesting. Tell me about him."

"He's been up here in the Northwest all his life," Sawtell obliged. "He's been a drover, a gold prospector, a sea captain, a lugger owner, a diver, a hotel licensee, a storekeeper, and many other things. He's black of hair and eyes, and he could strangle a big man with one hand almost . . . although he must be getting on for fifty. He owns property in Broome, and I wish I was as high as he is from the bread line. Told Pedersen once that he wanted to settle down and where better to settle down than at Dampier's Hotel? Said he must have something to do and why not run a bar? Seems to have given Mrs. Cotton every satisfaction. He never married, and he seems to have taken charge of her and the boy. We have nothing against him. If it wasn't for the say so of two identities who were in the bar that night and provided Black Mark with an alibi, I'd think seriously about him."

Bony suppressed a yawn and rolled another cigarette.

"The fingerprint man gained nothing from Mrs. Eltham's house," he said. "According to her domestic, no one of her friends paid her a visit for almost a week prior to her death, and the house was cleaned and dusted daily. Respectable woman . . . the domestic?"

"Yes. What d'you reckon about those nightgowns? That seems to be a common denominator in the two crimes," put in Inspector Walters.

"It does," Bony agreed. "Another is the tidiness of the victim's bedrooms. They are not, however, common denominators of the two women, but of the one killer. The fact that both women were widows may or may not have significance. I cannot see any. One woman was rigidly moral, according to the Official Summary, and the other was not rigidly moral. One victim lived alone. The other was surrounded by her staff and her guests. The Perth homicide men certainly went deep into the background of these two women, and they could not dig up a motive for killing them. They do state, however, that in view of Mrs. Eltham's gentlemen friends all being 'loaded with tin,' as the phrase goes, it is possible that she rebuffed an admirer who was not blessed with this world's goods. If that should prove to be right in fact, then his name will not be among those listed. By the way, have you a list of her friends?"

"Yes, I have," answered the sergeant. "I'd like to compare it with the C.I.B. list."

"We'll do so tomorrow. We will also compile a list of the attractive widows of Broome. It would be too bad if another widow were strangled."

The paperweight of rainbow stone being toyed with by Inspector Walters crashed to the desk.

"Unless your murderer has cleared out of Broome he will almost certainly strike again," Bony went on. "Having struck twice, he won't be able to prevent himself. At this very moment he is puffed with vanity. He has tasted supreme power, and that is a draught of which he will never be satiated. No motive? Oh yes, he has a motive. The gratification of hate, the gratification of the lust to kill, is a motive. That motive is an effect, and when I have discovered the cause, I shall have discovered his identity."

"Meanwhile, he may murder another woman?" Walters said sharply.

"Yes, meanwhile he may do so. In these two murders he has superbly covered himself, and yet he has begun to spin the web about himself, despite all his cunning. His unconsciously performed work in that respect is not, unfortunately, sufficiently

23

advanced for me to view the plan of the web he will inevitably make clear with, say, his sixth or seventh murder."

"Damnation!" exploded Walters, and Sawtell stopped in the act of lighting another cigar. "Six or seven murders! Here in Broome!"

"Easier for such a tiger-man to get away with six or seven killings here in Broome than down in Perth, or in London or New York. Here everyone knows everyone. Here almost everyone visits almost everyone. Were the floors of Mrs. Eltham's house swept and the dust and debris sent to Perth for analysis? No, they were not.

"So, what? We are placed on the horns of a dilemma. If we safeguard all the attractive women of Broome from attack, the killer bides his time till the safeguards are removed. If we do not take every step to guard the attractive women of Broome, he strikes at will until he gives us a clue to his identity, or, gentlemen, until I can build his identity with my own discoveries and my own methods. Should he claim another victim, I shall be hurt about it."

"So will the victim," Sawtell said, his face a mirthless grin.

"I am being neither coldly selfish nor facetious," Bony said severely. "You people were on the job when these two crimes were committed. The homicide men from Perth were on the job within twenty-four hours after the second murder was committed. Neither you nor they located a clue, can put forward a reasonable motive, or have by deduction thrown the searchlight of suspicion on any person.

"No blame is attachable. The circumstances are such that a psychologically cunning maniac has got away with two major crimes. Doubtless he would have baffled even me. He might strike again and still baffle me, but if he does strike a third time, I shall at least be right on his tracks. We have five or six days to prepare for that next strike."

The coldly level voice ceased. Sawtell asked why the five or six days' grace.

"Because the murderer struck on both occasions when there was no moon. He doesn't accept a chance of being observed.

24

We have time to formulate plans. We have time to prospect for the diamonds of truth. Our killer doesn't accept a chance. We must. And the responsibility will be all mine."

"Devote yourselves to your normal routine, and continue to accept me as your guest. I have faced problems as difficult, and have carried responsibility as great. No man ever rose to greatness who feared responsibility. I have never feared it . . . which is why I am now Detective Inspector Napoleon Bonaparte. You, Walters, and you, Sawtell, have had to climb gates to reach your positions. I have had to claw my way over Everests."

The voice which had contained a note of ringing triumph died away, and in the silence the two men smoked with stoically concealed embarrassment. They had discussed this half-caste before his arrival, food for discussion having been provided by Mrs. Walters' sister, married to a detective sergeant in Bony's own department. A little luck, a discerning mind, a charming manner, were the ingredients, they had decided, which constituted the recipe of the fellow's success. They knew better now. They recognised the giant, the giant who had burst asunder all the bonds placed upon him, through the accident of his birth, by the Lilliputians of custom, privilege, snobbery, and jealousy.

He was smiling at them, now on his feet.

"It's ten-thirty," he said. "What about sneaking quietly to the kitchen and boiling the kettle for a brew of tea."

25

Bony slept soundly that first night at Broome, and he was reading the reports and statements gathered by the Perth detectives when he heard Mrs. Walters calling her children to breakfast. They came racing in from the compound where they had been watching Abie breaking in a horse: the boy's eyes alight with admiration for the aborigine, and the girl's face glowing with admiration for the horse.

"Now eat your breakfast and don't talk too much or you'll be late for school," Mrs. Walters told them. But they were anxious to tell Bony about the horse and the breaker, and he nodded encouragingly.

"How far away is the college?" he asked eventually.

Two miles, he was informed, the journey being done by the boy on his bicycle. The girl walked to her school, which was much nearer. She told Bony that she liked her school, and the boy said that his was not bad, as though he were a connoisseur of public schools.

"We're having our Activities Day on Sat'day," he announced with pleasure. He nodded acceptance of his mother's correction of his pronunciation of the word Saturday, and hastily went on to tell more of Activities Day. "Will you come? Pop'll be driving Mum and Nan, and there'll be plenty of room in the car. Good afternoon tea on the lawn an' all that. Old Bilge's bound to do a bit of spruiking, but he isn't too bad."

Bony looked his doubt, and Nanette entered the lists.

"Yes, do go, Mr. Knapp. I'm sure you'll enjoy it. Won't he, Mum?"

"Mr. Knapp will be too busy, I expect," replied Mrs. Walters, although the invitation was confirmed in her eyes.

"On Saturday, is it?" asked Bony. When assured that it

26

was, he nodded, saying: "Since the forty-hour week came in and no one works on Saturday, why should I? Yes, I'll be delighted to go. I assume there will be an exhibition of handcrafts?"

"Oh yes, Mr. Knapp," both children answered. "Stacks of all sorts of things. But the afternoon tea's the best. It's a beaut. You can eat as much as you want."

Inspector Walters came in and sat down to breakfast. The boy and girl rose from the table and each removed their chair to back against the wall. Mrs. Walters smiled at them, and the inspector said:

"You get down to work, Keith. You've been slacking lately. And ride that bike on the road and not on the sidewalk . . . or else."

"All right, Pop. Say, Mr. Knapp's gunner go to Activities Day on Sat'day."

Mrs. Walters uttered the beginning of an exclamation. Her husband nodded his interest. Keith, who realised his error, reddened, and deflatedly left by the rear door, the girl taking the passage through to the front. Walters chuckled:

"Young feller is in for a surprise today," he remarked. "I wrote a complaint to Old Bilge about Keith's 'gunners' and 'jists.' What the devil we are paying terrific fees for, I don't know. Just as well the boy isn't boarding and out of our reach for a term at a time."

"I hope you weren't too sharp with Mr. Rose," said Mrs. Walters. "He has a very big job with all those boys, and he does take a tremendous interest in them."

"Don't worry, Esther, I was polite enough. I don't expect the headmaster, or even the form masters, to be listening all the time for errors of pronunciation, but when it becomes a conspiracy to distort and torture the language, then they should know about it." To Bony he said: "You gunner be—— Oh damn!"

They broke into laughter, and for Bony the day began well. He said he was going to be very busy, and might even ask for a portion of Sawtell's valuable time. All the morning he spent

27

studying the reports and statements compiled by the Broome police on the two murders, and checking them with those he had brought with him from Perth. After lunch he began the compilation of his Case History, and at four-thirty he called on Dr. Mitchell, by appointment.

Dr. Mitchell was short, rotund, red of face, and rapid in speech.

"Sit down, Inspector. If I can help in any way . . . Ah, I must remember. Inspector Walters said you wish to be known as Mr. Knapp. A drink? Or will you wait a moment for tea?"

"You are very kind, Doctor. Tea, if it's no bother."

"None at all. It's on the way. I'm delighted at meeting you. Heard of you from a pal of mine, Dr. Fleetwood. He was concerned in the case of that author feller being murdered with coffin dust. I took him up on the point. Don't believe it can be done, but he says that Professor Ericson is sure it can, following his series of experiments. Now, I suppose, you want to talk about strangulation, eh?"

"That is the reason for my call on your time," Bony gravely agreed. "I have studied your report, and I find there are one or two points concerning which I would like further information."

"Righto! Go ahead!"

"Thank you. Perhaps question and answer will serve best. It is correct that death from strangulation may occur instantaneously?"

"It is. Sudden and violent compression of the windpipe often causes immediate insensibility and death. I am not certain, but I think it probable that those two women strangled here in Broome died without a struggle, such was the brutality with which they were slain."

"Your report states that they were killed by the hands of the murderer, and not by a rope or string or anything of that kind. Would you say that the murderer's hands were exceedingly powerful?"

"Without hesitation."

"Another question, Doctor. You describe the precise inju-

28

ries suffered by those women, and I am not concerned so much by that as by the answer to this question. Were the hands of the murderer short or long fingered? I admit your difficulty."

Dr. Mitchell took thirty seconds.

"I cannot be definite," he said. "I'm sorry. A guess any good?"

"It would help."

"I might have been able to be sure about it had the question been asked before or immediately after the post-mortem. My guess is that the man's hands are neither long nor short fingered, and that the palm is longer than average. Meaning that the measurement from finger tips to the base of the palm is longer than average. Is that clear?"

"Quite. Now with reference to the man's fingernails. Can you tell me anything about them?"

"They were trimmed. I'd say they were well kept."

"That is not your guess?"

"No. It is my opinion based on the areas of ecchymosis."

The door was opened by a lubra who brought in a tea tray. She wore a white cap and apron over a brown frock, silk stockings, and flat-heeled shoes. She regarded Bony with momentarily startled large black eyes, set down the tray on a table at the doctor's elbow, and retired.

The doctor poured the tea, and Bony regarded his hands. They were sun-tanned, large and capable hands. He rose and walked to the door, opened it and reclosed it.

"Pardon my rudeness," he murmured. "I thought the girl had left the door ajar, and I want our conversation to be confidential."

"That's all right," the doctor breezily conceded. "That lubra can hardly understand a word of English. Take sugar?"

"Were there any marks on the shoulders of either victim?" Bony asked, sipping his tea.

"Yes. There were bruises on Mrs. Cotton's shoulders. Why?"

"Well, d'you think they were killed when standing or when lying down?"

"Don't know. Does it make any difference?"

Bony was evasive. He put another question.

"Mrs. Cotton was five feet and eleven inches in height . . . tall for a woman. If she was killed standing by a man of lesser height, I'm inclined to think that his wrists would bear down very hard on her shoulders. Do you think the marks on her shoulders were caused by that?"

Dr. Mitchell regarded Bony intently. Then he nodded, saying:

"She was strangled by a man behind her. She could have been standing, and he could have borne heavily on her shoulders with his wrists."

"Thank you. Mrs. Eltham was five feet and nine inches in height, and, you stated, she was strangled from the front. Would you be good enough to demonstrate on me how, in your opinion, the murderer placed his hands about the necks of his victims?"

"Oh yes, I'll do that," the doctor agreed. "I've already worked out that for myself. Sometimes, you know, a strangler uses one hand across the windpipe and the other at the back of the neck to counter the pressure. This fellow encircled his victim's neck with his two hands, in the first case with his fingers meeting at the jugular vein and his thumbs together at the spinal column, and in the second case the position entirely reversed. Thus we know from which side he strangled."

"What is your opinion now on the question of the position of his victims when killed? Standing or lying down?"

"Well, it seems that they must have been killed when standing. Is it important?"

"Yes," Bony agreed. "It has significance. Will you demonstrate those holds now?"

He stood up and turned his back to the doctor. He was five feet ten inches, and the doctor was three if not four inches shorter. When the large and capable hands were clasped about Bony's neck, the wrists were distinctly heavy on Bony's shoulders close to the base of his neck. Bony asked the demonstrator to bear downward more heavily on the wrists, and without increased pressure of the hands the weight placed severe strain on Bony's back and knees.

He was smiling when they faced each other, and the doctor demonstrated from the front. As his hands encircled Bony's neck, Bony attempted to lift a knee towards the doctor's groin, and the little man chuckled and easily threw him off balance.

Well satisfied with his interview with Dr. Mitchell, who would not permit him to leave too quickly, and who appeared hungry for details of Bony's career, Bony strolled back toward the Police Station. The sun was westering, and a soft cool zephyr met him from over the salmon-coloured sand dunes. The wind was a little stronger when he came to a break in the sand dunes, and he stood gazing out over the turquoise sea which bore on its placid surface one dark brown sail.

It seemed then so impossible that far beyond the horizon, far away in the sea wastes to the northwest, could be born a monstrous wind which with its strangling hands could destroy little stout ships and every soul aboard them. It is said that no insurance company will do business with lugger owners and their crews, so treacherous is that beautiful and serene section of the Indian Ocean.

Well, who would believe that here in this little drowsy town of comfortable bungalows and windowless shops, cut off from civilisation by hundreds of miles of virgin land, there could flourish a human being capable of being ecstatically triumphant when feeling through his hands the life of another seeping into the vacuity of death?

Turning to continue his way, Bony saw Mr. Dickenson.

Chapter Five: THE DERELICT OF BROOME

Mr. Earle Dickenson sat on the public seat placed in the shade of a poinsettia tree from which he could view the sea. He was tall and thin, and his beaked nose appeared always as though frostbitten. His hair was white and abundant and was carefully brushed back from a noble forehead. The pointed white Vandyke beard greatly added to the air of distinction, but the general effect was ruined by his disgracefully old and soiled clothes.

The Asians accepted him with the tolerance accorded to all beggars, dogs, and crocodiles. The white members of this very mixed community looked upon him with marked disfavour and, as has been noted, had made several attempts to have him kicked out of town.

Culturally, Mr. Dickenson was superior to anyone residing at Broome, excepting possibly the masters of Cave Hill College. He had travelled much off the tourist routes of the world and had associated with all manner of men. He had really lived the years of his long life, and there was no doubt his constitution had successfully defied John Barleycorn. Proof that the children loved him was provided by the fact that never a child had been known to be rude to him.

On this particular afternoon Mr. Dickenson was depressed, a condition caused four times every year by financial embarrassment. His credit had been dead for half a generation, not one of the hotels consenting to advance even one whisky unless paid for. So depressed was he that when Bony sat down on the other end of the seat, he did not withdraw his moody gaze from the shimmeringly blue Indian Ocean.

Bony was aware that in every city the police are greatly assisted by the informer, and that every small town has its "town drunk" who can be equally helpful. The "town drunk,"

32

however, is a different proposition to the city slum informer, and must be handled expertly and sympathetically . . . especially sympathetically.

"This view should enchant an artist," he remarked.

Mr. Dickenson slowly turned to regard the speaker, and what he saw did not quickly captivate his interest. The slim, dark man at ease on his own seat was presentable enough, but . . . a stiff whisky and soda would . . . When Mr. Dickenson again turned to regard his seat companion, the examination was made with prolonged calculation. The fellow was dressed in faultlessly creased gabardine trousers and an expensive tussore-silk shirt. His shoes were good and brilliantly polished. A stranger, too. He might be worth touching.

"It is not always so . . . enchanting," he said. "You have chosen the best time of the year to visit Broome. It is, I think, the twenty-sixth of June. Correct me if I am in error."

"You are quite right. Is the date important?"

"Merely that it is precisely four days prior to an important date."

"Indeed," murmured Bony.

"Should you be in Broome on June the thirtieth, I would be in the happy position of suggesting a drink."

"Which infers that you are not in that happy position today."

"Alas, my dear sir."

Two boys came riding bicycles along the road, obviously returning from school, and both respectfully called out:

"Good day, Mr. Dickenson!"

"Good day to you, young men," replied the old man, waving his hand, which Bony noted was long-fingered and clean. To Bony he said: "You are visiting?"

"Yes. I am staying for a few weeks."

"To appreciate the place, you must stay at least a year. There is none other like it in the world, and on that point I speak with authority. Should you have an interest in such matters, you will find the white section of the community of exceptional psychological interest. The whites are entirely lacking

33

in the spiritual attributes making for personality. Observe this person approaching."

The person was arrayed in white duck and wore a white sun helmet. He was well nourished. His gaze did not deviate from a point exactly to his front and distant probably a million miles. His facial expression was that of a Yogi meditating in a blizzard. Having watched him pass on, Mr. Dickenson laughed, a rumbling deep in his chest, and he said:

"Ninety-nine per cent of them are like that, atrophied from the frontal bone upward. I think it is due to the climate in alliance with temperance. To defeat this climate, to keep oneself mentally alive, one must drink. Moderately, of course. At which of the hotels are you staying?"

"I am staying with Inspector and Mrs. Walters. Mrs. Walters and my wife went to the same school."

"Indeed! Nice people. I have found Walters generous and understanding. His duties do not permit him to become mentally defunct. That man who passed us is a solicitor. Plenty of money. They all have plenty of money. They made it the safe way, financing and trading with men who gamble with ships and their very lives. They stay snugly ashore, and when the willies come they huddle in their palatial bungalows while brave men, both white and black, go down in the jaws of the sea. In no part of the entire world is snobbery carried to such astonishing limits. Yes, I like the Walterses, man and wife. Sawtell, too, although he is inclined to bully me on occasions."

"They have been very busy lately, I understand," Bony observed. "Two murders added to their routine work." Mr. Dickenson's interest appeared to wane, and Bony stood up. "Might I suggest an appetiser before dinner?"

Mr. Dickenson was on his feet in four fifths of a second.

"Regretfully, sir, I cannot meet kindness with kindness until the thirtieth."

"Then on that day I will be your guest. Shall we go along?"

As they advanced to the veranda steps of the Port Cuvier Hotel, Bony's companion buttoned the neck of his old shirt. On the wide veranda a number of languid people seated at

34

small tables were being served by a youth in the uniform of a steward, and, when they were mounting the steps, Mr. Dickenson remarked loudly:

"You'll find this place more respectable by day than by night. The sins of society are never practised in broad daylight . . . not in Broome."

Hostile eyes stared at them. A woman tittered. Bony and his companion sat at a vacant table. Bony surveyed the drinkers. They were a cosmopolitan crew, giving the impression that they were acting in a film of blood and murder in any one of a dozen Asiatic ports. The steward came to stare down at Bony and regard Mr. Dickenson with supercilious disdain. Bony turned to Mr. Dickenson.

"What is your fancy, sir?"

Mr. Dickenson named whisky . . . with soda. Bony ordered beer, and Mr. Dickenson said he would regret his choice. The steward brought the drinks, and Bony did regret it before the steward left, and called for gin and vermouth.

"Always stick to spirits, and never take more than two drinks unless you see it coming out of the bottle," advised Mr. Dickenson. "I've seen men who were careless in that regard climbing telegraph poles, or swimming out to sea looking for a shark, or doing sums on the sand with a pointed stick adding up how many scales there are on a groper."

"What do the people do for a living?" Bony asked.

"They live on each other, like the fishes," replied Mr. Dickenson, his voice raised. "The Asian divers and the Asian lugger crews risk their lives to bring ashore the wealth of pearl shell, and the whites loll about in security like the harpies of old."

Mr. Dickenson made it plain that his opinion of these people of Broome was not good, and Bony sensed that he was getting back a little of what he had received. After the second drink he rose from the table, and instantly the old man followed suit. The whisky had banished Mr. Dickenson's depression, and as he walked some little distance with Bony, he was almost stately.

35

"Have you lived long in Broome?" Bony inquired.

"Many years, Mr.——"

"Knapp. You, of course, are Mr. Dickenson?"

Mr. Dickenson nodded, and Bony asked another question:
"I suppose you know pretty well everyone in Broome?"

"I think I may claim to do so." The old man chuckled. "I
know much more about a lot of 'em than they warrant. A man
of my age, and I'm eighty-two, is entitled to likes and dislikes.
I have found something most admirable in out-and-out sinners and something which sickens me in mealymouthed saints.
The saints, I have noticed, become . amateur sinners . . .
when it is dark. Give me the hearty sinners. You know where
you are with them. Well, I turn off here. I thank you for your
hospitality. I trust that you will grant me the honour of returning it on the thirtieth."

Mr. Dickenson almost bowed. Bony almost bowed. With no
further word, they parted, in Bony's mind the phrase: "Saints
become amateur sinners after dark." Mr. Dickenson would be
well worth cultivating.

Before dinner he interviewed Abie, the black tracker. Abie
was feeding the horse in course of breaking in, and Bony's approach was to admire the horse and compliment the aborigine
on the work already done on it. Although the evening was
cool it hardly necessitated the military overcoat Abie wore
over his shirt and trousers which were tucked into stockman's
leggings, whilst the heavy military boots and the wide-brimmed
felt hat seemed to be adjuncts entirely out of place. Still, Abie
was a police tracker, and as such he was a personage among
his kind. "Same white-feller soljer."

The cicatrice down the left cheek had doubtless been caused
by a knife and thus gave no indication of Abie's position in his
tribe, but the hole in his tongue, revealed when he laughed
with pleasure at Bony's compliments, was decided proof that
he was a medicine man.

"You bin camp here?" Bony asked, and Abie pointed to the
stables and said, "Him bin camp alonga horse."

"You bin come on plane-feller, eh?" was Abie's question in

36

turn, and, when Bony nodded, he asked: "You all same white-feller p'liceman, eh?"

"No. Just looking round. You bin police tracker long time?"

"Long time."

A medicine man! Wily, knowledgeable, secretive. Influential with his tribal fellows for sure. Would be an excellent tracker when put on the scent, tireless and relentless.

During dinner Bony gained further glimpses of the picture of Broome, a picture he must clearly see to find a fault which would indicate the trail he must follow. His questions were put with purpose, and the information, some of it of no apparent value, was stored and indexed in his mind.

There was a French Catholic Order which conducted a school for native children. There were the churches of three denominations. The Shire Council was debating a proposal to raise the rates, and a meeting of protest was scheduled for the following week. There was a flourishing Women's Association, the president and driving force being Mrs. Sayers. There were three stores, two situated north of the Post Office and one down in Chinatown which supplied all the Asians and re-fitted and victualled the luggers. This one was owned by Mrs. Sayers, but Mrs. Sayers did not run it. She had a manager to do that for her. Yes, he could obtain cigarette tobacco there. Being Friday night, they wouldn't close before nine.

The sun was gilding the tops of the poplars when he strolled southward to Chinatown, and there was reason for his measured step and meditative expression.

Progress in his investigation was slow. In fact, he had barely begun to progress. The trail was cold, as cold as desert sand at the dawning. His remarkable gift of patience would be taxed, and the temptation to hurry, to take chances, would be keen because of the probability that the confident killer would strike down another victim. Haste would be worse than foolish, for should his opponent know who was seeking his tracks, the fellow might well remain quiescent, waiting for the redoubtable Napoleon Bonaparte to depart from Broome.

The sun had set when he reached Chinatown, a place having nothing of Orientalism about it. Large and empty iron buildings once crammed with pearl shell, ship chandlery, and stores now gaped at him. Women of many Asian nations watched him, and their children raced along the dusty sidewalks bordered by iron-constructed shacks and sun-blistered boards bearing the remnants of Chinese names. Twenty-two pearling luggers, and there used to be three hundred! And the twenty-two luggers with their divers and crews far away on that now green Indian Ocean wantonly courting the night.

Bony found the general store, a large iron structure having no windows but long open slits under the eaves ribbed with iron bars. Mounting the stout veranda steps, he crossed the weathered veranda and entered to be met with glass showcases, stacks of merchandise, and shelves loaded with everything from bolts of cloth to synthetic Manila rope and firecrackers.

No one was interested in him. He enquired where he could obtain cigarette tobacco, and was waved away in a southeasterly direction. That brought him into a maze of women's frocks, and a girl who was assisting a woman to choose shoes waved him on to the northeast. Following this course, Bony came into the grocery department where, after waiting whilst two young men discussed a weighty problem concerning a horse named Juniper, he was served with his requirements.

On emerging from the store, he almost bumped into Mr. Dickenson.

"Hullo! Good evening!"

"Ah! Mr. Knapp! I see you have been shopping. I, too, am on a similar errand for my landlady. Did you meet Mr. Lovett?"

"No. Who is Mr. Lovett?"

"The manager. A very keen businessman." Mr. Dickenson might have been a keen businessman too. "This store, you know, belongs to a lady, a Mrs. Sayers. Her husband left her very well off, and she had been well provided for by her scoundrel of a father."

"A hard woman?"

38

"Hard in the getting of money; soft in the giving of it away." Mr. Dickenson's tired grey eyes twinkled. "If I could write books, I could write ten about her. When you see her, you remember that once I took her pants down and smacked her. She was then very small, of course. I've watched a lot of 'em grow up in Broome, when Broome wasn't what it is to-day."

"The Mrs. Cotton who was murdered was the licensee of a hotel called Dampier's Hotel, wasn't she?"

"That was so," replied the old man.

" 'Way out of town, isn't it?"

"Five miles out."

"Could one hire a car to run out there for a drink one evening?"

"Oh yes, certainly," answered the suddenly alert Mr. Dickenson. "For three pounds you can hire a taxi for the evening, and the driver will guarantee to bring you back before one in the morning and assist you into bed."

"H'm! An excellent arrangement. I think I'll spend an evening there tomorrow. Would you care to accompany me?"

"It would give me great pleasure, Mr. Knapp." Mr. Dickenson was extremely regretful. "However, I fear I could not accept before the thirtieth."

Bony exhibited disappointment.

"Perhaps . . . A suggestion, of course. A small loan to tide you over?"

"You are magnanimous, sir."

"Then shall we agree to meet outside the post office tomorrow evening at, say, seven o'clock? I will arrange for the taxi."

Mr. Dickenson bowed slightly and stiffly. He made no reference to the "small loan," made no attempt to "touch," and Bony liked him for that. The old man entered the store almost jauntily, as though the meeting with Mr. Knapp had energised his self-respect.

Chapter Six: ACTIVITIES DAY

Firstly because the children so enthusiastically asked him to go, and secondly because the opportunity would provide a clearer picture of the people of Broome, Bony decided to give the afternoon of this Saturday to visiting Cave Hill College. At the last moment Inspector Walters found he could not spare the time; and so, dressed for the occasion in a light grey suit with soft felt hat to match, Detective Inspector Napoleon Bonaparte, Master of Arts and Master of Himself, drove the inspector's private car with Mrs. Walters beside him and the children in the back seat.

"I do hope you will enjoy it," she told him. "Most of the people will be friendly, but some won't. If you stick by me I'll manage to catalogue them."

Mrs. Walters looked her best and was happy knowing that she did. They passed Mr. Dickenson, who rose from the public seat beneath a shady gum to bow and wave in acknowledgement of the children's greeting.

"The majority of the townsfolk will be there, I assume," Bony said.

"Nearly everyone, and a lot of people will be in from the stations outback. It's quite a function, you know."

They left their car with many others parked outside the school grounds. Bony was pleasurably surprised by the size and architecture of the main building standing beyond well-kept lawns. Built of warm brownstone in early colonial style, it faced the ocean from its superior elevation and yet subtracted nothing from the hacienda style of the French Catholic Mission further along the coast.

With Bony on one side and her children on the other, Mrs. Walters passed through the iron-pillared gateway and sauntered along the main drive, talking vivaciously and entirely satisfied. The main school building of two stories had its every large window protected by an iron shutter, now raised and providing protection against the sunlight.

The lawn fronting the building was gay with colour: men in tropical white and wearing sun helmets, women in bright dresses and many having coloured parasols, and here and there masters wearing their black gowns and, much more numerous, the boys in light grey suits and caps of black and white rings. From the roof of the school, flags flew from four tall white poles. Cave Hill College was *en fête* to receive parents and friends.

Mr. Sylvester Rose, Princes College, Aberdeen, B.A., Adelaide University, M.A., and several honorary degrees, welcomed the guests. He detached himself from a group of ladies and came forward to greet Mrs. Walters. He carried his mortarboard under his arm, and his gown swung out behind his sturdy figure. Nearing sixty years of age, he moved with the virility of a man much younger. His face was square, and his hair barely tinged with grey. The hazel eyes were large and alert, and the forehead was broad and high.

"Welcome, Mrs. Walters, welcome!" he said, his voice carefully modulated. "So glad you have come to our Activities Day. And such a fine day, too. Your husband . . . I do not see him."

"Unfortunately, Mr. Rose, he was detained at the last moment. He was looking forward to coming, too. Please meet an old friend of my sister, Mr. Knapp."

"How d'you do, sir?"

"Well, thank you. And you, sir?"

"I am always well," stated Mr. Rose. "You are indeed welcome. We hope to show you the handwork done by our boys. Come along now and find seats. In a few minutes we are—not 'gunner,' Keith—we are going to serve afternoon tea. Good afternoon, Miss Nanette."

"Good afternoon, sir," replied Nanette, with creditable poise.

Mr. Rose begged to be excused to greet other arrivals, and a woman hurried forward with smiling face.

"Hullo, Esther! So glad you've come. I've been hoping you would. You look well."

Bony was presented to Mrs. Merle Simmonds, and informed that Mrs. Simmonds and her husband lived on a pastoral property named Tallinbah, eighty miles out of town. Then he was being introduced to her husband, a large man who appeared very tough until he smiled and warmly shook hands. Simmonds knew where to find vacant chairs, and he kissed Nanette and told Keith he hoped the "arvo" would soon be served.

It was all bustle and colour to cram a large canvas with interest for Bony, whose knowledge of the psychology of men and women was deeper than exteriors. Here on this brilliant lawn beneath the pure sky, here among these chattering people might be the man who experienced hellish ecstasy when his hands gripped a woman's throat. Fine feathers do not make fine birds.

It was a passing thought, for against this background Bony was quite happy. Simmonds knew Brisbane. Simmonds had been at St. Peters, Adelaide. Simmonds had carried his swag in Queensland looking for work. Simmonds flew his own aircraft. Simmonds was natural. Bony liked him. He liked Mrs. Simmonds too. She and Mrs. Walters made a good pair. And when he was presented to three young Simmondses, he liked one of them and held judgement on two.

Without warning, he was being formally presented to Mrs. Sayers. This afternoon she was arrayed in porcelain blue, and her hair was slightly more auburn than it had been at their first meeting in the Police Station office. Without doubt her dressmaker was more successful in cut than in influencing her clients in their choice of colour.

"Pleased to meet you, Mr. Knapp," trilled Mrs. Sayers. "Didn't have much of a chance the other day." Bony gave his inimitable bow and offered his most charming smile. "How are you keeping?"

"I have no cause for complaint now, Mrs. Sayers," he murmured. "When accepting Esther's invitation, I had no idea I would meet so many beautiful women in Broome." For a tenth of a second her brown eyes hardened with suspicion, but, seeing no guile, she accepted the bold compliment.

"You must come and have tea with me before you leave, Mr. Knapp. You too, Esther. You bring Mr. Knapp, and don't disappoint me." She almost giggled. "Heavens! I haven't talked to anyone sensibly for ages."

Mrs. Sayers floated away, and Mrs. Simmonds chattered to Mrs. Walters. Simmonds spoke of his old school, and Bony mentioned the Brisbane High School and the university whilst thinking that Mrs. Sayers might not be so superficial as she wished the world to believe. She was a widow. She was still attractive. Her name was on the list of The Widows of Broome.

A youthful master entered the circle. He was obviously keen on his work. He accepted Bony with interest. Another master came, one much older, lean and stooped. He did his best to conceal how bored he was with the show. Teaching had got him, had sucked him like a vampire, and there was not much left for the profession to drain from him.

"What's he like in school?" Bony softly asked Keith. The boy scowled and said that "Old Stinks" was "a swine" in handing out lines.

"Not like Old Bilge," conspired Bony.

A grin replaced the scowl.

"What is that master's name?" Bony asked, indicating a large-framed, florid man talking to a smaller man of serious mien.

"He's Mr. Percival," whispered Keith. Slipping a hand across his mouth to prevent the outburst of laughter, he added: "We call him Happy. 'Cos he never smiles. Always creepin' and sneakin' around to report to Old Bilge."

Five minutes later Bony was shaking hands with Mr. Raymond Percival, M.A., Ph.D. Mr. Percival seemed to tower above him, and his grip was almost painful. His dark eyes would have bored into Bony's mind had not Bony been on

43

guard, and, Bony decided, no juvenile culprit would long withstand their probing. Following the swift examination, Mr. Percival's reaction became negative.

Despite the conversational handicap, Bony continued to sum up the people gathered on the lawn. All the "best" people were there. It was easy to separate the goats of Broome from the sheep of the Interior. Some of the men eyed him with interest; others with contemptuous hostility. Bony thoroughly enjoyed himself.

Boys appeared wheeling rubber-tired trolleys bearing tea urns, multitiered cakes, and mounds of delicacies. Each trolley was in charge of a boy wearing a chef's cap, and his assistants served the tea whilst the "chef" cut and served the cake. They displayed tremendous *élan* in the task of waiting on the guests.

"He's a wonderful man, really," someone was saying. "Matron told me that all he thinks about is his boys. Puts himself out no end to gain their confidence and be a father to them."

"Wonder he never married," another woman said. "Should have done, you know, and had boys of his own. Quite presentable, too, in addition to his position. Can't say I'm wildly enthusiastic about him, although Fred thinks the world of him. Says he's the best headmaster the school could possibly have."

"Percival must have felt the thump when Rose was appointed over him," observed a man. "Not a pill I'd like to take."

"Poor Mr. Percival. And such a brilliant man, too. How are your boys getting along?"

"Very well. Socially the boys are well trained here, don't you think? The masters might supervise their washing more strictly. I noticed that our Tom's neck is perfectly disgraceful, and I'm sure he hasn't scrubbed his teeth for a month."

"It's funny you should mention that," a new voice broke in. "My husband complained that our boys never wash their necks. It seems that it's not done! They merely step through the shower from one side to the other."

Bony regarded Keith. He was polished like a lord's door

44

handle, but then he was a day boy and came under his father's inspection. Abruptly the hum of conversation died away, and, glancing round, Bony observed that the headmaster had mounted one of the garden seats.

"Ladies and gentlemen," he cried, in his best Assembly manner. "I propose that we proceed to Sayers Hall, where the work of the boys is now on display. It has been judged by Mr. Marshall Gallagher and Mrs. Sayers, to whom is due our united thanks." Soft hand clapping. "We, the staff, and the boys of Cave Hill College wish to express our deep appreciation of your continued interest in our activities, and we trust that the result of this year's labours will please you, and further we promise that we will endeavour to do even better next year.

"Much of the basic material to which our boys have applied their creative gifts has been brought in by the aborigines as an expression of their gratitude for the boys' discarded clothing, which is carefully collected and distributed among the several missions. You will agree that boys do grow. Often I regret that they grow up too quickly, and it does seem that before we can reach candid understanding of our small problems, they are of age to leave us. But our boys never lose their affection for their school, nor we our affection for them. Again, on behalf of the staff and my boys, I thank you."

Bravo! mentally applauded Bony. Quite a natural little speech despite the old-school-tie touch, and with the small crowd he entered the school and so came to Sayers Hall.

On benches, tables, and desks were arrayed the exhibits, and they were well worth inspection. There were cigarette boxes, needlework boxes, inkstands, and penracks of polished mulga wood. Larger workboxes were studded with the extraordinary variety of shells gathered from the reefs. Boab-tree nuts were carved and painted with commendable skill, and paperweights of all shapes and sizes were carved from the rainbow stone which has the appearance of a chocolate cake layered with cream. There were emu eggs of light green and of dark green cut to reveal the deeper pure white shell in designs and

45

figures of the aborigines' legends. Stencil work, carpentry, and leatherwork were well represented, and many of the coloured drawings and mosaic work must surely have satisfied the arts master.

"What happens to the exhibits . . . eventually?" Bony asked a heavy man in white drill.

The gentleman stared with expressionless eyes deep-set in a pasty face . . . and turned away. The curtain dropped instantly before Bony's eyes, but the smile entered them again when Mrs. Simmonds hastened to explain that all the exhibits were sent to Perth shops and the money received was paid into the mission funds. Thanking her, Bony nonchalantly regarded the man's large hands, maintaining his gaze until the gentleman thrust them into the side pockets of his white tunic.

The boys came into the hall and mixed with their parents, Keith excitedly leading his mother and sister to see his exhibit, which had gained a Class B certificate. A few minutes later Mr. Percival stood on the platform to speak, and his speech, if slightly pedantic, was given with a voice more pleasing than that of his chief. He called upon Mrs. Sayers to present the prizes, and Bony wondered how it was that Mrs. Sayers was given so much importance.

The prize giving accomplished, and the lady receiving an ovation following her speech, the usual votes of thanks were proposed and seconded, and what Bony decided was a very pleasant interlude drew to a close.

"Quite a good show," remarked Bill Simmonds when they were again on the lawn.

"I thought the general level of the exhibits very high," Bony agreed. "I'm glad I came."

"It's always worth while, you know. We've come in every year, almost, since the school was built. A great acquisition to the Northwest."

"It must be. When was it built?"

"Eighteen years ago. Someone got the idea that Broome has a wonderful climate for growing boys. Then it was remembered that the expense of sending children down to Perth was

46

too heavy, as well as the worry of their welfare on the way down and home again at the end of term. A private company was formed, and a hundred thousand pounds was subscribed in no time . . . almost half of it by Mrs. Sayers. She backed a gold mine. She generally does."

"There was no difficulty in staffing the school?"

"At first, yes. Percival was appointed the headmaster, but somehow he didn't quite suit and he was superseded by Rose. It made him a little sour. He's Rugby and Cambridge. Rose didn't go through a public school. But Rose is a born organiser, and he understands boys. Not a bad sort, Old Bilge."

"I understand Percival is known as Happy," remarked Bony.

"That's so," Simmonds chuckled. "Can't beat the kids for burrowing under surfaces. They don't like Percival, but he's a damn good schoolmaster all the same. Now don't forget, if you should ever pass Tallinbah without calling in, I'll be after you with a shotgun."

As he drove Mrs. Walters and the children back to the Police Station, Bony thanked her profusely for a most entertaining afternoon.

Johnno was from Java. For several seasons he had worked underwater as a Number Two Diver, and when paralysis tore into him one afternoon, he decided to quit diving and run a hire-car service. The service consisted of one old car, but in transporting people to and from the aerodrome, and the stores, he did surprisingly well. His speciality was conveying gentlemen to Dampier's Hotel.

Precisely at seven he appeared at the Post Office to take up Mr. Dickenson and Napoleon Bonaparte. He stopped with complaining tires, agilely alighted, and opened the door for his passengers, smiling as though they were his dearest friends. He was small and electrical, and he wore khaki drill shirt and shorts with an air of naïve grandeur.

"There's no need for abnormal speed, Johnno," remarked Mr. Dickenson as he took his seat. His worn clothes were less conspicuous against the upholstery of the car, but given a top hat to crown his head, he could have been the President of France. The car swept into high speed, and Johnno lounged over the back of the front seat to converse with his passengers and steer with one hand.

"As long as the wheels stay on we may arrive," remarked Bony.

"Arrive!" echoed Johnno. "I always arrive. Peoples say, Johnno, you arrive at nine o'clock, two o'clock, any ole time, and I arrive. Peoples like to arrive. I like to arrive. We all arrive."

"Then keep on the road," advised Mr. Dickenson.

The offside wheels were gouging into the soft earth off the narrow strip of macadamised roadway, and Johnno brought the car to the path prepared for it, and laughed. Sweeping past the southern boundary of the airport, with its control tower and hangars and white boundary markers, they were running over a natural earth road of the Northwest. The road skirted the dry tidal flats of the Dampier Creek, the surface almost white and powdered with the dust which rose like belching smoke behind the car. When the track turned suddenly into the scrub and the ground was sandy and red, the "smoke" was rising high above the trees so that anyone in Broome chancing to look out would know that Johnno would presently arrive, barring accidents.

It was quite a good road for the Northwest, and safe at ten miles an hour. All Johnno had to do was to keep the wheels in the twin ruts made by motor traffic, but at thirty miles an hour this is somewhat difficult. Kangaroos leisurely hopped across in front of the car. Bush turkeys ran, then stopped to look their astonishment, and the several species of cockatoos shrieked their defiance at Johnno and his car.

By the time they reached the big red gums bordering Cuvier Creek, Mr. Dickenson was grim, Bony was inclined to keep his eyes shut, and Johnno was still laughing. He pulled up with screaming brake drums at the veranda steps of the large and rambling one-storied structure which had been the Mecca of thousands of travellers over the last sixty years. Johnno stood at the door he had opened for his passengers, his good teeth emphasising the dark velvet of his creaseless face.

"What time you wish to leave?" he asked.

Bony turned to Mr. Dickenson, and the old man raised his white brows and considered.

"Perhaps at eleven," he said tentatively, and Bony agreed.

"Very well. I arrive at eleven," predicted Johnno. "You pay now, eh? Yes, three pounds. No worry then going home about money. You enjoy yourselves. Money is hell. You sing and you laugh, and you leave everything to Johnno. And if you are a bit too, too merry, Johnno will put you to bed when you arrive."

"Fair enough, Johnno," Bony said, chuckling, and from the veranda he turned and watched the car disappear into the scrub beyond the pall of red dust.

49

The topmost branches of the creek gums were bedecked with rubies by the setting sun, and the remaining branches of a tall dead tree were outlined in white by cockatoos preparing to roost for the night. As this land is north of Capricorn, the twilight is ever short, and Bony wanted to view the hotel yard before the light failed. He made the universal excuse, and Mr. Dickenson led the way through the building to the rear door.

It was a spacious yard of plain red earth enclosed with a paling fence. Along one side was the narrow building devoted to single bedrooms and invariably occupied by male guests. At the far end stood the garages and stables, whilst a divisional fence marked off a large plot of lawn bordering the creek along the third side. The yard was scrupulously tidy, and the entire establishment was indicative of good management.

Swept of all litter though it was, the tracker would have had an easy task to indicate to his white superiors the footprints of Mrs. Cotton's murderer had the man who had found her and all those in the hotel who had trooped out at his alarm not smothered them with their boots. On recrossing the yard, Bony found himself familiar with the scene from the sketch plan prepared by Sergeant Sawtell.

Here was the "Spot Marked X," to reach which Mrs. Cotton must have come from one of two doors at the rear of the house. Her bedroom faced the lawn beyond the division fence, and midway in that fence was a small wicket gate on which was the word "Private." She could have walked through that gate, or her body could have been carried through it by her murderer. If the latter, then why? If she had been killed in her room, then why was her body brought out to the yard and left there sometime before eleven-thirty? The theory that she had walked in her sleep was the only reasonable explanation.

No footprints left in the yard by the murderer, and no fingerprints of a man in her bedroom. Sawtell had been able to prove that. A half-caste girl was taking washing from the line beyond the division fence, and she was laughingly beseeching a small aboriginal boy not to turn the tap from which water would flow through a hose to the sprinkler. An aborigine trundled a barrow loaded with wood from the stack across the yard to the kitchen door, and he shouted to the girl to hurry with the clothes and laughed at Bony as though it were a fine joke for the imp to play.

There were only five men lounging in the main bar. Two oil lamps suspended from the ceiling had recently been lit, their wicks not yet turned up. Behind the bar stood a giant screen composed of large pearl shells from which all the dross had been removed and the screen itself fashioned into the likeness of an oyster shell. Spaced between the bottles on the shelves were polished tortoise shells and framed pictures of luggers. In the angle stood a potted palm growing from the terrible teeth of a tiger shark resting on a small occasional table. The entire front of the bar could be raised on hinges, but tonight was bolted down to the main struts.

"What's it to be?" asked Mr. Dickenson, his poise sure in the possession of Bony's "loan." They breasted the bar. A young man came from the five men at the far end, and he appeared uncertain until he caught sight of the pound note the old man put down on the counter.

"How's things, Pop?" he inquired cheerfully after scrutinising Bony.

"My name is Dickenson, young man," returned Mr. Dickenson in the tone of one accustomed to authority. "Had I begotten sons, they would have been respectful to their elders."

"Suits me, if that's how you feel about it," countered the barman with no change of countenance. "Thought you didn't get your quarterly interest until the thirtieth."

Mr. Dickenson flushed, and Bony softly interposed.

"Wonder where I've seen you before. Could have been in Sydney."

The barman shook his head.

"Never been in Sydney. Don't recall having met you. What's your name?"

"Knapp. What's yours?"

51

"Blake."

The barman left them to attend to the other customers, and as Bony made some remark to his companion in vice, his mind was busy with its card-index system.

"He's a swifty," said Mr. Dickenson.

"Face is familiar. Been here long?"

"First time I've seen him behind the bar. He came in from the cattle country up north. Thanks, I will have another."

Bony nodded to the barman, who drifted back to them, pouring the drinks better than a novice. He said:

"Might have seen me out in the Territory sometime."

"Likely enough," agreed Bony. "I've been around."

"In for a spell?"

Interest in the question was not evident in the light grey eyes, and Bony almost succeeded in turning up the card in his mental index. He said casually, "Just travelling," and escaped explanation by the entry of two men into the bar.

"Not very busy tonight," he observed to Mr. Dickenson.

"Not so far. Early yet. I've seen two hundred men drinking here, and ten people serving 'em as fast as they could. Great pub. Wish I had it."

"Who does own it?"

Over the rim of his glass, Mr. Dickenson regarded Bony with a singular expression.

"The late Mrs. Cotton's estate owns the property," he said. "You've heard of Black Mark, I'll warrant. He's the present licensee. Black Mark's an out-and-out sinner, and out-and-out sinners don't strangle people. They knock heads off when they're in a rage, but they never close wind pipes on a dark night. The feller who strangled Mrs. Cotton was no out-and-out sinner . . . in the daytime."

"H'm! Seems sound psychology," agreed Bony.

"It is. Mrs. Cotton was a fine woman, and her husband was a fine man. Pity the police didn't catch her murderer. The other one didn't matter so much, but she was entitled to her life."

"What's your personal opinion of the murderer's race?" asked Bony. "White or black?"

"White, for sure. I know nothing of the inside of these matters." The old man regarded Bony steadily. "The Asiatic does run amok with a kris. He does slip a knife into you for some reason or other. He'll even strangle . . . but with a cord . . . and for a reason. The police know more about these Broome murders than I do."

Mr. Dickenson drank his whisky, dabbed at his lips with a tattered but clean silk handkerchief, and called the barman. His nose appeared now somewhat less frostbitten, and his eyes were decidedly brighter. Time passed pleasantly. The bar remained almost empty, and the barman was having an easy evening. His card would come up eventually. Mr. Dickenson said, conversationally:

"I believe I saw the man who murdered Mrs. Eltham."

"Indeed!" Bony's reaction was not unlike that of a cat on sighting a bird. The barman served the drinks, talking the while to a man about a herd of cattle on the move to the Wyndham Meatworks. When he had again left them Bony waited before being impelled to say: "You actually saw him?"

"Yes. Not that night he strangled Mrs. Eltham. Another night. I mention it because through you I might assist the inspector." Mr. Dickenson solemnly studied the magnificent shell screen. "I'm careful to avoid connection with trouble. You would not mention my name?"

"No, certainly not." Bony made a swift decision. "I'll return your confidence. My business in Broome is to reveal the murderer of these women."

"The thought did occur to me. I like paying my debts. I owe a debt to Inspector Walters, and another to you, sir. What I am going to tell you, you understand, is from one friend to another. I am a peaceful man."

"The children, when they greet you, support that claim."

"I thank you. The night I believe I saw the man who killed Mrs. Eltham was last Tuesday week. I was then suffering from lack of funds, and also my heart was behaving badly. Angina pectoris, my doctor says. I find relief in whisky, but at this time I was out of funds. I'm afraid I am not like the squirrels who gather in summer the food to sustain them through the winter."

Bony nodded politely, and Mr. Dickenson lit a cigar and with the other end smoothed into place the beard about his mouth. Humour was faintly betrayed by his eyes when he continued:

"Throughout my winters, when I am bereft of the where-withal to ease a painful heart, I am compelled to have recourse to a practice which is really abhorrent to me. I have found that ten drops of battery acid in a small tumbler of water is efficacious, but this method of relief is restricted by suspicious people, with whom Broome is overcrowded. Anyway, I recalled that Mrs. Eltham possessed a car, and that the car was still within the garage at the rear of her house.

"Having been on the premises but not, of course, inside the house, at the time of the murder—with many other rubber-necks—I had noted that the padlock securing the garage door was a common one, and I gambled on possessing a key which fitted. Accordingly, when the Perth detectives left Broome, I sneaked into the yard from the rear at about three in the morning. It was very dark, as a sea mist was thick over the town. I had filled a small bottle with the battery acid, and was congratulating myself on having obtained sufficient to last me a whole week, when I fancied I heard movement inside the house. You see, I had relocked the garage door, and was passing along the path at the side of the house on my way to the front street. I was wearing rubber-soled canvas shoes for the occasion. And so I sat me down with my back to the veranda base and waited to see who would come out, either by the back or the front door."

Mr. Dickenson ceased speaking whilst the barman refilled the glasses. The hair at the back of Bony's head was stiff. Here, possibly, was the flaw in the picture for which he so patiently sought.

"All I could make out of the man who left by the kitchen door and passed me by within a yard was the blurred outline of his figure against the sky. If my old eyes weren't sharp, I wouldn't have seen even that. Although I was squatting down, and the fellow passed so close, I'm sure he was a big man. He was wearing a felt hat, like a stockman's. I saw one arm, and it seemed abnormally long. And that was all I did see."

"How did he walk?" asked Bony.

"That I couldn't see. As I said, I was sitting down like Br'er Rabbit, and the night was dark."

"D'you think he was carrying anything . . . large?"

"I didn't get that impression. He wasn't a Comic Cuts burglar getting away with the swag; leastways, I don't think so. He locked the kitchen door after him, because I went to find out. D'you know what I think?"

"Tell me."

"If he wasn't the murderer, who returned for something he had forgotten, then he was one of the woman's friends who went in to take some small thing which might prove his visits to the house."

"That was the night following the departure of the detectives?"

"That was the night."

Despite examination of Mr. Dickenson, nothing further was brought out. Having given his information, the old man determinedly evaded adding to it. He drank like the gentleman he surely was, but his capacity astonished Bony. The evening mellowed, and Bony's guest was in the mood to discuss the people of Broome in general, with additional biographical details of certain personalities. Time passed so swiftly that Bony was astonished when Johnno appeared.

"I arrive, eh!" he exclaimed. "Yes, one drink for me. Then we depart. Yes, plis. Brandy, Dick."

Mr. Dickenson was tired, and Johnno assisted him down the veranda steps to the car. The night was black and white with no mezzotint. One could have read a newspaper in the moonlight and be completely concealed in the shadows. Bony slid in beside the old man, and Johnno, loudly braying with the hooter, departed at top speed.

The homeward journey was fast. Mr. Dickenson was not nervous. He sang a little. He quoted poetry. Abruptly, he drew Bony's head to his mouth and whispered:

"I might know that feller again. As he passed me, I could hear his teeth clicking as though he were in mortal fright."

Bony was about to press a question when Johnno turned back to shout something of the evening, and the car went into a bad sand skid. It almost collided with a tree and almost turned over. Mr. Dickenson chuckled, and Johnno laughed but thereafter gave his attention to his driving. Eventually he was instructed to put the old man down at the Post Office, where Bony also alighted and dismissed Johnno with a handsome tip.

Mr. Dickenson insisted on shaking hands before parting from Bony, and Bony sauntered to the Police Station, where he found Inspector Walters in the kitchen, in his dressing gown and reading a novel.

"Well, you drunkard," he greeted Bony.

"I found your derelict quite good company," Bony said, so happily that Walters was suspicious. "Brought home a little memento of the evening."

"A glass! We've plenty," objected Walters.

"But a special glass. Before my last drink, I wiped off all the fingerprints. When the filled glass was handed to me by the barman, I picked it up by the base to empty it, and I've held the glass by the base all the way back, despite an ugly skid."

"That barman important . . . Black Mark?"

"It wasn't Black Mark. Black Mark didn't appear. The fellow's name is Richard Blake. I'll send his prints to my Department. Sawtell can take them." From his hip pocket Bony extracted a bottle of beer, and without comment the inspector left his chair for glasses and bread and cheese.

Chapter Eight: A PUZZLE IN SILK

The house occupied by the late Mrs. Eltham was a typical Broome bungalow, set well back from the road and partially concealed by ornamental trees. The cement drive ran directly past the house to the garage at the rear, and from it a cement path paralleled the house front, skirted its far side, and joined the cemented yard between house and garage. Off the yard was a small grass plot on which was erected a rotary clothes hoist.

The storm shutters enclosing the encircling veranda being bolted down, the house presented a windowless aspect and was without individuality. It was owned by someone in Perth, and was still under police control. According to Inspector Walters, no one had entered it after the homicide men had returned to headquarters.

Arriving at the rear door, Bony opened the case he had brought and tested the handle for fingerprints. The door handle was clean of any prints. With the key obtained from Walters, he opened the door and tested the inside handle. It, too, was clean. Had substantiation of Mr. Dickenson's statement concerning the man he had seen leaving the house been necessary, it was provided by the clean door handles, which should have produced fingerprints of the last investigator who locked the door.

Elated by the probability that it had been the murderer who had returned to the scene of his crime, Bony stepped into the house and sought the light switch, the storm shutters making the interior almost dark. Closing the door, he sat on a kitchen chair and rolled a cigarette whilst noting everything within visual limits.

Like many of these tropical bungalows, the house proper was devoted to bedrooms, the encircling veranda space being

57

used for general living purposes. The storm shutters having been down for many days, the air smelled slightly musty, and yet within the mustiness was the fragrance of perfume.

This part of the veranda was obviously used as a kitchen and dining room. It was clean and tidy. There was not much furniture, but it retained evidence of having been well kept. On the wash bench were the utensils used by Mrs. Eltham at supper that last night of her life. The floor was covered with apple-green linoleum neither new nor yet worn.

Before moving on, Bony knelt on the linoleum and brought his eyes close to its surface. He could see his own shoe tracks, but none other, and with a finger point he established the film of dust which had settled after the visit of the unknown man. The same degree of dust was on the wash bench and the furniture.

Passing on round the corner of the house to the next veranda section, Bony located the light switch and found himself in the lounge. Small, soft rugs graced the floor. Glass-fronted cases were filled with expensive books. Two seascapes in oils rested on easels and seemed to be reasonably well executed. Both pictures bore the initials of the dead woman. The magazines on a small occasional table, the conch shells used as ash trays, pieces of costly china and crystal, and the curtains and lamp shades, bespoke the tastes of a cultured woman having money to indulge them.

Confident that none had seen him enter the house, and that the lights could not be noted from either the front street or the rear laneway, Bony again sat down and made another cigarette. He was prepared to conduct a long and unhurried investigation of this dwelling, for the man who had spent some time here after the police had finally gone must have left something of himself or some evidence explaining the reason for his visit. Discovery of the motive for that nocturnal visit might well lead to the motive for the murder of Mrs. Eltham. It might lead even to the identity of the murderer.

With all their training and their scientific aids, the homicide experts had failed to prove the identity of the murderer or even put forward a likely motive for the crime. On what rested that double failure? The astuteness of the murderer, in small degree, and the type of community in which he lived, in large degree. The mental lethargy of people all familiar with each other prevented them from noticing the unusual, and thus provided the cloak of secrecy for a killer who planned all his moves.

The problem was to discover the motive having a common denominator covering the murder of two women dissimilar in morality, circumstance, and background. The victims were alike only in being widows. Several motives could be assumed for the murder of one, or that of the other, but there was no motive to be applied to both crimes.

Old Dickenson had provided a splendid lead and, if handled rightly, might give others. This lead might break the wall confronting the man who now sat and smoked a cigarette in Mrs. Eltham's lounge, the man whose maternal forebears had bequeathed him patience which has no limitations.

Had one of Mrs. Eltham's men friends killed her? There were nine listed by the police, but the list could not be accepted as complete. No one of these nine men had visited Mrs. Eltham immediately prior to the night of her death. That was proved by the fingerprint expert. He found no male fingerprints, and according to the domestic, she had, with Mrs. Eltham's assistance, cleaned and polished the entire house the day before Mrs. Eltham's death. Each of the nine men knew nothing whatever of the interest in Mrs. Eltham of the other eight. That proved she had been an excellent diplomat. There was nothing whatever among the dead woman's papers pointing to any other man in Broome. The homicide people were satisfied with the statements and integrity of those nine men, and the Broome police who knew them personally were equally satisfied.

The homicide men had gone through this house like soldier ants through a native village. They had removed all letters and other documents, and they had taken the nightgown found beside the bed to be tested at the headquarters laboratory for fingerprints. Other than the prints of the dead woman and the domestic who had washed and ironed the garment, there were none. That the murderer wore fine rubber gloves was considered certain.

This house contained four rooms. There were no connecting doors, each room opening to the veranda. One was unfurnished. Two were furnished with a single bed. Mrs. Eltham's room was large and well furnished, and contained a double bed. Each room had the usual glazed window, in addition to which was the universal fly screen on the inside fastened with a snap lock.

The door of Mrs. Eltham's room was closed, and Bony tested the handle for prints and found it clean. Within was sufficient light enabling him to locate the electric switch, and he operated that with the point of a match. It, too, was clean of prints. Bony reclosed the door and stood with his back to it.

Beyond the bed was the window with its fly screen closed and its lace curtains drawn aside. The bed was exactly as when the body had been found on it, the top sheet folded over a blanket and counterpane and the whole partly turned back, as though the woman had been on the verge of getting into bed when attacked. On the door side of the bed was a small woolly mat on the far edge of which was a pair of embroidered slippers. Over the bed's foot sprawled a floral linen dressing gown, and on one of two chairs lay a flecked tweed skirt, a lemon-coloured sweater, a satin brassière and slip, and silk stockings.

When Bony moved, the dust-filmed mirror reflected his actions as he bent over the bed, when he opened the door of the wardrobe and saw the packed dresses on hangers, and when he gazed upon the dressing-table appointments and noted the dust on them and on the glass surface. There were no signs that a struggle had taken place in this room, or elsewhere in the house. There had been no signs of a struggle in Mrs. Cotton's bedroom, either. The murderer had had time enough to remove all signs of a struggle in Mrs. Cotton's room, and here he had much more time to do so. But why? The killer could have caught the woman by the neck and could have possessed sufficient strength to prevent any disorder. But why the laying-out of the body on this bed after the nightgown had been ripped from neck to hem?

Bony sat on the vacant chair and made another of his extraordinary cigarettes. He scrutinised every point of the picture illumined by the light falling from the brier-pink shade. He tried to re-create the dreadful drama of that night of May fifth, tried to feel the woman's growing alarm and swift horror when she heard the stealthy steps on the veranda or within this dark room. There was no cord switch with which to switch on the light without leaving the bed. To do that she needs must leave the bed to reach the switch beside the door. Had she seen her murderer? He had choked her from in front. Had she been caught and strangled before she could reach the light switch? Or had she left the room to investigate the stealthy footsteps when attacked? Questions! The answers would have made the picture much clearer.

For what had the man, seen by old Dickenson, come into this room? This was a question having much more of urgency than those others. Find its answer and a great step would have been taken by this patient and relentless tracker of men toward *his* quarry.

Gradually Bony came to feel that there was a flaw in the picture of the room. When fully conscious that there was a flaw, he sought for it and could not see it. There was nothing wrong with the bed. There was no significance in the arrangement of the dressing-table appointments. The woman's clothes lay over the other chair in the order in which she had removed them. The small clock on the bedside table had stopped at two thirty-four. Whether it had stopped in the morning or the afternoon could not be proven. There were no pictures on the walls, and all the personal photographs had been removed by the police.

Presently Bony's restless eyes were directed to the bowl of dead flowers on the chest of drawers. On wilting to death, the flowers doubtless had changed the position they had occupied when alive. The stalks were not of the same length.

Those flowers had been originally arranged by a woman, and, moreover, a woman with artistic tastes. Most women are expert in arranging flowers. Marie, Bony's wife, spent a goodly portion of her time with flowers, and he had often watched her bringing a kind of orderly symmetry from chaos.

The dead flowers ought not of themselves to have fallen into a compact mass toward one side of the bowl. When the homicide men came, the flowers would not have been dead. They might have lifted the flowers to ascertain if anything had been dropped into the water. They might have moved the bowl to examine it for fingerprints. It was then that Bony recalled upsetting a vase of flowers on his own dressing table whenever a drawer was rebellious.

He examined the dust on the surface of all the furniture, leaving the chest of drawers till last. The evenness of the dust film on the chest convinced him that it had been wiped after the fingerprint men had left.

On pulling out the right-hand top drawer it stuck slightly and the dead flowers spilled from the bowl. He went through the contents of all the drawers comprising bed and table linen, curtains and towels. All but the towels had been ironed. The ironed articles had been opened out, for the folds were not exactly as ironed, and that could have been done by the investigators, who also could have disarranged the flowers or even upset them.

There were drawers fitted to the dressing table, and he looked into them. Other than face creams and powder, wads of handkerchiefs, packets of cigarettes, and stockings, there was nothing to interest him. Within the wardrobe, in addition to the rack of frocks, there were several hats on a shelf, a drawer containing gloves, and a compartment containing shoes. Nothing of interest there.

Again in his chair, he made another cigarette and again examined the over-all picture of the room. There was something wrong, and patiently he sought to locate it. Being a woman's room it defeated him, although a married man of many years. He wished that his wife were there, sure that she

62

would have seen or understood what was wrong with it, what made it incomplete. Being merely a man, he was puzzled by something which to a woman would have been glaringly obvious.

"Give!" he murmured. "Give!"

Not the least important, there was still the floor. He took from his case a powerful torch, and began on the floor about the chest of drawers. The floor was less dusty than the veranda spaces without. He found innumerable flower petals at one side, proving that they had been swept off at one end of the chest. He found a bobby pin near the foot of the bed table, and he found a flaky object which at once captured his interest.

It was not easy to lift from the floor, but having done so, he rose to his feet and stood directly under the electric light to look at it on the palm of his hand. It was like a large fish scale, but had nothing of the fish scale's polished surface and strength. When he dented it with a thumbnail, the dent remained. When he pressed hard with the nail, he could not divide it. The surface was pitted as though with a fine needle. It was a dull white in colour.

Fully thirty minutes he spent crawling around the floor. He found two more flakes, another bobby pin, a number of long hairs, five spent matches, parings from a pencil, and shreds of silk. These objects he placed in specimen envelopes from his wallet.

Again on his feet and contemplating the bed, he knew what was missing from this woman's bedroom. The clothes-laden chair shrieked it. He looked down on the floor between the door and bed, for there he had found the wisps of silk. There was no silk in the chest of drawers. He rolled back the bed-clothes and lifted the multispring mattress. There was nothing beneath it save the canvas sheet protecting it from the wire bed mattress.

The murderer had ripped Mrs. Cotton's nightgown from neck to hem and had left the garment beside her body. He had similarly torn Mrs. Eltham's nightgown and left it lying

63

on the mat beside her bed. What had he done with Mrs. Eltham's underwear?

Bony passed to the wardrobe and removed the frocks and suits, and in a far corner he found a large bundle wrapped about with blue silk. His eyes were as blue as the silk covering of the bundle, and he broke it open on the bed and disclosed scraps of silk of several colours: cream, black, daffodil yellow, and green. He could see where a knife had sometimes been employed to start the rip completed by hands.

He sorted the pieces into the respective colours, his mind thrilling with the ecstasy of the hunter who has come within range of the hunted. Having smoothed the pieces of black silk, he proceeded to place them in position to prove the type of garment they had once been. He worked on the cream pieces with the same result, and troubled no further with the remaining scraps of silk.

There was no mention of this bundle of torn silk in the reports compiled by the Broome police, nor was mention made of it in the General Reports compiled by the men from the C.I.B. Had the bundle been in the wardrobe when the police went through the room, they could not have missed it.

After the homicide men had left and the house was finally shut up, the murderer had returned. Motive! It was coming . . . coming from the little bits and pieces . . . coming from those desecrated items of silken underwear . . . a strange and terrible motive for murder.

Chapter Nine: MEDICAL INSPECTION

It was four o'clock when Bony entered the Police Station by the rear door and discovered Mrs. Walters baking scones. He sniffed with exaggerated noise, saying:

"Ah! Hot buttered scones! And strong hot tea!"

"Where have you been all day?" Mrs. Walters asked accusingly.

Bony placed the sugar sack he had brought with him on a side table.

"Merely pottering about. Plenty of butter, now."

"You haven't had lunch?"

"It wasn't convenient. I'm glad now . . ." And sniffing again loudly, he sat down at the floured table. "Six buttered scones and two cups of tea, and I won't want any lunch. Who would?"

"Did your mother have any more like you?" asked Mrs. Walters, buttering hot scones.

"I don't know," he replied. "You see, I was abandoned by her and found under a sandalwood tree. You get along with that baking. I've something to show you."

"Have you?" Mrs. Walters looked at him intently. "This is the last tray to go into the oven, and I'll clean up in no time."

"Good! I want to ask a question and not be slapped for it. Promise not to slap?"

"I promise."

"All right. Do you wear silk underwear?"

"What a question! Very often. Why?"

"I'll tell you in a moment or two. Excuse me."

With a scone in one hand and a teacup in the other, and his mouth whitened by flour, Bony hurried along the passage to the office door. He made sure no member of the public was doing business, and was pleased to find both Walters and

65

Sawtell, with a third policeman, working at their desks. He had already been introduced to Constable Clifford.

"Mrs. Walters wants you, Inspector, and Sergeant Sawtell . . . at once," he called from the doorway.

"What the hell——" Walters began to explode, but Bony had vanished. He and Sawtell left their desks, like dutiful children, and obeyed the summons. Bony closed the door.

"I understand," he began, "that when Lily Mallory, Mrs. Eltham's domestic, reported that she couldn't get into the house, you, Sawtell, went there and broke in. Almost immediately afterwards you telephoned Walters, and he joined you in the house. Did either of you then or subsequently examine the floor of the wardrobe in Mrs. Eltham's room?"

"No. We waited for the Perth men to get here," replied Sawtell. "But I was present when the C.I.B. man stripped the wardrobe of all its contents from top shelf to floor. Why?"

"Did you see a bundle of rags pushed into a far corner?"

"No. There was nothing of the kind there."

"I find that satisfactory," murmured Bony as though to himself. "Now look . . . all of you."

From the sugar sack he took the bundle wrapped in blue silk and opened it out on the side table.

"Examine those pieces of silk, Mrs. Walters, and tell me what you think about them."

She handled the coloured pieces, lifting a strip of lime-green silk to which was a hem of fine lace. The three men silently watched her fluttering hands, the eyes of both Walters and Sawtell hardening as they understood the significance of this wilful destruction.

"Oh!" exclaimed Mrs. Walters. "Oh, what a shame! Such lovely undies, too. Why, it's almost new."

There was indignation in her dark eyes when she turned to Bony.

"I found that bundle in a corner of Mrs. Eltham's wardrobe," he said. "Thank you for your confirmation of what it represents. It's expensive material, is it not?"

"Very. I very much doubt that it was purchased here in Broome . . . not since the war."

66

"Black-market goods, perhaps," contributed the inspector. "Could have been brought in by a lugger. What's it all mean?"

"That Mrs. Eltham's murderer destroyed all her silk underwear. Can you spare an hour to run me out to Dampier's Hotel?"

"Certainly. What's breaking? Come on, out with it."

The inspector's face was almost ferocious.

"D'you know what happened to Mrs. Cotton's personal effects?" persisted Bony.

Walters referred to Sawtell, and the sergeant replied:

"I believe all her personal effects were stored in her bedroom and the room locked up."

"Good! We'll run out there at the first opportunity. Was Constable Clifford ever inside Mrs. Eltham's house . . . after she was found, of course?"

"Yes. He was often there with us."

"Ah! This case is beginning to break," Bony cried, and none had seen him so excited. "I'm glad I came to Broome on two counts. One because I am your guest, and the other because you gave me a real puzzler of a case. Now, Walters, do something for me immediately. Ring up Dr. Mitchell and tell him your wife has taken a bad turn and to come at once."

"But Esther's all right," objected Walters.

Bony sighed, and Mrs. Walters snapped:

"Go and do what he asks, Harry. I'm having a real bad turn."

The inspector stamped away. Sawtell grinned, and Mrs. Walters looked impishly at Bony. They said nothing, but could hear the inspector at the telephone in the office.

"Have you ever charged anyone with destroying women's clothes?" Bony asked Sawtell.

"No, and I've been here fifteen years."

"I've known of it, but not in connection with homicide," Bony said. "This fellow is exceptionally clever. He works with silk or rubber gloves. No fingerprints. We'll send these remnants down for expert examination, but I think they'll find

67

only my prints or those of Mrs. Walters. How long has Constable Clifford been with you?"

"Almost two years."

"Married?"

"No."

"Well, engaged?"

"I don't know that one," averred Sawtell. "He's efficient and ambitious. We've found him a good bloke. He boards with us."

Inspector Walters returned to say the M.O. was on his way.

"I'm sitting back. You can make the explanations," he said to Bony.

Three minutes later Bony began the explanations to Dr. Mitchell, who was certainly astonished to find Mrs. Walters looking quite sweet in her cooking apron.

"Inspector Walters brought you here under false pretences, Doctor," he said. "However, I believe that the real reason will prove to be of such interest that you will readily forgive him. You see, we're so positive that you will assent to help us in clearing up these murders at Broome."

"Naturally. Anything I can do. Lead me to it," pleaded Dr. Mitchell, setting down his bag.

"We thank you, Doctor," murmured Bony, producing his pocket wallet. "I believe I know what these objects are, but I require that they be definitely identified. Look!"

From the specimen envelopes he shook free onto the table the three small flaky objects he had retrieved from the floor of Mrs. Eltham's bedroom. The doctor bent over them. He tested one with a fingernail.

"They are particles of human skin," he announced. "They come from a person afflicted with psoriasis, a disease of the skin for which there is no known cure."

"Is its incidence rare or otherwise?"

"Neither common nor rare," replied Dr. Mitchell. "It's more prevalent in southern climes than in the tropics, I think. I know of four cases of it here in Broome. Patches of skin become dry and flaky and can be rubbed off or will fall off. It's

68

not a notifiable disease, for it's not contagious. In fact, many doctors tell the sufferers that they will outlive their medical advisers, for it occurs much more often than not in healthy people."

"Does it favour, if I may use the word here, one sex particularly?" asked Bony.

"No, I think not. It's no respecter of persons. Redheaded people are sufferers equally with blonds and brunettes. As I stated, there's no known cure, and there is no known cause. Because its effects are not serious, medical science hasn't given much attention to it, both time and money being so urgently needed for the defeat of considerably more serious diseases."

"And you know of four cases of it in Broome?"

Dr. Mitchell nodded and lit a cigarette. Bony pursed his lips, and the doctor, guessing what the next question would be, said:

"I'll give you their names in strictest confidence, and in the hope that the information may lead to the identity of this strangling beast. Mind you, there are doubtless others in Broome who, knowing there is no cure, rely on the chemist for ointment to give relief."

"There is a chemist in Broome?" promptly asked Bony.

"Yes. He might know of other sufferers. I'll enquire if you wish."

"That's kind of you. Well, now, the next step. The persons afflicted with psoriasis: is it all over their bodies?"

"In the majority of cases, not entirely. Most of them have it only on parts of the body, on their legs or their arms or on their backs. Those specimens of sloughed skin have, I think, come either from an elbow or a knee, where the skin is coarser than elsewhere."

"Every sufferer, then, would not show it on the face and hands and forearms?"

"That's so," agreed Dr. Mitchell. "In those cases the disease would not be observable without the patient's consent."

"Have you got it?"

"I . . . oh no. Thank goodness."

"Would you consent to prove that?"

The doctor declared he would be delighted to prove it, and Bony explained his reason for establishing a fact, telling where he had found the portions of dead skin and pointing out that the doctor had been inside Mrs. Eltham's house. Turning to Mrs. Walters, he asked:

"If you will permit the use of a spare room . . ."

"Certainly, Bony."

"Then I will inspect your carcass," Bony said almost gayly. "Now don't run away, my dear Walters. It'll be your turn next."

"Be damned if it will," snorted the inspector. "You can take my word for it, backed up by the wife, if you want it."

His eyes clashed with the half-caste's calm gaze, and Bony said:

"I regret that in this matter I cannot accept the word of any person known to have been inside Mrs. Eltham's house prior to, by one day at least, her demise, and subsequent to it. When it's proved that everyone known to have entered the house is free from this psoriasis, then I can logically assume that those particles of skin fell from the body of the man I am seeking for double murder."

He was absent with the doctor for five minutes, and on returning from the bedroom to which they had retired, he nodded to Walters and the inspector went in to be examined by the doctor, went without demur. Sawtell followed him, and they brought Clifford from the office to undergo the same inspection. When the inspection of the Police Force was concluded, Bony asked who removed the body of Mrs. Eltham to the morgue. The local undertaker and an assistant had done that, and the doctor was able to vouch for the undertaker, who was his patient. The assistant was a Malay, and therefore free, for the disease does not occur in that race.

"Well, that covers everyone, with the exception of the homicide men," Bony decided with satisfaction. "We'll write an air-mail letter to the chief of the Perth C.I.B. and have him establish if those three men he sent up here are free from psoriasis. If they are, then our search for a murderer in a population of some eight hundred people can be reduced to, what d'you say, Doctor, a round dozen?"

"Probably less than a round dozen."

"Well, I am truly grateful to all of you for your willing co-operation. By elimination, and by finding tiny bits and pieces and fitting them together, we shall eventually come to see the cause of horribly tragic effects. If you will let me have those names, Doctor, and any others provided by the chemist."

"The names of my patients I'll write now," said the doctor, producing his prescription pad. Rapidly he tore off the sheet, scribbled, and presented it to Bony. Bony slipped it into a pocket and accompanied the little doctor to his car.

"It's truly good of you to be so helpful," he said when the medico was behind the steering wheel.

"Anything I can do, well, it's my job in a case like the one you're handling. I'm a little nervous that the swine might kill again."

"Have you studied psychiatry?"

"Yes. That any help to you? Somehow I think it might be."

"I think that too. I'd like to talk one evening soon."

"Do. Any time after seven. Give me a tinkle in case I'm out. Busy place this . . . for me. Cheerio!"

Thoughtfully, Bony returned to the station office.

"Who's on that list?" asked Walters, and Sawtell evinced keen interest.

Bony produced the scrap of paper. He looked round. Constable Clifford was not present.

"Mrs. Janet Lytie," he read out, and paused.

"Old dame who runs a teashop," supplemented Sawtell.

"Miss Olga Templeton-Hoffer."

"Starchy old bird who nurses a martinet of a father. Go on."

"Master Leslie Lee."

"Schoolboy about fifteen. Next."

"Mr. Arthur Flinn."

"Oh! Might be worth keeping tag," Sawtell said.

Bony placed the paper in his pocket wallet.

"The doctor has added a fifth name," he almost lisped, and watched for the effect. "The fifth name on the list is Albert Mark."

There was a long pause, and then Sawtell breathed:

"Black Mark."

"I'd like to run out and see him before dinner," Bony said.

Chapter Ten: A PETTY THIEF

Black Mark heaved himself away from the dinner table and strode through the empty bar to stand on the front veranda and pick his teeth. When you came to look at him properly, you had to admire the barrel of a chest, the vast shoulders and the powerful arms, and the nether portion encased in gabardine trousers. At first you did not note these things, because you had to withstand the shock received from the wide, square-cut black beard, the mop of fine black hair, the bold black eyes and the strong black brows. Only a very drunken man or a small child would have the daring to be rude to Black Mark. What had made him so prominent in the northwest of Australia was that, in addition to abnormal physical strength, he was intelligent.

He was continuing to pick his teeth when the police jeep stopped and three men came up the veranda steps.

"Evening, Mark," said Walters nonchalantly.

"Evenin', Inspector. Evenin', Sergeant."

"This is Mr. Knapp," proceeded Walters. "Personal friend of mine from over East. Criminologist, and all that. Might be able to help us solve these murders."

"Glad to meet you, Mr. Knapp," Black Mark said in a voice thrice the volume of a normal man. "You're welcome to what you can see and find out. I'm an inoffensive man, as the inspector will back me, but I'd be mighty obliged if you could point out the man who murdered Mrs. Cotton. Point him out privately."

Bony smiled easily, saying he would keep it in mind. He asked what had been done with Mrs. Cotton's personal effects.

"Well, nothing was touched in her bedroom bar the bed linen," obliged Black Mark. "Probably you know that the

73

body was taken from the yard and laid on the bed, where it remained most of the day. After the body was removed, I took all her things and locked 'em up in her bedroom. Being her executor, I had the solicitor out here and that's what he advised me to do. Later on the d.s from Perth looked in, but they didn't do much."

"Were you with the Perth detectives when they entered the bedroom?" asked Bony.

"Yes. I went in with 'em. They were interested mostly in the window fastenings. Like to look at the room?"

"I would."

Black Mark conducted them to a large, well-furnished room containing a stripped double bed now laden with all kinds of woman's possessions. There were several trunks of the kind seldom seen today, and a treadle sewing machine, and a dozen or so silver trophies won by Mrs. Cotton's husband.

Bony examined the window. It was one of the casement type and quite large. The usual fly-netted screen was fitted on the inside. It was not possible to force the window from the outside without breaking the glass. With the window open, the screen provided a degree of protection, for unless the netting was slit the catch lock could not be turned back.

"Who brought the body here from the yard?" Bony asked.

"I did, with a man named Jenks taking the feet."

"The door wasn't locked . . . then?"

"No. There wasn't even a key in the door."

"How often did Mrs. Cotton walk in her sleep?"

"Very seldom," replied Black Mark. "Not once in six months, I'd say. Seems to have done it when she was overtired. She never wandered far, and usually woke up by herself and went back to bed."

"On that night Mrs. Cotton was killed, the bar was busy, I understand," Bony went on, calmly regarding Black Mark. "Was the noise in the bar particularly loud?"

"Yes. We had a bit of a party. Five prospectors in for a spell."

"So that if Mrs. Cotton had cried out for help, either here

74

or in the passage without, or even in the yard, you would not have heard her?"

Black Mark hesitated, seemingly reluctant to agree.

"What about the staff?" persisted Bony. "Could they have heard a cry for help?"

"I don't know," Black Mark replied. "I been thinking along that line, and I've questioned the maids and the cook and her husband. They reckon that if Mrs. Cotton had sung out they would have thought it was someone in the bar."

"So that it was comparatively easy for anyone to walk into the place, knock on Mrs. Cotton's door, push her back into the bedroom, and strangle her?"

Very slowly Black Mark said, softly for him:

"I'm afraid it was. But she was found in the yard, remember."

"When the Perth detectives were here, did they examine the contents of the dressing table, and the drawers of that tallboy, and the inside of the wardrobe?"

"They looked into those things but they didn't take anything out."

"Sawtell . . . did you, or Pedersen?"

"Yes, just looked into the drawers. Black Mark was with us. We were trying to find if anything belonging to the dead woman had been stolen. Everything seemed in order."

Bony opened the door of the wardrobe and burrowed his head and shoulders beneath the hems of the close-packed rack of dresses, and later on both Walters and the sergeant admitted they were not surprised when he brought out a bundle wrapped in a piece of linen.

Sawtell obeyed Bony's order to remove the books from a small table, and on the table he broke open the bundle.

"What the hell's that?" demanded Black Mark, his eyes almost glaring at the strips of torn and ripped silk of several colours. "Looks like women's silk underthings."

"I think, Mr. Mark, that Sergeant Sawtell will take charge of these pieces of underwear," Bony said, an edge to his voice. "You have not seen them before?"

75

"I certainly haven't," declared the licensee furiously. "I don't get it."

"Tell me, was Mrs. Cotton a woman of tantrums? Is it possible that she tore these garments in a fit of temper?"

"No, of course not. Mrs. Cotton was a fine woman, and sweet-tempered, excepting when she had good cause to blow up. She wouldn't have done all that. Why, she went to market good and hearty only the week before she was killed because someone stole a nightdress of hers off the drying line."

"Stole her nightgown!" echoed Bony, his eyes blazing.

"Too ruddy right. Said it was one of her best silk ones. We have some pretty hard doers drinkin' here, but we never had no thief before that nightdress was pinched."

"What about the aborigines? Are they trustworthy?"

"No, they're not. But they wouldn't have pinched it, or pinched anything else, because they know one of 'em would tell us."

"Can you recall the date that the garment was stolen from the line?"

"Yes. Let me think. Mrs. Cotton was murdered on the night of April twelfth. That was a Thursday. The nightdress was stolen on the Sat'day before. We were extra busy that day. We had the Football Club picnicking out here, and the Buffaloes were having their Annual Outing. There were a lot of school kids, too. Most of all that lot went back to town at sundown."

"Most of them?"

Black Mark reminded Bony of an outraged porcupine. His hair and beard were distinctly uncurled.

"Fifty or sixty of the men stayed on till nigh midnight," he answered.

"Were many of them strangers to you?"

"Yes, they were. I don't know everyone in town. But they wouldn't pinch a nightdress off a clothesline. No one does that sort of thing up here in the Nor'west."

"H'm! Fetch me a broom, please."

Black Mark looked his astonishment and made no comment. While he was absent, Sawtell rerolled the silk items into a bundle and wrapped that in a pillow slip. On Black Mark's return with the broom, Bony ordered them all outside whilst he swept the floor. There might have been sufficient dust to fill an eggcup. There was nothing but the dust, so far as the human eye could detect, but Bony gathered it into a specimen envelope.

"Take us out to see the clothesline," he requested.

They were conducted to the yard and through the wicket gate to the strip of lawn over which were stretched two long wire lines. When loaded with washing, the lines were kept aloft by forked poles. The inspector said:

"There would be no reason for anyone just visiting the hotel to come here, would there?"

"No," answered Black Mark. "As you saw, there's a notice on the little gate reading 'Private.' "

"But anyone crossing the main yard could easily see the clothes on the line," Bony pointed out. "Who did the washing that day, d'you know?"

"Two lubras from up the creek. The blacks have a camp there."

The party stood under the two long lines. The young man who had served in the bar that night Bony and old Dickenson had visited this place emerged from the hotel and walked across the yard to enter one of the single bedrooms. He did not openly evince curiosity, but he missed nothing.

"The maids working here at the time Mrs. Cotton was murdered: are they still employed by you?"

"One is," replied Black Mark, continuing to bristle. He added, with strange diffidence in view of his mood: "Her name's Irene. She's a half-caste."

"I'd like to talk to her. Bring her here and then leave us."

The licensee rolled away to the kitchen. " 'An out-and-out sinner,' " quoted Bony, and completed it with: " 'Out-and-out sinners don't strangle women in the dark.' "

"He's got psoriasis," Sawtell said.

"But, according to police report, he proved a watertight alibi for the night Mrs. Eltham was killed."

"Many murderers have put up a watertight alibi," growled Walters.

"And Black Mark has got the pub licence," argued the sergeant.

The black-bearded man appeared, followed by the girl Bony had seen being teased by a small boy at the water tap. She looked frightened. She was a slim girl about twenty, and had her nose not been so broad she would have been good-looking. Bony stepped forward to meet her, and his smile banished her nervousness.

"I want to talk to you, Irene," he said. The others drifted away through the wicket gate. Bony proceeded to the far end of the grass strip to the bank of the creek, and the girl followed. "You and I, Irene, are people apart. We understand each other, and we can speak of things to each other without being considered foolish. What we talk about, no one will know. O.K. with you?"

"Yes, O.K. with me," she assented, her voice soft and her accent pure. Curiosity mastered her. "What part of Australia d'you come from?"

"From Brisbane, Irene. I happened to be over here on holiday, and when I heard about Mrs. Cotton I thought perhaps I might be able to help Inspector Walters. Did you like Mrs. Cotton?"

The large, doelike eyes filled with tears.

"Mrs. Cotton was . . ."

"All right, Irene. I thought she was a good woman, and that's why I want to find out who killed her. Did the police question you much?"

The girl wiped her eyes with the small handkerchief she slipped from the pocket of her white apron.

"Sergeant Sawtell asked a lot of questions," she replied. "About when Mrs. Cotton went to bed that night, and what we were all doing."

"Well, then, of what we are going to talk you will say nothing to anyone. Do you remember Mrs. Cotton losing a nightgown off the line?"

78

"Oh yes! It was one of her best ones."

"Can you tell me which line it was pegged to, and about where?"

"In the middle of that one next to the kitchen."

"How much other washing was on the line that night?"

"Not very much. You see, it was a Saturday."

"Oh! A Saturday?"

"You see . . . What's your name?"

"My wife calls me Bony. You can call me Bony, too."

Irene smiled, and then she was good to look at.

"All right, Bone-ee. You see, the lubras from the camp up the creek come to wash twice a week. They wash on Mondays the sheets from the guests' rooms and the staff's, and the other things from the dining room and the kitchen. Then they come again on Saturdays just to wash for Mrs. Cotton and Mr. Mark."

"Then Mrs. Cotton's washing was the only woman's washing on the line that day?"

Irene nodded, and Bony gave her the cigarette he made and lighted it for her.

"Thank you, Irene. You've no idea who might have stolen Mrs. Cotton's nightgown, have you?"

"Oh no! I would have told her if I had."

"Yes, of course you would. Why was the washing hung out so late?"

The girl burst into low laughter, and Bony beamed. She said:

"Old Mary Ann had a baby Friday night, and she wouldn't let one of the other lubras take her place, saying she'd washed for Mrs. Cotton especially for ten years and she wasn't going to miss out that Saturday. She wasn't feeling so good in the morning after the baby was born, but she got here about three in the afternoon, she and a young lubra called Juliet. There was no drying wind, you see, and when night came the clothes were still wet."

"Yes, of course, they would be. Had that ever happened before . . . in the winter months?"

"I don't remember so."

"It doesn't matter." Bony swiftly followed up, expertly preventing the girl's mind from wandering from the subject in hand. "Who stripped Mrs. Cotton's bed and tidied her room after her body was taken away?"

Irene said that she "fixed" the bedroom and stripped the bed. Yes, she had then swept the floor. No, she noticed nothing wrong with the room or the bed. No, Mrs. Cotton wasn't in a bad temper that night, or drunk, or anything like that. Mrs. Cotton never got drunk, and she was a kind mistress to everyone who worked for her. When she heard about Mary Ann's baby she told Mary Ann to go back to camp at once, but Mary Ann began to cry and said she was all right and that Juliet would be sure to spoil Mrs. Cotton's best undies.

"Well, then, having fixed the bedroom, did you look into the wardrobe for anything to be washed?"

"No," replied Irene. "All I did was to put two dresses into the wardrobe."

"Didn't you notice when you fixed the room that there wasn't any of Mrs. Cotton's silk underwear about?"

"Oh yes, I noticed that."

"Did you tell Sergeant Sawtell about it?"

"Oh no! Sergeant Sawtell took it all away: Mrs. Cotton's nightie, and her day undies."

"How do you know about the undies . . . that the sergeant took the undies away?" persisted Bony.

"I don't know. He took the nightie, and he would have taken the undies," was the naïve reply.

"Yes, I suppose he would do that," admitted Bony. "You never saw a bundle of old rags in Mrs. Cotton's wardrobe, did you?"

"Old rags!" laughed Irene. "Mrs. Cotton wouldn't have any old rags in her room. Soon as anything got raggety, off it went to the blacks' camp."

Bony jumped to his feet and the girl rose with him.

"Well, Irene, thank you very much. Now remember, don't say anything about what we've been talking. All that's a little secret with you and me. What size stockings do you wear?"

She mentioned a size-five shoe, and that she liked nylons but they were too dear for her. Bony assured her that if he could obtain them, nylon stockings she should have. Then he said:

"By the way, before I go. On the Saturday the nightgown was stolen there were a lot of people out here from the town. D'you remember anyone particularly who came in here from the main yard?"

"No. Oh no. No one would dare come in here," Irene replied.

"Then do you remember seeing anyone leaning over the fence and taking notice of what was inside?"

The girl began to shake her head. Then, beneath the light brown skin, the blush could be seen. She nodded and, after hesitation, said:

"Yes, there was that Mr. Flinn. When I went out last thing before dark to see how the clothes were drying, he was leaning on the back fence. He called to me, and I wouldn't go."

"Oh! You don't like Mr. Flinn?"

"I hate him. He's been after me for a long time. Mr. Mark said he'd knock his bloody head off if he comes after me again."

"Dear, dear!" murmured Bony. "What language! Well, Irene, I must be going. I'll not forget about the stockings. Shoe size five. Good-bye."

"Good-bye . . . Bone-ee!"

He waved to her from the wicket gate and then sought the Broome police, finding them with Black Mark on the hotel veranda. The licensee accompanied them to the jeep, and before climbing into the vehicle, Bony said to him whilst holding his black eyes:

"I've had a little chat with Irene. She knows nothing about those torn garments found in the wardrobe. You really would like to know who strangled Mrs. Cotton?"

"You're just telling me."

"I may tell you one day . . . on several conditions."

"Name 'em."

"That you will say nothing of those torn silk garments, that

81

you do not question Irene regarding what she and I have been talking about, because I've told her not to tell you. And also that you will keep to yourself the fact that I am a friend of Inspector Walters and the fact that I am interested in who strangled Mrs. Cotton."

Black Mark expanded his chest, and the chest appeared to lift the fringe of his beard.

"Goes with me," he said.

With the passing days Bony became increasingly perturbed. Time, he had said so often, was his greatest ally, but in this matter of double homicide, Time as an ally had to be ignored because the double murderer took count of Time only as measured by the moon. And now the moon was growing old and the period of darkness long.

Bony sat at the table in his "office," a secluded corner of the station veranda. The table was littered with notes, and two small conch shells were disgracefully full of cigarette ends.

Were it not for the ageing moon, he would have been fully satisfied with his progress in this investigation. His patience wasn't wearing thin, but the moon was being now so anaemic that on the next morning it wouldn't rise before two thirty-eight. Additional measures would certainly have to be taken to safeguard further possible victims of this strangling maniac.

At eleven, when Mrs. Walters brought him morning tea, she found him slumped into the chair turned sidewise to the desk and one leg resting on a corner of it. Failing to notice her approach, he was all activity when he did, thanking her for troubling about him, and then asking if she could spare a few minutes.

Mrs. Walters gladly assented to give him all the minutes he might want, and on making her comfortable in a chair on the far side of the table, he said:

"I am finding so much femininity in this investigation that often I wish I were a woman, with all a woman's knowledge of other women, and all a woman's knowledge of men. Women can see deeper into others of their own sex, and much deeper into men than men can. You have been so helpful that I am going to pester you for further assistance."

"I shall be only too glad to help in any way, Bony," she told

83

him, and so eagerly that he smiled his appreciation. "When you use the word femininity, I understand just what you mean."

"I thought you would. Now just listen while I run over a few items, some of which are not known to your husband or to Sawtell. And what we say let it remain between us. Now, then. On Saturday, April 7, Mrs. Cotton's personal washing was left all night on the line because the lubra turned up late that day. The next morning a silk nightgown belonging to Mrs. Cotton was missing. It has never been recovered. A few nights later, on the twelfth, Mrs. Cotton was found dead in the hotel yard, and subsequently, I found in her wardrobe all her silk underwear torn to shreds.

"A few weeks later, history is repeated. One May third Mrs. Mallory, who served Mrs. Eltham, washed her laundry. The clothes not being dry at nightfall, they were left on the line. During the night a silk nightgown was stolen. Two nights later Mrs. Eltham was strangled, and, subsequently, I found her silk underwear ripped and torn and bundled inside her wardrobe. Both women, you will recall, were found in a state of nudity, and beside each body was the torn nightgown they had been wearing when killed. Those nightgowns were ripped only once. What do you make of all that?"

"I think that he killed those women because he feared them."

"Psychiatrists have gone very deep into the human mind, and they admit there is yet a very long way to go. One fact deducible from that destroyed feminine underwear is that the destroyer is an introvert, one whose sex life was so unbalanced by circumstance that he has been transformed into a homicidal maniac. Such a person can continue the social round, or in business, and yet be entirely unsuspected by those with whom he associates."

Bony paused to give Mrs. Walters opportunity to comment, and when she remained silent, he asked a question which astonished her:

"Have you at any time in your life met a man who, superficially, was charming and yet revealed something in himself which frightened you?"

"Yes," she replied.

"In Broome?"

"No. It was before I was married and came to Broome. I have met men I have instinctively known I could not trust. There seemed to be something evil despite their agreeable manner."

"H'm! Have you met a man of that type here in Broome?"

Mrs. Walters' mouth became tight and her dark eyes clouded.

"Remember, we're talking in confidence," Bony said.

"Well, there's a man in Broome with whom I'd not want to be alone. The man is Arthur Flinn. He was the man who ignored your question of what happens to the exhibits at Activities Day, and Mrs. Simmonds told you they were sent to Perth for sale."

"Ah! So he is Arthur Flinn." Deftly Bony changed the subject. "How many widows are there in Broome who are comparatively young and able to afford expensive silk underwear?"

"Well, there's Mrs. Sayers for one," replied Mrs. Walters without hesitation, and Bony drew forward a slip of paper and jotted down the name. "Then there's Mrs. Watson and Mrs. Clayton and Mrs. Abercrombie. And we must include Mrs. Overton. That's five."

"Thank you. Of those five widows, who would do their own washing or have it done at their homes?"

"I think no woman in her senses would send silk clothes to a laundry," replied Mrs. Walters. "Anyone able to afford such a luxury could afford to have it washed by a lubra at home, or do it herself."

"Yes, I suppose so. Are there any other widows . . . additional to the five you have mentioned?"

"Several I could name, but they are not in the upper circle occupied by the five and those two unfortunates."

"You are kind to be so patient with me," Bony said smilingly. "A few more answers and I'll let you out of school. Do you know any of those five women intimately?"

"Oh yes. I'm on visiting terms with Mrs. Abercrombie and Mrs. Overton. And, of course, Mrs. Sayers. I don't know Mrs. Watson so well, although I've met her often at school functions. Mrs. Clayton is a bit standoffish, her husband having been an author."

"Er, I can understand that," Bony hastened to say. "Well, I think we'll take steps to protect those five widows. I'll talk to your husband about it. How often d'you leave your washing out all night at this time of year?"

Mrs. Walters took time to consider.

"Seldom during the winter months. Perhaps once in every four weeks . . . due to a wet wind coming in from the sea."

Bony stood up, saying:

"I'm grateful for your co-operation, Mrs. Walters, and now I'll be slightly better armed to tackle your husband. He's been quite sore with me because I haven't told him how I knew someone had been in Mrs. Eltham's house after it was finally shut up."

"Yes, I know, Bony. Harry hates mysteries."

Bony chuckled. "I just love them," he asserted. "I find a good mystery the very breath of life."

Five likely victims! When Mrs. Walters had left him, he compared his list from her information with that supplied by Sergeant Sawtell. The five were on Sawtell's list, and from Sawtell's memoranda Bony jotted down information concerning his five. Mrs. Sayers lived alone in her house, but in a room off the rear yard lived a man named Briggs, who was her chauffeur and general man about the place. A woman came daily to cook and do the housework. Mrs. Overton lived entirely alone. Mrs. Clayton lived with her daughter, aged fourteen. Mrs. Watson lived with two small children, aged respectively four and three. A married sister spent much time with her in the evenings. And Mrs. Abercrombie had for a companion a woman much older than herself. Mrs. Overton seemed most open to attack, but then Mrs. Cotton had been surrounded by people.

It was all very well to place a guard over those women.

Such a precaution would surely be noted by this Mr. Hyde, who would then select any unguarded woman. It was all very well to assume that he had a predilection for widows. Assumption was as far as anyone could go along that road.

There was one road Bony was reluctant to take. This killer of women had stolen the nightgowns belonging to his intended victims. The theft seemed to be a prerequisite to murder. The five widows could be interviewed and requested to report immediately they suffered such a loss, but could they be depended on not to gossip about such a request from the police? Bony thought not. It was useless to do anything unless absolute assurance could be obtained that official interest in nightgowns on clotheslines was not transmitted ultimately to the ears of the killer.

And yet, were another victim claimed by this murderer, it would be just too bad. At lunch, when listening to Nanette's bright chatter, he decided to ask the five widows to report a theft from their clotheslines. After lunch he decided to drop this plan for another, and at no period of his career had he been so unsure and so hesitant in reaching a decision.

During the afternoon he sat with Inspector Walters in the office.

"Have you a spare map of the town?" he asked.

Walters said there was one, and after a short search produced it.

"Mark on it, please, in red ink, the position of the houses occupied by the Widows Sayers, Overton, Abercrombie, Watson, and Clayton," he requested, and without comment Walters did so. He gave Bony a full five minutes' study of the position of the five houses before saying:

"Am I thinking what you're thinking?"

"I am trying to plan how to protect those five women without the man we want knowing it. I thought it might be wise for one of us to interview each of those five women and ask them to report at once when they had a nightgown stolen from their clothesline. I still think that course would be the exercise of wisdom, but it has a grave defect. We can receive no guar-

87

antee that one or more will not gossip about it, and gossip in a place like Broome means blaring radiobroadcasting. However, it would seem that the best we can do is maintain an unobtrusive surveillance over those five houses and then, when washing at one of them is left out, to wait by the clothesline."

"That seems the best thing to do."

"Could you arrange for Clifford and Sawtell, with you and me to take turns, to maintain watch on those five clotheslines?"

"Yes, of course."

"Good! Get Sawtell to begin by taking a walk this evening."

"Certainly. And Clifford can do it tomorrow . . . between sundown and dark?"

"Between sundown and dark. If only I am permitted time, I'll so build the fellow's personality and background that I'll be confident in handing you sufficient proof on which to charge him. Time is so essential, and yet the danger to one of those five widows is real, so real that I am made nervous. Now what do you know about Arthur Flinn?"

Inspector Walters produced a report and read from it.

"Flinn, Arthur Willoughby. Probable age forty-eight. Believed to be a bachelor. Pearl dealer by profession. Resides at the Seahorse Hotel, in Chinatown, and has an office in Chinatown which is not now open for business. Came to Broome in 1945. Has stated that he came from Sydney, where he lived during the war, and that he carried on his business in Darwin for ten years before the war. Has stated also that he was born in Australia and that he possesses independent means."

"Thanks," murmured Bony. "I'd like to telegraph Darwin for a checkup, but we cannot even trust the postal officials during this hunt for our Mr. Hyde. Write to Darwin by air mail. They may know something of him. Will it go tonight?"

"Early tomorrow. Should have a reply the day after. Is he important?"

"Flinn is one of Dr. Mitchell's psoriasis patients. On the evening of April seventh, during the night of which Mrs. Cotton's nightgown was stolen, he was seen resting against the back fence of the hotel. You will remember the flakes of dead skin I found on the floor of Mrs. Eltham's bedroom. Admittedly, there was no dead skin amongst the dust I swept up from Mrs. Cotton's room. Dr. Mitchell examined it through his microscope and failed to detect any. The room was thoroughly cleaned by Irene, the girl at the hotel, immediately after Mrs. Cotton's body was removed. That collection of dust proves only that the murderer did not return on a night after his crime to destroy Mrs. Cotton's silk underwear. It proves that he did it on the night he murdered her. He had time to rip and tear Mrs. Eltham's underwear the night he murdered her. Why he did not, but went back after a week or two to do it, I cannot tell you."

"I remember seeing Mr. Flinn doing quite a lot of walking about Broome during the evenings," succinctly added Walters. "Why not keep an eye on him?"

"A friend is already doing that for me."

"Tell."

"Mr. Earle Dickenson is obliging me."

"But he must be drunk," objected the inspector. "It's the beginning of the new quarter."

Bony smiled whimsically.

"Mr. Dickenson is obliging me by not becoming drunk. Should you see him when making the round of the widows' houses, you might be forgiven for thinking he was drunk. I can assure you he is cold sober, and is taking a strong and beneficial interest in this murder investigation."

"Well, well, well! You'd make a hell of a good temperance reformer."

"Alas, I may have made a rash promise. I promised old Dickenson that when we have nailed our murderer he and I will get blind blotto at the Dampier Hotel."

"I might be with you too. Now I think I see through a brick wall. The evening before you visited Mrs. Eltham's house, you and old Dickenson went out on a bender to the Dampier Hotel. Now lemme think. Four days after the Perth mob left Broome, old Dickenson was taken off to hospital suffering from acid poisoning. He could have gotten the battery acid from Mrs. Eltham's car. He could, that night he stole the battery acid, have seen . . ."

"You're destined for the C.I.B.," Bony said with a chuckle, but Walters remained serious.

"What did old Dickenson see? Go on, tell, Bony."

Bony related Mr. Dickenson's adventure on that night he "borrowed" Mrs. Eltham's battery acid.

"Clicking teeth, eh!" pounded Walters. "Faulty dentures, might be."

"Or action resulting from great mental disturbance. I'd like to make our Mr. Arthur Flinn intensely angry."

"Otherwise it doesn't get us anywhere?"

"It may eventually. It's a big piece among my bits and pieces. Ah, here comes the postboy."

The youth having departed, the inspector sorted the mail, flicking several letters across his desk to Bony. He spent two minutes with the contents of one official envelope and on returning his attention to Bony found him gazing at the ceiling. Bony said:

"C.I.B. reports that no one of the three men sent up here is suffering from psoriasis. That reduces a problem still further, for the chemist's list of sufferers is confined to two women, a boy of sixteen, and a man who has been away with the pearling fleet for eight or nine weeks. My own office in Brisbane reports that the fingerprints on that glass I purloined at the Dampier Hotel are those of Ronald Locke."

"Is . . . that . . . so," Walters drawled. "Is . . . that . . . really . . . so? Sawtell! Our Richard Blake is Ronald Locke."

The sergeant came to his feet as though actuated by invisible wires.

So Richard Blake was Ronald Locke, and every policeman in Australia saw red when he thought of Ronald Locke. Bony was no exception when walking through Broome after dinner.

Ronald Locke was, in 1940, the head steward in an exclusive club. Although only twenty-six years of age, he was remarkable for his charm of manner and perfectibility as a gentleman's gentleman. At his trial, witness after witness testified to his excellent character. He was tried and convicted and sentenced to death for strangling a girl of eighteen because, to use his words, "She nagged at me to marry her before the baby was born." It so happened that a few months before this trial the Executive Council in another State had commuted a death sentence to life imprisonment because "the murderer had a low intelligence." That produced severe criticism by the press, but it was much more severe when the Executive Council of the State in which Locke committed his crime reduced the death sentence to ten years' imprisonment . . . "because of his previous good character." To make matters worse, Locke was released on probation after serving only half his commuted sentence . . . and promptly disappeared. In an editorial of a metropolitan newspaper, quoted in every *Police Gazette* all over Australia, it was stated: "Justice is mocked when, following a fair trial conducted by a learned judge before a jury of intelligent men who find the accused guilty, politicians commute the sentence because the murderer has a low intelligence or had, previous to his crime, a clean record. Are murderers to be hanged only if they have high intelligence or have been previously convicted for stealing apples from an orchard?"

Bony's interest in a murderer swiftly waned once he had finalised his investigation of the crime, but even he had been exasperated by the interference of vote-catching politicians with the course of justice. His sympathies were ever with the victim, and the victim's dependents, and now that he had this Ronald Locke in reach, he was in no haste to have him brought in and charged with breach of parole. Locke couldn't get away, not far, in this Northwest so pitiless toward the fugitive.

It was natural for both Walters and Sawtell to jump to the belief that Locke had killed Mrs. Cotton and Mrs. Eltham, but this youngish man of only thirty-two did not fill the frame into which Bony was building, with his bits and pieces, the murderer he sought. The barman at Dampier's Hotel would not, however, be ignored.

Bony was unconscious of whither his legs were taking him, and he was unconscious of the resplendent car which glided to a halt beside him, until the vibrant voice of Mrs. Sayers came like a soft blow:

"Hello, Mr. Knapp! What's she like?"

"Oh! Good evening, Mrs. Sayers. To what lady do you refer?"

Mrs. Sayers was seated beyond the lowered rear window, her eyes mischievous, her hair not quite as auburn as on Activities Day. Behind the wheel lounged a man uniformed with distinct nautical flavour. He was chewing hard and looking straight ahead, and his lean and weathered face was as crinkly as a prune.

"The lady you were dreaming about, of course." Mrs. Sayers giggled. "But I won't pry. When are you coming to tea? I'm dying to find out what's behind those big blue eyes."

Bony chuckled.

"You remind me of Red Ridinghood," he said. "I would be happy to call tomorrow afternoon, if convenient."

"Do. About three. Bring Esther with you. I want to make up for abusing her husband for not catching the murderer. Nice old stick, but I like 'em pliable."

"You will find me pliable, I think. Like the elm, I bow to every storm."

92

"Was I . . ." Mrs. Sayers again giggled. "Was I a storm that afternoon in the police office?"

"Perhaps a little one . . . in a teacup. Harry Walters has been greatly worried lately, and after all, he is not a common detective."

"No, of course he isn't. Well, bring Esther tomorrow, and I'll make it up. Good-bye!"

Bony stood back and, being hatless, bowed. He watched the car glide along the road without a pang of envy.

Recalled now to the business in hand, to make himself *au fait* with the layout of Broome, he continued on his way, passing the gate through which Mrs. Sayers' car had disappeared. The house was particularly spacious. Set well back from the road, it was almost surrounded by wide lawns on which, each side of the house, grew a huge palm tree. Beyond the right-hand palm could be seen a clothesline.

Bony passed on to enter Chinatown by a different route and came to the Seahorse Hotel which, were it not for the iron shacks across the street, would have looked out over the entrance of Dampier's Creek to Roebuck Bay. On a seat at the edge of this sidewalk sat Mr. Dickenson, the old man appearing to be asleep. Ignoring him, Bony passed up the hotel veranda steps, and on the veranda was accosted by a man whose accent betrayed his northern European origin.

"Have a leetle drink, sir? Me and the flies don't agree."

"One with you and one with me," Bony dictated, and they entered the empty bar. To the left was a lounge furnished with tables and chairs, and there several Asians were entertaining their lady friends.

"Vot you have?" asked the man who couldn't drink with the flies.

"Beer, please." The drinks came up.

"You yust visitor here, eh?"

"Yes. Peculiar place, Broome. What's wrong with it?"

"Vong mit it? It's all vong. No boats. No men. No shell . . . only leetle. Look!" Bony was urged to look out through the doorway. "Millions of dollars . . . down in the sea . . .

and no boats, only few, to peek up dose dollars. One time plenty boats, plenty divers . . . Jap divers. Now no Jap divers. Now only few southern Asians, and some of dose now go back to their countries because Government don't like 'em. The Government say no dollars. Short of dollars. No dollars—no petrol. No dollars—no houses. Millions of dollars out dere . . . you know Kalgoorlie? I vork in Kalgoorlie gold mines. More dollars in sea dan in all Kalgoorlie gold mines."

"Well, then, what's wrong with the people?" Bony pressed, being uninterested in economics or politics. The lean and sun-burned man chuckled ironically.

"Der people! Look you, the price of shell today ees five 'un-dred and fifty pounds a ton. Before the var a hundred pounds a ton. Der people here don't vant more boats, more men, more divers. No nous. No, vot you say? No brain. Dey think if too much shell brought in, der market go bung. You go into luna-tic place and ask vot's vong with them. Same thing."

With difficulty, Bony left the Seahorse Hotel. On the side-walk, he pretended to trip, looked down at his shoes, and crossed to the seat, to which he raised a foot to tie the lace.

"Flinn inside?" he asked softly.

"Went through to his room a half hour ago," murmured Mr. Dickenson without moving. "He took lunch at the Port Cuvier, and afternoon tea with Mrs. Sayers. Left when Mrs. Sayers went out in her car."

"Thank you, Mr. Dickenson. By just keeping a general eye on him, we'll finally get his background."

Bony walked along the street running parallel with the creek, passing sheds and tiny houses seemingly full of coloured women and children. He took a turn left and came to the gen-eral store owned by Mrs. Sayers. The light of the westering sun tinted with gold the ugly iron buildings, and beyond the marsh skirting the creek the white gulls circled. Seated in his car parked outside the store was Johnno.

"Good day!" he shouted long before Bony could halt at the car window. "You take a walk, eh? How you like Broome?"

"Reasonably well," conceded Bony. "Doesn't anyone ever go out fishing?"

94

"Fishing! You want to go fishing?" With flashing teeth and sparkling eyes, Johnno expressed his delight and amazement that anyone like Bony would want to go fishing. "All right! You tell me you like to go tomorrow, the day after, and we go. I have nice friend with motorboat. We always arrive, but sometime the fish they are sleepy. Never mind. We have sleep too."

"I'll remember that," promised Bony. "Where are all the pearl buyers?"

Johnno almost choked with laughter.

"Pearls all finish," he managed to get out, and, having regained breath, he went on with his usual volubility: "One time plenty pearls. One time plenty divers. One time this place full up with people: Javanese, Malayans, Japanese. All plenty money." Shoulders and dark arms worked overtime within the confines of the car. "Gamble all night. Drink up all night. Eat up and drink up. Pearls, sometimes. Now, no pearls. Maybe one, maybe two in season."

"Then the pearl dealers don't do any business now?"

"No pearl dealers. All gone . . . back home."

"Isn't Mr. Flinn a pearl dealer?"

Johnno made a face and shrugged . . . Bony shied off Mr. Flinn.

"Well, I'll be getting along, Johnno. I'll let you know about the fishing, eh?"

"You tell me, and I tell my friend, yes," assented Johnno, and Bony passed on from the car to enter the store, which was about to close. He had gained the veranda when through the doorway came Mr. Rose and Mr. Percival.

"Remind me, Percival, that we contact Leggit on Wednesday morning about that special order," Mr. Rose was saying when he saw Bony. Both men were dressed in white drill and wore sun helmets and canvas shoes. Mr. Rose regarded Bony with a frown, but it vanished when Bony greeted him.

"You really have the advantage of me," Mr. Rose said, genuinely embarrassed. "You know, I'm such a fool. Where did we meet?"

95

"This is Mr. Knapp," interposed Mr. Percival. "Mr. Knapp came to our Activities Day with Mrs. Walters."

"Ah! Of course, yes. I must be growing old." Mr. Rose smiled broadly. "We are so apt to do that. Are you enjoying your stay in Broome, Mr. Knapp?"

"Very much so," Bony replied. "It has the atmosphere of the Orient, don't you think? I hope to remain another week."

"Splendid! We would be pleased to see you at the school one afternoon, wouldn't we, Percival. About half-past four. Take you around and we'll plead with the matron to give us tea. By the way, Percival, remind me that I reply to Inspector Walters' complaint about the 'jists' and 'gunners.'"

Mr. Percival, large and florid, gave no indication that he heard this request. His face was expressionless, but his eyes were very much alive as he watched Bony's reactions to Mr. Rose. Bony expressed his delight with the invitation to the school and, following the adieus, went on into the store, to stand behind a mound of dress lengths and watch the departure of the two masters in Johnno's service car.

An odd pair, he thought. The headmaster serenely omnipotent; the senior house master silent and watchful. Bony made his purchases and was the last customer to be let out of the store for the day.

The Police Station office was closed too, and he returned to find Walters reading a newspaper in the kitchen. On his entry the inspector put down his paper and eyed Bony sternly. Bony proceeded to roll a cigarette.

"I think we'll forget about the information from Brisbane," he said. "For a little while, anyway. It would be just too bad to pull that fellow in for evading conditions of his probation, send him back to the East, and let slip through our fingers the man who did murder those women."

"He strangled one woman," Walters said coldly. "He could have murdered the two here."

"Quite so, but we have no evidence against him . . . yet. I remember the trial quite clearly. There was no evidence that Locke collected women's nightgowns and destroyed their silken

96

underwear. I have another reason for keeping Locke in cold storage."

"How are you going to explain the delay in returning him to his State?"

"Explain!" Bony looked at Walters with pained eyes. "Explain to whom?"

"You damn well know who. The Department, of course."

"The Department! Oh, don't let that bother you. It will be my kettle of fish, as they used to say when my grandfather was alive. My dear man, if I bothered to make explanations to my superiors, why, I'd require the services of two stenographers to answer the 'please explains.' Hullo, Sawtell!"

Bony, noting the smallness of the sergeant's eyes and the tightness of his wide mouth, knew that the blow had fallen. Sawtell strode to the two men seated at the table, and from a side pocket drew a scrap of pink silk which he placed on the table. He began to speak as though giving evidence in court.

"I was passing along the laneway at the rear of Mrs. Overton's house, and I thought I saw something brightly coloured lying near the back door. I could see that the back door was closed. There was no smoke rising from the chimney. In view of the plan set out this afternoon concerning five women, I did not proceed to the back door from the rear lane, but passed on round the block till I came to the front of the premises. Near the front gate which was closed but not locked there is a small letter box. The morning delivery of mail was still in the box.

"I thought I had better investigate. I knocked at the front door and no one answered. It was locked. I then proceeded round the house to the back door, where on the ground I found this piece of torn silk. I knocked on the back door and received no answer. I tried the door and found it locked. Under the circumstances, I thought I'd better report before investigating further."

Bony turned over the relic of silk. It was about ten inches in length, and two inches at the narrow end, widening to three inches.

"I hope we're wrong," he said softly. "Let's go."

"What about Abie?" asked Sawtell.

"Leave him until we know more," Bony replied, his voice sharp and unusually authoritative.

They met Keith coming in from the street, and without halting, the inspector told him to tell his mother they would be late for dinner. Walking abreast, with the slighter figure of Bony in the centre, an observer would think he was being taken to jail, for the expression on the three faces was wooden and no man spoke. Other than a few children and two women, the street was empty.

Arriving at the front gate to Mrs. Overton's house, Bony felt satisfaction on seeing that the driveway was composed of cinders. There he saw many footprints, including those made by Sergeant Sawtell. There were the prints of a woman's shoes, those indented by a boy, the prints made by a man's naked feet, and those left by shoes size eight. The insides of the heels were worn, and there was a circular object adhering to the left sole.

The bungalow was smaller than average. Along the front the storm shutters were raised. The front of the veranda itself was enclosed by narrow painted battens making a small diamond pattern. The house either side this property could only barely be seen beyond the ornamental trees and the division fences of board.

"Front or back?" asked Walters.

"Back. No answer to our knocking, we break in."

A cinder path skirted the house, and Bony asked his companions to walk off it. The same tracks he had seen on the drive were on this path. He noted that there was no veranda along this side of the house, and therefore no shutters. At the rear the cinder path ended at a cemented area between the house and what appeared to be a combined woodshed and laundry. Beyond the cement, another path wound onward to disappear among scattered ti-tree bush.

Bony pounded on the kitchen door.

"Let me push it," urged Sawtell when no one responded.

"Wait."

Bony bent down and placed an ear to the keyhole. He was then sure that what he thought he heard was fact. Within the house was a peculiar noise, a sound not unlike water gurgling down the outlet of a bath. For ten seconds Bony listened. The noise continued, and there was strange rhythm in it.

"Have either of you a gun?" Bony asked.

Walters shook his head and Sawtell said he always relied on his hands. The sergeant stood before the door, raised a foot and shot it forward with such force that the door crashed inward and was almost torn off its hinges. It seemed that the three men entered at the same instant.

Bony jumped to a window and let up the spring blind. They were in an ordinary kitchen, off which was the bathroom. A passage ran through the centre of the house, and beyond the far end could be seen the battens enclosing the front veranda. The kitchen was small and tidy. On the floor lay a small Pomeranian dog, its flanks working, and from its mouth issuing the noise like water draining away from a bath. There was blood on the patterned linoleum beneath its jaw, and its eyes were partially closed.

Sawtell looked into the bathroom and followed the Inspector and Bony into the passage. Bony opened doors. The first two gave entry to small bedrooms. The left front-room door was open. It was the lounge. The door opposite was closed. Gripping the door handle only with the tips of forefinger and thumb, Bony opened the door and pushed it inward.

The interior was quite dark. Bony struck a match, and the tiny flame revealed a white bed. He edged round the doorpost and found the light switch, and with the corner of the matchbox pressed upon the small knob. There was no resultant light.

"The master switch," he directed, and heard one of the

policemen run onto the veranda. Waiting in the darkness, he flailed his mind for evidence of failure in himself, for having omitted something which should have been done and which might have prevented what he thought he had seen in the flickering light of his match.

The light blazed on, and behind Bony the inspector cried thinly:

"He got her! The swine!"

The room was made to appear smaller than it was by the furniture, of which there was too much. There was a three-quarter-size bed. The bedspread was rose pink, and it, with the blanket and top sheet, was folded back. Lying on the bed was a woman. Her body was naked. She was lying on her back, her legs straight, her arms close to her sides. The face and neck were in sharp contrast to the whiteness of the rest of the body, and the white pillow was equally as sharp in contrast with the woman's rather long black hair. She must have been in her late twenties, and quite good-looking.

That the woman was dead was obvious. Beside the bed was the woman's nightgown. Bony stooped for it. It was ripped from neck to hem, and with it he covered the body.

"In the wardrobe, Sawtell," Bony said whilst gazing upon the outline of the pathetic figure masked by cream-coloured silk. "No disorder in the room. The arrangement of the bed-clothes precisely the same. She must have been off the bed when he strangled her, or if he strangled her on the bed, then he removed the body to tidy the bedclothes. He is controlled by habits which are powerfully dominant when he's mentally normal . . . if he is now ever normal, which I much doubt. I see him as a man unable to tolerate untidiness. Have you found the bundle, Sawtell?"

"Yes," replied the sergeant. "In a far corner of the ward-robe."

"We won't examine it now. Bring a broom, please. This murderer could be anything except a sailor, a workman, or a bushman. He's neither an Asian nor an aborigine."

"He could be a club steward," cut in Inspector Walters.

"Yes, he could be. He could be a ship's steward, a gentleman's valet, or a senior noncommissioned soldier whose duty for years was the maintenance of camp cleanliness. That dying dog gets on my nerves."

"Looks as though the killer bashed it. What am I supposed to be doing?"

"There's nothing much you can do, Walters," Bony said decisively. "We can go through the place for fingerprints, but we won't find the prints of the murderer. I do know that he wears your size in shoes. I do know that his stride is twenty-one inches . . . the same as yours. I do know that he wears the heels of his shoes more rapidly on the inside than the outside . . . like you do. Further, I know that his weight is approximately your weight, and I have observed that you keep your desk meticulously tidy."

"Damnation! You going to frame me?" demanded Walters.

"I am going to frame this murderer if I have to track him ten times round the world. Ah, thanks, Sawtell. Both of you stand outside while I sweep the floor."

As they had done at Dampier's Hotel, the two men watched Bony sweep the entire floor of this room and saw the dust and debris gently swept onto a sheet of paper.

"There's no need for microscopic aid," he said, holding the paper that they might see what he had collected. "The man with psoriasis was here. You establish how he entered the house, Sawtell can get on with the photography."

Walters and the sergeant departed, obviously glad to break into action. Bony took the broom to the kitchen and swept that, the debris being added to his collection of specimens. In it he found no large piece of sloughed skin, but did see specks of what might be similar particles. On the floor here, as well as on the passage and bedroom floors, were the tracks of the man he had seen first on the front drive. The round object adhering to the left sole had left its imprint on the linoleum more plainly than the outline of the sole.

Nothing could be done for the unfortunate dog. It was unconscious, and every bone in its body seemed broken.

The day was departing with its usual haste in this latitude, and Bony hurried outside to examine the path running away to the rear gate. On this path he found the tracks of the man who had been inside the house. At one place only did he see the print of the naked feet, and that proved that the shoeless man had passed this way after the other. There were no children's footprints, and no prints of a woman's shoes. Here and there were the tracks of the little dog.

Bony came to the gate, a wicket gate in the wire fence. Beyond the fence was the usual laneway, and beyond that a wide paddock covered with patches of wire grass. There still remained sufficient light to enable Bony to see that the man who had been in the house had passed through the gateway and then crossed the lane and entered the paddock. The barefooted man had done the same. It was clear he had followed the other.

Bony returned to the house where, in the kitchen, Sawtell said that the murderer had forced the scullery window to gain entry and had left by the kitchen door, taking the key with him. Walters arrived from the front, and mentioned the doctor in a manner indicating recognition of Bony's authority in this case.

"Will you return to the office, Sawtell, and ring the doctor. Return at once with the printing gear. Leave by the front door and return that way. Leave Abie till the morning. The light's gone now."

Sawtell left, and Inspector Walters bent over the dog.

"Finished, I think," he said savagely.

"I'm afraid so," agreed Bony. "The doctor will put it to sleep, I expect. Must have been done last night sometime . . . about eighteen or twenty hours ago. Probably the dog barked when the killer climbed in through the window, and he picked it up and smashed it on the floor. The animal can't weigh more than five pounds."

They sat down, Bony to roll a cigarette and Walters to light a pipe.

"This is hell," remarked the inspector. "When is it going to end? I wonder. More work, more worry, more interference from Perth. The newspapers all over Australia will be screaming for results. The entire C.I.B. will be sent up here."

"In the morning, Walters, you have Richard Blake, otherwise Ronald Locke, arrested."

"Ah!" There was grim satisfaction behind that "Ah!"

"I know now that Locke did not murder Mrs. Overton," Bony went on. "However, I don't intend that the entire C.I.B. or any section of it shall be sent up here to Broome. This is not the place, and such is the psychology behind these murders that teamwork on a large scale would be a definite hindrance. We three, yourself and Sawtell and me, with Clifford to assist, form an efficient team.

"Our immediate objective must be to lull the murderer into thinking he has again got away with it. We will arrest Locke on the charge of breach of his parole. There is no need to put him into court here. Clifford, or another of your constables from outside, can take him down to Perth by air, and he can be held there for several weeks before being sent back to his State. Meanwhile, I'll advise the C.I.B. to hold Locke and set out my reasons.

"We will not state to the local press representative, or anyone else, the legal charge preferred against Locke, but we will say that Locke is the Ronald Locke who strangled a girl back in 1940. The people here in Broome and throughout Australia will jump to the same conclusion about Locke that you and Sawtell did. They will condemn Locke for the murder of these three women . . . everyone save the murderer. Results! The Broome people will not panic, we shall not be overwhelmed with abuse, and Locke will receive no more than his just deserts. I shall have an extension of time in which to finalise this case, and our murderer will be so elated that he won't be able to wait for another month and will strike again before the next moon rules the midnight sky. And when he does strike again, I shall be waiting for him."

Inspector Walters regarded Bony beneath glowering brows.

"If you're not waiting for him, I shall be finished," he said softly and deliberately.

"And I . . ." Bony looked steadily at Walters. "And I will be more than that. I shall have failed for the first time in my career, and for the last time. My career will be ended, for my pride will have been destroyed. If I fail in this case, the pride which drove me on and up to the summits of many Everests of achievement will vanish, and all the influences so powerfully and continuously exerted on me by my maternal ancestors will inevitably draw me back to the bush, to become, as so many others like me, a nomad, a pariah."

For a short space they sat in silence broken only by the laboured breathing of the dog. Inspector Walters, Police Administrator of one tenth of the continent of Australia, had need to be no mean psychologist. He understood exactly where this remarkable man stood, the courage he had from youth to defeat all those terrific obstacles, and the pit always before his feet. He regretted having spoken of his own career. If the murderer successfully struck again, Henry Walters could say farewell to promotion, might even be relegated to a less important post. That would be little, indeed, to what this strangely named half-caste would receive for failure to locate the man who killed the widows of Broome.

"Sorry I spoke like that," he said gruffly. "It's a good move, letting everyone think we have arrested Locke for these murders. You're the boss. Use us up. Sawtell and I will be liking it."

In the eastern sky three horizontal bars of high-level haze were tinted and polished like the great oyster shell brought to Broome, and the morning star audaciously tried to bedazzle the ancient and emaciated moon. When the cloud bars were stained gold by the dawning, Bony arrived at the end of the laneway passing the rear of Mrs. Overton's house and sat down to await the day.

The night fought valiantly with the day, with inevitable result, and, the battle decided, Bony arose, took up his tin of bait and fishlines and, instead of following the laneway, climbed through the fence and went looking for mushrooms. Inside the grass paddock opposite Mrs. Overton's back gate he came to a wide ribbon of blown sand on which, as he had hoped, were the footprints of the man wearing a size-eight shoe with a circular object adhering to the left sole, and the print of the man without foot covering.

Beneath the fishlines, Bony produced a bottle of water, plaster of paris, a fruit tin, and a small trowel, and within six minutes had taken a cast of each man's footprints. With these concealed beneath the fishing gear, he proceeded parallel with the lane until he reached its far intersection, intending to skirt the building block and so reach Mrs. Overton's house by the front gate.

He was on his way, well pleased with the "mushrooms" he had gathered and confident that he had not been observed. He had climbed through the fence at the far end of the paddock when he met Mr. Dickenson.

"You are out early this morning," stated the old man. Mr. Dickenson glanced at Bony's tin and advised fishing from a point about a hundred yards down the creek from an old lugger. Bony gravely thanked him, and asked why he was out so early.

"I can manage with about four hours of sleep," explained Mr. Dickenson, adding: "When I'm in normal health and my heart is not troubling me. After seeing our friend retiring to bed last night, I felt that I had had a busy day and deserved relaxation. I felt the need of more of the relaxation this morning, but I recalled our little agreement. Flinn won't appear until around ten o'clock."

"What time last night did you cease to keep watch on Flinn?"

"What time? When the Seahorse closed at eleven. Flinn was then on the front veranda. He was tight."

"Pardon my pertinacity. How did you manage to observe Flinn retiring to bed?"

"I went round to the rear yard and I saw him in his room undressing."

"Thank you. Can you tell me to what degree he was intoxicated?"

"About as drunk as you were that night we returned from Dampier's Hotel."

The smile born on Bony's face was killed by reproof.

"Then Flinn couldn't have been tight. I wasn't."

"Flinn was tight. I watched him drinking whisky all the evening. That was an achievement of which I am not a little proud this morning. Flinn was quite able to undress himself. If you require a precise estimate of his condition, then he was twice as tight as you were."

"I was not tight. Inspector Walters will bear me out. Have you heard of the latest murder?"

"No. Who was the victim?"

"A Mrs. Overton."

"Indeed! A nice woman. Strangled?"

Bony nodded and Mr. Dickenson sadly shook his head. They might have been discussing juvenile delinquency. The old man asked if anyone had been arrested for this latest crime, and Bony told him that Clifford had left for Dampier's Hotel to bring in Richard Blake for questioning.

"That young fellow might be the guilty party," Mr. Dickenson conceded, thoughtfully gazing at Bony's fishing gear. "Is it known when Mrs. Overton was murdered?"

"The night before last. The murderer also almost succeeded in killing her little dog. It had to be destroyed."

"A pity. It was an affectionate little animal but not, I imagine, anything of a watchdog. Yes, it could have been young Blake. He was in town late the evening before last, and I remember that he was in town that night Mrs. Eltham was murdered. Did you ever see Mrs. Overton alive?"

"No."

"Doubtless you have seen her body. She would in life have been physically strong. Blake is not a large man, or powerful. Still . . ."

"You doubt that it was Blake?"

"I would require clear proof before I would believe it."

"It was not Blake, you think, whom you saw that night leaving Mrs. Eltham's house?"

"That is what I believe."

"Does your opinion alter when I tell you that Richard Blake is Ronald Locke, the Sydney murderer? You may remember the case."

"I remember the case. It does not alter my opinion. Do we now relinquish our interest in Mr. Flinn?"

"No. We maintain our interest in Mr. Flinn . . . you and I. I'm so glad you have assented to assist me. As you do, I don't think Blake is the man we want. However, his arrest will allay fear in the people of Broome, and I would be so pleased did you not make public your opinion just expressed, and further that you do broadcast the news item that Blake has been arrested for the murder of Mrs. Overton."

Mr. Dickenson stroked his Vandyke beard and permitted a twinkle to enter his eyes.

"It was, I think, Shakespeare who wrote: 'O, what may man within him hide, though angel on the outward side!' My friend, I like subtlety. Provided that he be not subjected to too much mental——"

"Between ourselves, Locke won't be charged with murder," Bony cut in. "But I want everyone, including this Broome murderer, to believe that he has been. You will understand why?"

"Perfectly. Further slight inconvenience for Locke will not come amiss. I will continue to take an interest in Flinn, and should you think I could be of assistance in other directions, call on me."

"It's very good of you," Bony said warmly.

"It's good of you, sir."

They parted, and Bony saw Mr. Dickenson enter the laneway which would take him past the rear of Mrs. Overton's house. Two minutes later he entered the house from the front, finding Sawtell in the kitchen.

"Coo! What you got there? Fishing lines?" asked the sergeant.

"Yes. I fish for men. An hour ago the inspector sent Clifford out for Locke. Would you like to dash off home for breakfast?"

"You must have seen blazing hunger in my eyes. Won't be long."

"Oh, don't hurry. I'll spend the time in meditation. Bring Abie back with you. Follow routine. What tracks he indicates, make a cast. They might be useful later on."

The sergeant having left, Bony wandered through the house. The doctor had reported that Mrs. Overton had been strangled by a man standing behind her, and such were the injuries that, in his opinion, it was the same man who had killed Mrs. Eltham and Mrs. Cotton. The body had been removed to the morgue by the undertaker and his Malay assistant, and the inquest would be held this day . . . to be adjourned as those previous inquests had been.

A plane for Perth was due to leave at nine, and Walters would now be preparing his reports for Headquarters to accompany Bony's personal letter to the Chief of the C.I.B.

Another plane was expected to leave about six in the evening, and Bony urged that Clifford take his prisoner down to Perth in that. It would leave them a man short in the team, but old Dickenson could step into the breach.

The time he was alone he spent going through the dead woman's papers. He read the letters found in the postbox. There were no locked drawers, and no safes, so that he had access to everything. He learned that Mrs. Overton was interested in church missionary work, and that she had contributed to missionary literature. There was a man in Melbourne who wanted to marry her and it appeared that her dead husband's mother approved. A legal firm in Perth managed her financial affairs. Nothing of importance, but several matters of interest. Two of Mrs. Overton's correspondents mentioned Mrs. Sayers, who, it appeared, was much admired by Mrs. Overton, and one writer referred to Mrs. Overton's attachment to the boys at Cave Hill College and her work at the Methodist Sunday school.

The dead woman's background was excellent. Bony studied a photograph of her . . . a Junoesque type of woman. She had lived a virtuous life in Broome, for that was on record, and there was nothing among her papers or within her home even to hint of anything to the contrary. To use current phraseology: why pick on her? That was the puzzler. Why pick on Mrs. Cotton? Excepting in her business, Mrs. Cotton had not been particularly interested in men. Mrs. Eltham was the kind of woman who does manage to get herself murdered. Where was the common denominator uniting these three women in the mind of a murderer? The victims of Jack the Ripper were all of one class. Landrau chose his victims among women having property. With those two series of murders there was a common denominator.

Hearing Sawtell's voice at the front, he gathered the letters and papers and thrust them into a drawer, and was standing on the cemented area between the rear of the house and an open-fronted woodshed when Sawtell appeared with Abie.

The sergeant joined Bony. The tracker, wearing his "uniform" of military greatcoat, stockman's felt hat, and military boots, remained just off the path running past the house to the cemented area.

"This feller bin alonga street," Abie said, pointing to the path. "He bin walk here," and he pointed to the cement.

"Take him into the house," Bony instructed, and Sawtell beckoned the tracker to the kitchen door and told him to: "Track 'em alonga house floor, Abie."

Abie having entered, the sergeant said softly:

"Won't find much. Too many of us tramping through the place."

"You never know," murmured Bony. "These fellows can do extraordinary things. Hop in and put on the light. He might pinch the settee or something."

Sawtell grunted and went inside. Bony stood at the edge of the cemented area and regarded the clothesline and wondered if Mrs. Overton, as those others, had lost a nightgown. He was hoping she had, for on that fact would rest the certainty that the murderer would steal a fourth nightgown before attempting his fourth murder.

The two men emerged from the house, and Abie said, again pointing to the path:

"That feller him bin in house. You bin in house. Mister Knapp, him bin in house. Mister Inspector Walters, him bin in house too. Doctor bin in . . ."

"Old Bill, the mortician, and Ally, his offsider, they bin in house," interrupted Sergeant Sawtell. "All right, Abie. You findum which way that feller go from here."

Exhibiting importance in every movement, Abie proceeded along the path to the back gate, his pace a jog trot, the upper portion of his thickset body angled forward, presenting a picture having much similarity with that of a hound held in leash. On reaching the gate, the two men were immediately behind him. Turning to them, the aborigine laughed. There was nothing to produce merriment: it was his reaction to his fancied position of importance in the eyes of big-feller policeman boss.

"That white feller who bin come in other gate and run-about house, he come along this gate. Him bin go . . ." White-feller words failed him, and he waved a hand towards the grass paddock. "Him bin go out there. P'haps him bin know-em Abie see which way, eh?"

"P'haps, Abie," agreed Sawtell. "What about other feller, eh? Other feller bin no wear-um boots, eh?"

Abie was clearly startled. He laughed again and ran back beside the path to the low scrub. He was tremendously excited, but Bony was not deceived. Bony was evincing interest in the late Mrs. Overton's distant clothesline when he heard Abie say:

"I no know-em that feller."

"You never seen him tracks before?" demanded Sawtell.

"I no know-em." Abie was decidedly dejected by the admission of failure. "Him bin China-feller, p'haps. P'haps him bin blackfeller camp in Chinatown."

"All right, Abie," Sawtell said cheerfully. "You bin good tracker all right. You show-um good track that feller come along here and go in house, eh?"

Carrying his tin of fishing lines, Bony sauntered away towards the Police Station. At the end of the lane, he glanced back to find that the sergeant had disappeared, probably to secure the house. Abie was rolling a cigarette, his felt hat slightly tilted to one side like Sergeant Sawtell's hat.

Half an hour later Sawtell entered the Police Station office. The local press correspondent had just left in a great hurry for the radio station. In one of the cells off the compound was lodged Ronald Locke.

"Let me see your casts, please," Bony requested, and Sawtell produced them. "I'll take a quick look at the impressions. Must memorise them."

Walters called the sergeant to his desk, and Bony carried the casts out to the damp earth about a rose tree. He pressed the casts to the ground and stood back to see them. The print of the naked foot he would, of course, never forget and would recognise again. The other, the shoeprint, caused him to frown. It was not the print of the shoe which was worn down on the inner side of the heel, although it was the same size. It did happen to be a left print, but there was no circular indentation showing that to the sole of the shoe some object had been adhering. It was, in fact, an excellent print of Mr. Dickenson's left shoe.

Chapter Fifteen: ABIE'S DEFECTION

Bony put the casts on Sawtell's desk.

"Where's Abie?" he asked.

"Dunno! Out in the yard, I suppose. You want him?"

"No." Bony remained standing. "When you made those casts, you are sure that you took them from the prints pointed out by the tracker?"

"Positive. I got Abie to run a line round them with his finger."

Bony turned away and sauntered through to the kitchen.

"You must be starving," Mrs. Walters remarked, and Bony, wrenching his mind from Abie, smiled and said that he supposed he was. She busied herself preparing his breakfast, and he crossed to the doorway and stood looking out over the compound. Abie wasn't in sight. Constable Clifford was locking the door of a cell, under an arm a pair of shoes. With a motion of his head, Bony invited the constable to join him.

"Are those Locke's shoes?" he asked, and was told they were, and that Sawtell wished to compare an imprint from them with the casts he had made under Abie's directions. "Let me see them."

Bony examined them. They were size seven. Those shoes had not made the impressions of Sawtell's casts, nor had they made the impressions from which Bony had made his casts. The casts were of a shoe size eight. Nevertheless, a man having a shoe size seven could wear a shoe size eight in which to conduct his murders.

"Thank you, Clifford. Tell the Inspector that when convenient I'd like to have a word with you here."

Clifford departed for the office and Bony sat down to breakfast. He said nothing to Mrs. Walters as she served him, and she could see that he ate automatically. She was washing the dishes when he rose from the table and carried the china to the washing bench. Picking up a drying cloth, he proceeded to dry the dishes as she washed them.

"What do you know about Mrs. Overton, her friends, her relations?" he asked.

"Not much, Bony. No one here knew her husband; he died before she came to Broome. She was making a trip round Australia and decided to live here permanently. I think there was a man in her life somewhere."

"Yes, he lives in Melbourne. His name is Bryant. You've never met him here?"

Mrs. Walters shook her head and hoped that her guest would not drop her favourite china toast rack.

"Mrs. Overton was well liked in Broome," she said. "Quite a friend of Mrs. Sayers. Worked hard with the Methodist church and their Sunday school and among the boys at the college. The young people all liked her. She had a way with children round about twelve and thirteen."

"Did she entertain much?"

"Not a great deal. She didn't drink, but she never outwardly disapproved of people who do. Although she never served liquor in her own house, she often attended parties where drinks were laid on."

"The people she invited to her house, would be of the elite of Broome, I suppose?"

"Oh yes."

"Is Arthur Flinn among the elite?"

"Yes," Mrs. Walters frowned. "I was at one of Mrs. Overton's afternoon teas when he appeared. I don't think he was quite welcome. Just an impression, you know. I remember thinking that his effect on me was probably the same with Mrs. Overton. There are some men, Bony, who seem to want always to paw a woman. You know the type, perhaps."

"Yes. Go on, please."

Mrs. Walters laughed mirthlessly.

"Women are peculiar," she averred. "They can't stand some men even touching them, and they seem to like it from other men. One afternoon when the radio was playing a dance tune, Sergeant Sawtell was in here and he grabbed me in his arms and made me dance. Had it been Arthur Flinn, I'd have screamed."

"Thank you. Let's move away from the unpleasant Flinn. Now, can you tell me if Mrs. Overton employed domestic help?"

"I'm not sure about that. I'm inclined to think not."

"Well, then, did she have a woman in to do her washing?"

"I'm not sure about that, either. Mrs. Sayers would know."

Bony was placing the dried dishes in the correct place in the kitchen cabinet when Clifford returned from the office.

"Cup of tea?" asked Bony, swinging round from the cabinet. The constable betrayed his astonishment and looked at Mrs. Walters, who said:

"Of course he'll have a cup of tea. Anyone will have a cup of tea here at any time."

Clifford appeared uneasy as Bony brought the cup and saucer and the milk from the safe. Being waited on by an inspector was a new experience.

"Was the arrest effected without incident?" Bony asked.

"Yes. I got hold of Locke and told him he was wanted, and that he'd better not raise any argument about it. Black Mark wanted to know why I was taking him . . . when I had him in the jeep. They didn't know about Mrs. Overton at Dampier's Hotel."

"What was Locke's reaction?"

"He was quiet enough. Said it would catch up with him sometime."

"Meaning?"

The grey eyes in Clifford's tanned face flickered.

"I don't know. He could have referred to the breach of parole or to these murders. Full of conceit, and, I'd say, a born liar."

"No one interrogated him yet?"

"No."

"Where's the tracker?"

"In his camp in the stables, I think."

"Thanks, Clifford. When you go back to the office, mention to the sergeant that I'd like to be present when he does interrogate the prisoner."

Bony left for the compound, and in the sunlight he took time to roll a cigarette. The stables then were to his right, the building erected long years before the coming of motor transport to the Northwest. On the left were the nine cells. They could be counted easily enough. Each door was an iron grill from floor to roof.

Without haste or hint of purpose, Bony strolled to the stables. There was a chaff room stacked with fodder, a saddlery room containing polished harness, and seven horse stalls. The stalls were vacant. Skirting the stalls, Bony came to a loose box, and within the loose box the tracker lay asleep on old blankets laid out on straw. Abie had removed his greatcoat and military boots.

Beyond the loose box was a doorway in this end of the stables, and quietly Bony stepped past the sleeping aborigine and went out. He found a tap, and a tin dish on a wooden case, and about the case the water had moistened the ground, and the ground revealed the prints of Abie's naked feet. They were identical with those on the paths skirting Mrs. Overton's house. It was one of the strangest twists in an investigation Bony had ever encountered.

Bony went on to sit in the shade cast by the tree beneath which he had first seen Abie with a petrol-saturated rag about his head. What was that ebony-skinned gentleman up to? He had been following the man wearing the size-eight shoes to the left sole of which was attached that circular object, the man who had, without the smallest doubt, entered Mrs. Overton's house and strangled her. Proudly wearing boots all day, it seemed that Abie preferred to walk in naked feet by night.

That Abie had the ambition to become an aboriginal Holmes was a thought instantly to be discarded as fantastic. Whatever purpose Abie had had in trailing a murderer, it was much stronger than the ambition to become a great detective, because the time of the act was opposed to his racial instincts. Assessing Abie's standing in relation to white civilisation, Bony placed him much nearer the wild blacks than those who have become famous in pulpit and art. The motive driving Abie out into the dark night must have been powerful, when instinctively he would cling to the protection of his camp. The danger from evil spirits to blackfellows who wander from the campfires at night had been instilled in Abie with his mother's milk.

More extraordinary was Abie's deliberate deceit when instead of pointing out the tracks left by the man who had murdered Mrs. Overton, he had drawn a mark round the track made by Mr. Dickenson, who had not walked through the laneway before parting with Bony in broad daylight. Abie would bear watching.

Sawtell and the constable appeared in the compound, and Bony went to meet them.

"Going to have a word or two with Locke," announced the sergeant.

"All right. I'll go with you," Bony said.

When at the cell door, they could see the prisoner seated on the board bed. Clifford unlocked the door, and they passed in, the constable remaining outside. Sawtell gave the man his shoes. Locke thanked him, easily and without betraying emotion.

"I suppose you know why you're here?" asked Sawtell.

"Oh yes," replied Locke, without looking up from lacing the shoes.

"What were you doing in town the night before last?" Bony questioned.

Having laced the shoes, Locke stood up. He was clean and neat. His eyes were light grey and revealed nothing. Goodlooking, the cleft chin and the sensuous mouth would certainly appeal to undiscerning women. Coolly, he asked Bony:

"What have you to do with me?"

"That'll be all on that line, Locke," snapped Sawtell roughly.

"All right! I was in town on the spree. What about it?"

"What were you doing in town on the night that Mrs. Eltham was murdered?" was Bony's next question.

The light grey eyes blinked back the flash of fear.

"I wasn't in town that night."

"But you were, Locke," Bony insisted. "What did you do that night?"

"You're not trying to frame me for that murder, are you?"

"What an idea!" exclaimed Bony, and Locke shouted angrily:

"Then what's behind these questions? I didn't throttle those women. All I did was to clear out of New South Wales instead of reporting every week."

"Where were you on the night Mrs. Cotton was murdered?"

"In the bar. I was in the bar all evening drinking with the mob. The sergeant knows that. He checked up on me like on all the others."

There was indignation on the man's face and in his voice, and Bony was not happy about it. Abie had crossed the compound and was standing just beyond Constable Clifford.

"On the night before last, you were in town," Bony said loudly. "Sometime during the night before last a Mrs. Overton was strangled."

The small, effeminate mouth trembled. There was horror in the light grey eyes, horror born of realisation that having once escaped the hangman in New South Wales, there would be no escaping the hangman in Western Australia. No one in Australia, no one at all, would ever believe that he who had strangled a girl in Sydney had not strangled three women in northern West Australia.

"I didn't do it," he said, his voice a whisper. Then, in startling contradistinction, he shouted: "I didn't do it! I didn't do it!"

"Pipe down," ordered Sawtell. "You'll be treated fairly. We'll be taking you to Perth this evening on the plane."

Bony left the cell, Clifford opening the door. Abie's eyes were wide, and Bony tried to look into them and failed. The sergeant came out and, seeing the tracker, roughly asked him what the hell he was doing there and to clear off and bring in a horse named Nancy and get on with his job of breaking her in. The aborigine shuffled away in his heavy boots, and Bony said to Clifford:

"See that Locke has cigarettes."

He felt that he had made slight amends to the prisoner, who had not been charged with murder and yet was sure he would be. A man in white drill trousers and white sports shirt appeared.

"Anything fresh, Sergeant?" he asked Sawtell.

"No, only that the prisoner will be taken down to Perth on tonight's plane."

"Ah! Who'll be his escort?"

"Clifford, I expect."

"Thanks. My paper will appreciate that. Everything clinched, I suppose, about these murders?"

"What are you talking about?" demanded Sawtell.

"You know." The stranger to Bony became persuasive. "Give us a break."

The sergeant regarded the correspondent sternly. He said with significant deliberateness:

"Officially, I don't know anything. We're sending Locke to Perth for holding on the charge of breaking the terms of his parole."

The correspondent was satisfied.

"Yes . . . ah yes. Yes, I understand," he said, and believed that he did. Twenty minutes later the radio was flashing the news to Perth that a man had been arrested in connection with the Broome murders, and thirty minutes later Bony sat down with Mr. Dickenson on the bench in front of the Port Cuvier Hotel.

"Mr. Flinn inside?" he enquired.

"Went in an hour ago," replied the old man.

"How are you standing up to it?"

"Standing up to it? Good! Gives me something to do."

"I'd like to switch you to a more important assignment,"

Bony said. "They've brought in Locke, and he'll be taken down to Perth tonight. The newspaper correspondent thinks that Locke is the man wanted for these murders. Now, Mr. Dickenson, I'm more in need of your co-operation than ever. I cannot be everywhere at the same time."

"Well, whatever I can do . . ."

"I appreciate your help, Mr. Dickenson." Bony broke off to light a cigarette. The old man gazed across the street at the busy hotel, and his expression revealed the price he was paying to assist Bony. Inherited instincts and the early influence of the class of society from which he had fallen were still with him.

"I think we'll let up on Flinn for the time being," Bony went on. "Having to send Clifford to Perth with Locke will make us still more shorthanded. I'd like you to undertake another assignment this evening, an all-night one."

The old man removed his gaze from the drinkers on the hotel veranda to regard his bench companion.

"I can see quite well in the dark," he said. "I have seen much of Broome life after dark."

"Much, I think, which I might find of value. Could we meet, say at seven o'clock, this evening? Outside the Post Office?"

"That would be convenient to me."

"Well, then, it might be as well to get a little sleep this afternoon." Bony stood up, and Mr. Dickenson said:

"I'll do that. Do you think it permissible to take a little relaxation before I turn in?"

Bony did not betray his doubt of Mr. Dickenson's will power to withstand much longer the siren voice of Mr. Barleycorn. However, he acted with wisdom.

"I do think it permissible. We have both earned a couple of sustainers."

Chapter Sixteen: FORCES ORGANISED

The Police Station office was closed. Walters had gone off to receive Dr. Mitchell's post-mortem report and to attend the funeral of Mrs. Overton. He expected a large number of people to be at the graveside. Sawtell, having spent the morning in the murdered woman's house testing for fingerprints, was at his own ill-equipped laboratory at home, and Clifford was making enquiries concerning Mrs. Overton's domestic arrangements.

Before Bony was a list of five names headed "The Widows of Broome." An ink line ran through the name of Mrs. Overton, and the ink line appeared to magnify the remaining four names—Sayers, Clayton, Watson, and Abercrombie. With Clifford's departure for Perth and Constable Pedersen still away in the bush, the police strength in Broome this coming night would be only two.

The horns of dilemma continued to prod Bony and make him extremely uncomfortable. The build-up of the murderer was so tenuous, so vague, that it was difficult to see his picture. The psoriasis clue was indefinite, because even had Dr. Mitchell been ordered to inspect every man and woman in Broome it would achieve only the identity of every sufferer and not indicate the one among them who strangled women in their homes. First establish the murderer, then the sloughed skin found in the homes of two of his victims would be added proof of his guilt. The four women must be guarded every night henceforth, but if the murderer discovered the precautions taken he would not walk into any parlour.

However, there were four widows, and there must be four guards: Walters and the sergeant, himself and Old Dickenson. He could hope for time and luck, and he would certainly need both. Meanwhile, he had letters to write for Perth, and was making a request to the superintendent in charge of the C.I.B. when he heard someone knocking on the back door.

Mrs. Walters' footsteps sounded in the kitchen, and quite clearly he heard her exclaim:

"Why, Mr. Percival! Will you come in?"

Then Mr. Percival's voice:

"Thank you, Mrs. Walters. Just for a moment or two. Mr. Rose delegated to me the matter of your husband's complaint regarding some of our boys' slovenly pronunciation, and I thought I would call in about it."

Mrs. Walters explained that the front office door being locked she regretted having to ask the visitor to walk through her kitchen to reach the lounge, and Mr. Percival said Mrs. Walters was not to bother as he could not stay more than a minute.

"You know, Mrs. Walters, boys are boys all the world over," he said with his clear enunciation. "I've been with them all my life, and I know them inside and out. When thrown together as they are at school, they are both faddists and copyists. You have without doubt noticed that Keith takes up something with enthusiasm, and with equal enthusiasm drops it to take up something else."

"Oh yes, Keith is like that. Nanette is different."

"Yes, I suppose she is." Mr. Percival cleared his throat. "The point I am trying to make is that this deliberate mispronunciation of which your husband rightly complains is probably the result of one boy showing off, as we call it. It's extremely silly, but it's merely a fad which is bound to pass. When I was at school we gave certain words an entirely different pronunciation to that in normal use. We thought it clever, and no doubt our boys think this clever too. I lectured the entire school on the subject the other day, and the staff has received instructions to correct the fault whenever it is heard."

"I'm glad to hear that, Mr. Percival. My husband . . ."

"I feel sure he will understand," proceeded Mr. Percival. "I've learned that the great majority of our problems are not after all so very serious if dealt with with a degree of

122

mental detachment. It is so easy to permit a problem to magnify itself. We at the college have made the training of boys almost a science. We endeavour to accomplish an ideal, which is why the boys at a public school appear to be turned out from one mould. We are very proud of our boys, Mrs. Walters, and we shall not be disappointed in your son."

"It's nice of you to say that, Mr. Percival," Mrs. Walters said happily.

"Well, I must be getting along. Mr. Rose is attending the funeral of poor Mrs. Overton. It is all very dreadful. She was such a fine woman, and we shall miss her. Always ready, you know, to assist us with our social activities. The boys thought a very great deal of her. Gloom hangs over the entire school. Am I correctly informed that the murderer has been arrested?"

There was no hesitation by Mrs. Walters, and Bony silently applauded.

"Well, a man has been arrested. Constable Clifford is taking him down to Perth this evening. My husband tells me very little about his official work, you know. Says I'm not to be trusted."

"A generality, of course. I am relieved . . . we all must be . . . that the perpetrator of these horrible crimes has been apprehended. We should, however, withhold personal judgement even in such time of stress to which we have been subjected. We have reason to be proud of the ethics and procedure of our British criminal courts. By the way, I have not seen Constable Pedersen recently. Is he still out in the bush?"

"Yes. We can expect him only when we see him," replied Mrs. Walters.

"Ah yes, yes. Our boys hero-worship him. His talks on bushcraft and the wild natives have made him extremely popular. Well, thank you, Mrs. Walters. I am glad that the little matter of the 'gunners' and 'jists' has been ironed out. We have been hoping to welcome Mr. Knapp at the school. Mr. Rose and I met him down at the store, and he almost promised he would call on us one afternoon."

"I will remind him. I'm sure he won't have forgotten."

"Thank you. I trust he is enjoying his stay at Broome."

"Oh yes, Mr. Percival." "Tell him I'm leaving shortly," willed Bony. "Tell him . . . tell him . . . tell him." Mrs. Walters said: "We shall be sorry when he leaves us." "Shortly . . . shortly . . . shortly," willed Bony, but Mrs. Walters said: "Good-bye, Mr. Percival. It was nice of you to call."

"Thank you, Mrs. Walters," and Bony knew he was then beyond the kitchen doorway. "Good-bye!"

Bony permitted his wrist watch to mark off a full minute before he left his "office" for the kitchen. He said nothing to Mrs. Walters and she was astonished to see him sink to his knees and squint across the surface of the linoleum just inside the doorway. Size eight were the shoes on Mr. Percival's feet.

"When talking to you, where did he stand or sit?" he asked.

"He stood just there," replied Mrs. Walters, indicating a point midway between the door and the kitchen table.

"A broom, please."

She brought him one, and he swept the floor and carefully retrieved the flotsam accumulated since it was last swept. The envelope containing it he marked with the letter P. Mrs. Walters looked her astonishment.

"I am cram-full of suspicion of everyone," he said, a clear twinkle in his eyes. "Mr. Percival wears the same size shoe as worn by the murderer of Mrs. Overton, but his shoes are not worn along the inner edge of the heels."

"They oughtn't to be, anyway. Mr. Percival's shoes were almost new, I should think," argued Mrs. Walters. "Oh, he couldn't be . . ."

"He could. So could Mr. Rose, or one of the other masters. Any man wearing a size-eight shoe could be the man I cannot drag forth from black obscurity. Look! If you permit that kettle to boil much longer it'll boil dry. D'you know what happens when a kettle boils dry?"

Mrs. Walters laughed outright and turned to take a teapot from the cabinet. Having made the tea, she said:

124

"Now I think back, it does seem that Mr. Percival asked a lot of questions, doesn't it?"

"Did he?" asked Bony innocently.

"You know he did. You couldn't help but hear what was said."

"I did hear something about the boys. You're not accusing me of spying, are you?"

"Oh no. I wouldn't dream of such a thing."

Bony smiled and went for the teacups. It seemed to Clifford, who entered at that moment, that Inspector Bonaparte did nothing else but serve him with cups of tea.

"Any results?" Bony asked him.

"Yes. Mrs. Overton did not employ anyone to help with the housework. Ah Kee, the laundryman, said he collected Mrs. Overton's washing every week. When I asked him if he laundered her silk things, he said no."

"All right! Anything further?"

"Nothing," replied Clifford. "I made enquiries of Mrs. Overton's neighbours on whether they had seen anyone lurking about at night, and they all replied that they hadn't. None of them said they had ever lost anything, although I hinted that we'd received reports of petty thefts."

"Good work," approved Bony. "Well, I suppose you want to make ready for your trip south. You'll find the sergeant at home. Report to him. Did you pass the cigarettes to the prisoner?"

"A large packet when I took his midday meal to him."

"Done much air travel?"

"Fair amount, sir."

"You will please me by returning as quickly as possible. We're shorthanded. I'll have a communication for you to present to the Chief of the C.I.B., who will facilitate your quick return. I'd like you to be in at the death."

That made Clifford smile appreciation of the compliment, and Bony returned to his office. He was still there when he heard the inspector's voice in the front office, and he waited five minutes before joining him. Walters was in dress uniform, and he looked bigger and even more efficient.

"The entire town was there," he said. "Some of 'em made it plain how pleased they were I had caught the murderer. I'll be lynched if another murder happens."

"That shall not happen. Will you guard Mrs. Watson's house all night?"

"No need. She and her children are leaving for Perth on the plane tonight. Be down there for a month."

Bony sighed his relief.

"I shall watch over Mrs. Sayers, and I'll get Old Dickenson to keep his eyes on Mrs. Clayton's house for the night. That leaves Mrs. Abercrombie, who has a woman living with her. They should be in the least danger."

"You'd say so if you saw the companion. Grows a moustache. Sawtell and I will take care of them. We'll take shifts. But what about you? Like us, you didn't go to bed last night."

"I'll manage. When d'you expect the relief constable from Derby?"

"In the morning. And Clifford should be back by tomorrow night."

Bony transmitted Clifford's report of his enquiries and left the inspector at his desk. He sought Mrs. Walters, from whom he learned that dinner would be at six. He asked to be called punctually at six, and lay down on his bed for two hours' sleep. He slept at once and woke refreshed, and at seven he joined Mr. Dickenson on the bench placed well in the deepening shadows of the trees outside the Post Office. Without preamble, he said:

"Now let us to the plough and furrow straight toward the distant who-and-how. Tonight I want you to plant yourself close to Mrs. Clayton's house, and stop there till dawn. Only if you observe a man trying to enter, or gaining entry, will you give the alarm. D'you know how to manage a Webley?"

"I am acquainted with concealable weapons," the old man said. "This walking stick I brought in case . . ." He snapped back a catch and withdrew the handle for about two inches to reveal the blade of a sword.

"Excellent!" murmured Bony. "However, under the cir-

126

cumstances I've outlined, it will be essential to raise the alarm. Take this revolver and raise the alarm by firing rapidly. Either the inspector or Sawtell will be watching Mrs. Abercrombie's house, and whoever it happens to be will join you in a couple of minutes."

"Supposing I shoot the fellow instead?"

"It would be against the fool law. You see a man breaking into a house in the dead of night and you can prove . . . what? That he's a murderer? Why, it takes about ten eyewitnesses to prove that he is breaking a window for the purpose of entering."

Bony rapidly itemised his many difficulties, accepting the old man into his confidence because of his innate decency and his will to fight for the remnants of his self-respect. Unfortunately, eighty-two is badly matched against forty and fifty, even against sixty.

"Tell me about Abie," he urged. "You mentioned having seen him walking about barefooted at night."

"I have so," said the old man. "Before proceeding with him, I want to say how greatly I appreciate your attitude to me in view of my present social position. Now for Abie. For several years I have suffered from insomnia, and I've sat long hours of night on these seats, observing much and pondering on the frailties of man and the deceitfulness of woman. I have on several occasions seen Abie prowling about at night without foot covering and without the overcoat which gives him such pride to wear. I have seen him entering and leaving house gardens, and I have been interested by the fact that no robberies were reported."

"Strange. What do you think of the theory that Abie was trying to trail someone?"

"Then I never saw the man being trailed."

"Very well, let's leave him for another person—Mrs. Sayers. From what you said the other day, you know something of her history. She sleeps alone in her house at night?"

Mr. Dickenson vented a soft chuckle.

"I've known her since she was eating pap in Old Briggs'

arms. She's a toughie, and I'll warrant she would give this strangling gentleman a run for his money. Still, even the toughies can be caught with one foot off the ground. If Old Briggs slept inside the house, you need have no concern for Mrs. Sayers."

"He sleeps in a place near the garage, I understand."

"Yes. Both of them are ruled by routine. Every night, including Sundays, Briggs leaves for the Port Cuvier Hotel dead on nine o'clock. At the hotel he has two glasses of beer and purchases a bottle of gin. He returns to the house exactly at ten. If Mrs. Sayers hasn't visitors, he closes the storm shutters and locks the front door, looks to the windows to be sure they're fastened, and leaves by the back door, which he locks and takes the key to his room. And before he gets into bed he's lowered the tide in his bottle down to an inch."

"You appear to have studied him rather closely," observed Bony.

"It's given me something to do. Look at Broome during the daytime. Hardly anyone is abroad. Sit and watch Broome at night and you will be astonished by the number of people. I could write a book about Broome. I might even be able to write two. Oh yes, I've watched them. I've been watching 'em for years."

"Has Flinn been on visiting terms with Mrs. Sayers for long?"

"No. About a year. He doesn't call on her often," replied the old man. "As I told you, he's a flash. I suppose you know he was one of Mrs. Eltham's midnight friends?"

"I did not know."

"Oh yes. So was that schoolmaster at the college."

"Indeed! Which one?"

"Percival."

"Interesting."

"There's another point."

"Proceed, please."

"One night about a month before Mrs. Cotton was murdered Percival and Mrs. Sayers had a hell of a row. What about, I don't know. He called on her when Old Briggs was away at the pub, and he hadn't been inside more than five minutes when I could hear her shouting at him to get out and keep out. Those were her words. She can be as vulgar as a fish-wife."

The dusk was deepening, and the stars were emerging to make their nightly bow. The western sky gilded the plane passing over the town, and neither man spoke of it or of its passengers.

"Having known Mrs. Sayers all her life, do you think her a woman capable of working with us?" Bony asked.

"She has brains, I must admit," replied the old man.

"And discretion?"

"If you mean to keep a secret, yes. What she lacks in subtlety she gains in courage."

"And Briggs?"

"If she ordered it, Briggs wouldn't hesitate to cut a throat."

"Thanks. Now let us to the plough I spoke of."

Bony glanced back once, to see the gaunt figure melt into the shadow of a tall tree.

Chapter Seventeen: BONY CAPTURES MRS. SAYERS

Mrs. Sayers invariably dined at six to permit her cook-house-maid to depart at seven. At seven precisely the cook reported and was dismissed, and the house was, figuratively, taken over by Luke Briggs. At eight forty-five Briggs invariably reported, asking if Mrs. Sayers required anything before he took his evening stroll.

Seen on his feet and without his chauffeur-*cum*-sea-captain uniform, Luke Briggs would have delighted Charles Dickens. He was quite bald. His face was the colour of teak and marvellously wrinkled. About five feet eight inches in height, and weighing in the vicinity of a hundred and thirty pounds, he could be taken for a Cockney chimney sweep or a racecourse tout. To guess his age, one could range from sixty to a hundred, and then be out at either end. For his evening stroll he wore rubber-soled canvas shoes, grey Harris-tweed trousers, and a coat much too long for him. The coat made him look like a soldier crab inhabiting a conch shell, but it was worn for a purpose—the inside pockets were capable of taking a dozen bottles.

When Briggs entered the lounge this evening, Mrs. Sayers was seated before her escritoire writing letters. He stood in the doorway, and it seemed that it required mental effort to stop his jaw from its fascinatingly methodical chewing.

"Anything you want, Mavis?" he said, and at once the chewing recontinued.

"No. Not now, Briggs," replied Mrs. Sayers without turning in her chair.

"We want a new booster coil, and while we're about it, we'd better have a new set of spark plugs—eight of 'em."

The jaw chewed whilst the woman's voice came across the room:

"Make the old things last another month."

The jaw stopped chewing. It was as though Briggs had to turn a switch, and it seemed a pity that he couldn't chew and speak at the same time.

"Impos!" he asserted. "You got an engagement at the college tomorrer afternoon at three. No coil, no car. No car, you walk."

"Damn you, Briggs. Go away. I'll telephone the store first thing in the morning."

Briggs departed along the carpeted passage to the rear quarters and left the house. On reaching the front gate, he noiselessly opened one panel and vanished in the direction of the Port Cuvier Hotel. Five minutes later Mrs. Sayers heard the front doorbell ringing. She stepped from the house proper, crossed the wire-enclosed veranda, and switched on the exterior light before opening the door.

"Why, it's Mr. Knapp!" she exclaimed. "Do come in."

"I offer many apologies and I have a hundred excuses, Mrs. Sayers."

"Well, you don't need them. I'm delighted to see you," Mrs. Sayers giggled. "And I'm all alone, too." Closing the front door, she conducted the visitor to the lounge, chattering about the weather and saying that his visit relieved her from a lonely evening. She made him sit in a chair requiring a crane to lift one out, and she chose the settee, pulling forward an ornate smoker's stand to serve both. "You didn't bring Esther with you?"

"They have been tremendously busy," Bony explained.

"You know, I'm so relieved that they arrested that terrible man. Poor Mabel Overton! It's so sad. She was a lovely woman, Mr. Knapp. So sweet-tempered. And why he murdered her I can't imagine. If they don't hang him for it, I'm going to raise hell."

Words. Behind the brown eyes lurked a question. They had already noted Bony's clothes, his hair, and every feature.

"Did you know her well?" he asked.

"Oh yes. We were friends for years. She was a good woman,

but not tiresome. She never drank like I do, or smoked or said naughty words, like I do. She had everything I haven't got."

"I find it difficult to believe that you lack anything, Mrs. Sayers," he said, smiling, and again glimpsed the question mark behind her eyes. This was a shrewd woman, a successful woman through recognition of those qualities she did lack. He said:

"I'm sure you do not lack the ability to keep a secret, once you decide it is worth keeping."

"When you're brought up in a place like Broome by a father who was a pearl buyer and a male nurse who's the son of the Sphinx, keeping secrets is second nature, Mr. Knapp."

"I would be honoured did you consent to share one of mine."

Again the smile unrelated to the brown eyes, and the giggle so unrelated to the character of this woman. "Dear Mr. Knapp, you intrigue me," she gurgled, and Bony flinched. Then, changing front so swiftly that he was astonished, she said: "Open up. If it's an honest secret that hurts no one, I can keep it with you."

"Thank you."

Bony imparted his real name, his profession and purpose in Broome. He said that the arrest of Locke was primarily intended to deceive the man who had murdered three women and who would probably attempt to murder a fourth. He asked Mrs. Sayers to give him her full co-operation, and pointed out that the extent of the required co-operation might be more than she was then visualising. Whilst he spoke in low tones, she listened without interruption.

"I'll co-operate, of course, Inspector," she said quietly. "Tell me what to do, and I'll do it. Ask any questions you like, and I'll answer them as best I can."

"I hadn't any doubt that you would consent to assist me, Mrs. Sayers. Now these are the things I would like you to do. One: go on calling me Mr. Knapp. Two: continue to live as you normally do. Three: take certain precautions against danger to yourself which I will enumerate later."

"Yes. All right, Mr. Knapp."

"Now for my questions. Did Mrs. Overton complain to you of a man's attentions to her?"

"No, not complain. She did say that Mr. Flinn proposed to her, but not what kind of proposal. She told me that she detested him."

"Indeed!"

"She was engaged to a man in Melbourne, you know. I was writing to him when you arrived."

"What is your feeling towards Mr. Flinn?"

"I think he's a nasty piece of work."

"He called on you the other day, I understand. A social call?"

"Hardly a social call," replied Mrs. Sayers. "He wanted to sell a small parcel of pearls, and he found out that I know more about 'em than he does."

"Thank you. You are being really helpful. Would you tell me just why you think Mr. Flinn a nasty piece of work?"

The brown eyes clouded.

"He reminds me somehow of a spider, and I hate spiders. Gives me the feeling that he wants to eat me."

"Well, let's get back to Mrs. Overton. Did she have any male friends?"

"No man special here. As I told you, she was engaged to be married."

"Did she tell you that she lost a garment from her clothesline?"

"Oh yes, she told me about that."

"Was it a nightgown?"

"Yes, a lavender silk one."

"When was it stolen, d'you know?"

"Yes. She told me she lost it Tuesday night. Does it mean anything?"

Bony related the circumstances of the theft each murder victim had suffered, and told of the finding of their silk underwear bundled into the wardrobes. Mrs. Sayers was now sitting stiffly upright, her eyes wide and her lips parted.

"These three crimes provide proof that in Broome is a man

133

imbued with a terrible hatred of women," Bony proceeded. "Each crime was planned with meticulous attention to detail, so that he made no stupid mistakes which a man nearer to normalcy would have made. However, he has been unable to evade doing those things which had become habitual long before he set out on his murder career. Thus his second murder indicated a pattern, and this pattern was made clear with his third murder. You realise, of course, that his three victims were widows?"

Mrs. Sayers nodded.

"They were able to purchase expensive silk underwear. From each he stole a nightgown. He cut and ripped to pieces their silk underwear. That, broadly, is the pattern in which is concealed his motive."

"Why kill three entirely different women?" asked Mrs. Sayers, and Bony secretly acknowledged her intelligence.

"That question is a difficult one. The first victim was a hotel proprietress, the second was a woman of blemished virtue, the third was much respected for her good works. I can find no common denominator."

"Well, the first sold drink."

"That's so. The murderer could have a hatred of drink."

"The second sold herself," itemised Mrs. Sayers.

"The murderer could hate immorality. For what could he hate the third? The third sold good works. I understand that Mrs. Overton was a keen church worker and intensely interested in child welfare. A man cannot hate both good and bad. Assuming that he plans to murder you. Why you? Pardon me for saying so, but you are neither good nor bad. It could be said that you are negative. Not that you are, of course, but by the same yardstick you are. Do you know a man in Broome who makes you uneasy, even frightened?"

"No man has ever frightened me. I've known plenty of the Flinn type. Frightened of 'em? I can take care of myself. Briggs taught me to do that when I was a little girl. I was caught one night on the beach by a Malay. He was in hospital for months."

134

"That was some time ago, I suppose," Bony commented.

"Yes, years ago. In the good old days the place was crowded by all nations. Money! Money floated on the wind, and what my father didn't manage to pick up my late husband did. You needn't worry over me, Mr. Knapp. I can look after myself."

"Briggs taught you jujitsu, didn't he?"

"Yes. How did you know?"

"When the Malay attacked you, everyone in Broome heard about it, I assume?"

Mrs. Sayers shook her head.

"No one knew about it bar Briggs and my father . . . and Old Dickenson. By hell . . . he told you, eh?"

"No. He did mention, though, that Briggs had taught you to take care of yourself. What I'm trying to establish is how many people in Broome know you were taught jujitsu by an expert?"

"Very few, if anyone."

"Might be an idea to go into training."

"You think the murderer might have a go at me?"

"It would be a certainty if he stole one of your nightgowns. You sleep alone in the house. Is there any communication with Briggs?"

"Yes, but I don't know if it's working. I can ring a bell in Briggs' room from my bed. I had it put in several years ago when I was ill."

"Do your friends know about this?"

"No. Why should I tell them? It never had any importance." Mrs. Sayers giggled. "Besides, imagine the gossip if Broome knew all I had to do to bring a man into my bedroom was to press a button."

Bony, managing with elegance to extricate himself from the chair, stubbed his cigarette and looked down steadily at Mrs. Sayers. She was older than Mrs. Overton had been and, he thought, the lightness of her make-up was distinctly to her advantage. Her arms were firm and well moulded, and wealth had certainly not coarsened her. She must have been strikingly handsome when a young girl.

135

"Mrs. Watson and her two children left for Perth today. You know that?" he said.

"Oh yes. I heard she had decided last week to have a holiday."

"I'm glad she went away. It reduces my responsibilities by one. Mrs. Abercrombie and Mrs. Clayton are two of them. You are the remaining responsibility."

"But I've told you you needn't worry about me."

"Mrs. Abercrombie has with her at night an elderly companion. Mrs. Clayton has her daughter with her. The daughter is only a schoolgirl, but Mrs. Clayton is safer than you are. I don't want to frighten you, but I do want you to understand quite clearly that you are my greatest responsibility. You would relieve me of much anxiety did you consent to adopt every safeguard against swift and silent and deadly assault."

Mrs. Sayers stood up, proving then that she was slightly taller than Bony.

"Whatever you say goes with me."

Bony smiled his thanks.

"Our plan of defence will not entail any inconvenience," he said. "We must have the co-operation of your man Briggs. Both you and he must not vary your usual living routine, or in any way indicate that you are on your guard. Even your cook must know nothing. Is that Briggs returning?"

"It'll be him. You'll have a cup of coffee or something?"

"Thank you. I suggest that you ask Briggs to come in here."

"He'll report as usual. He makes wonderful coffee, but I have to pour the brandy. I just love brandy in my coffee. Briggs introduced me to it when I was cutting my wisdom teeth."

"It appears that Briggs has been Jonathan to your David." Bony held a match to her cigarette, and their gaze held above the tiny flame. She felt the impact of his personality, and in the instant acknowledged the mental power which subjugated in everyone the consciousness of his mid-race.

"Briggs has been my father and my mother and my brother," she heard herself saying, whilst thinking how strange it was that not till now had she realised it.

Briggs stood in the doorway. His jaw was chewing. He turned the invisible switch and said:

"Anything wanted before I lock up?"

"Come here, Briggs. And don't keep on chewing like a mechanical figure in a toyshop!"

Bony suggested that they sit down, and Briggs listened whilst perched on the edge of a chair, the tail of his coat hoisted by the bottle in the back pocket. As Bony proceeded to outline what he had told Mrs. Sayers, the man's facial expression never changed, nor did the small bright black eyes waver from Bony's mouth. When Bony ceased speaking, he said:

"I been urging Mrs. Sayers to take proper care for the last two months. Things being as they are, I'll be doing sentry go round the house at night."

"You'll do no more nor less than what Mr. Knapp wants," interjected Mrs. Sayers. "In other words, Briggs, you'll do just what you're told to do."

"I'm listening." The eye farthest away from Mrs. Sayers was momentarily masked by the lid. The wink was the signature to a treaty of alliance against the willful and unpredictable Mrs. Sayers, *née* Mavis Masters.

When Bony bade his adieu at the front door, the communicating bell in Briggs' room had been tested and found efficient, the house had been secured, and every room had been investigated by Briggs . . . just in case Mr. Hyde had sneaked in whilst he had been out and Mrs. Sayers had been entertaining Bony. Briggs had gone to his room, locking the kitchen door and taking the key with him as usual. He had agreed not to prowl outside the house, not to drink the usual quantity of gin, and to sleep with the bell under his pillow. Mrs. Sayers promised Bony to lock her room door on retiring.

He heard her lock the front door, and instead of setting out to the Police Station, Bony sat all night under one of the palms.

Bony was shaving when he heard Mrs. Walters calling him, and on emerging from his room, showered and refreshed by three hours' sleep, she complained that the tracker had not come for breakfast.

"I'll see where he is," he volunteered. It was nine o'clock and the morning sunshine was hot. The sky lacked colour although it was cloudless, and the small flies were instantly a bother when he stepped down into the compound.

Abie was not at his camp in the loose box. His blankets were there, tossed into a heap, and the straps with which he fastened his swag were there too, but the military overcoat and the boots and the wide-brimmed felt hat were absent. Recalling that he had not seen Abie since the previous morning, Bony returned to the kitchen, where Mrs. Walters was placing bacon and eggs and toast before her husband.

"When did you last see Abie?" he asked the inspector.

"Abie! Don't remember. Why?"

"Abie didn't come for his breakfast when I called him," replied Mrs. Walters. "He came for his dinner last night."

"Out with the mare, I suppose," Walters said, evincing little interest.

"Not like a blackfellow to be away at mealtime," she pointed out, and Bony added:

"He's not in his camp or anywhere in the compound. I wonder what he's up to. By the way, those drawing pins fastening that calendar to the wall interest me. Where did you obtain them?"

"From office stock. All office requirements are sent up from Perth. Where's the interest?"

"I'll reveal it after breakfast. Anything of note happen last night?"

"Nothing. The women went off to bed at eleven, leaving the front door open. Talk! They talked for a couple of hours before going to bed, and for nearly two hours I could hear them talking to each other from their rooms. What did you do?"

"Sat under one of Mrs. Sayers' palm trees and communed with the stars. Earlier, she told me that Mrs. Overton had had a nightgown stolen."

"Crumbs!"

"It's the one item of fair news in this depression," Bony claimed. "Our man is running true to his pattern. If only I could see him in the picture I'm trying to paint. I'd take a chance then and act on a search warrant. If those three garments were found in his possession, we would have enough evidence for an arrest."

"In such case, would you advise the arrest?"

"No. We would have enough evidence to arrest for clothesline thefts but not for murder. These days you have almost to make a moving picture of the actual murder to have hope of gaining a conviction. Our next step is to watch for clothes left out all night, and continue to guard those three widows. A picture record! Quite an idea."

"Did you contact your assistant this morning?" Walters enquired, and Bony could not quite decide whether there was a sneer in the voice.

"I did. All was quiet on his front. I sent him home to sleep. He's been very helpful. Have you been in the habit of sending Abie out on night duty for any purpose?"

The inspector was astonished.

"You did not send Abie out trailing smuggling suspects?"

"Ye gods!" groaned Walters. "What are Sawtell and Clifford for?"

"Compiling statistics," Bony blandly replied. "I wonder where that black's got to this morning."

Walters pushed back his chair.

"Expect Sawtell will know. I'd better open the blasted office."

The sergeant arrived as he was unlocking the front office

door. Bony entered the office from the house passage, bringing with him his plaster casts.

"You know where Abie is this morning?" Walters demanded.

"No. Not on deck?"

"Absent without leave. 'Bout time you jerked that gentleman down to ground level." The inspector snatched up the telephone and asked for the airport office. He was told that the plane from Derby might arrive about eleven and the aircraft from Perth about one . . . perhaps. He asked Bony what his plans were.

"Well, all of us have earned a full night's sleep, and you two will be wanting bed before bedtime," he pointed out. "I suggest that on arrival Clifford and the constable from Derby be given the rest of the day off duty, and that they report to me at seven this evening . . . in plain clothes. I didn't tell you, Sawtell, that Mrs. Overton lost a nightgown. That confirms the pattern, and makes the watching of clotheslines a duty of paramount importance. Will the Derby plane bring mail from Darwin?"

"Should do. Time we had Darwin's report on Flinn."

"Might help. By the way, Sergeant, look at this shoeprint cast. What d'you make of the circular indentation?"

"Looks like he picked up a wad of chewing gum."

"Or a drawing pin," supplemented Bony, placing the convex head of a brass drawing pin over the raised protruberance on the cast. The pin had been filed off. The head fitted exactly. "This drawing pin was one of the four used to pin the calendar to the kitchen wall."

"What cast is that?" Sawtell asked sharply.

"The cast taken of the shoeprint made by the man who murdered Mrs. Overton," replied Bony.

Sawtell's eyes were small.

"I don't get it," he admitted, and passed to his desk from a drawer of which he took the left of the shoe casts he had made under Abie's direction. The shoe cast he compared with that made by Bony. They were of the same size but of different shape. The heel of Bony's cast was worn along the inside edge. The shoe from which Sawtell had made his cast was worn much at the back of the heel and there was a distinct hole in the sole.

"I still don't get it," Sawtell said.

"It's quite simple, Sergeant. I made a cast of the left foot of the murderer of Mrs. Overton. Your cast is of the left shoe worn by Mr. Dickenson. You say that Abie drew a line with his finger round the print of the man's tracks he saw on the paths and inside Mrs. Overton's house?"

"So he did," asserted Sawtell. "I was particular about that. Here, along this side of the cast, is the mark he made in the dirt."

"Come, Sawtell, I'm not doubting you," Bony hastily assured the now angry man. "And I'm sure you will not doubt my tracking ability. Abie deliberately pointed out to you false tracks, because Old Dickenson was not inside the garden nor was he inside the house. Now, then, let us compare the casts of the naked feet."

The comparison was made. The two sets of casts were the same.

"When you told Abie to point out to you the naked footprints he could not trick you, for there was only the one set. If you take these casts to the moist earth about Abie's washbasin, you will discover that they fit exactly."

Walters butted in:

"Two added to two make four," he said. "Abie, you said, had been walking around at night. Was he following the murderer that night, or was the murderer following him?"

"He was following the murderer," replied Bony. "If he knew then that the man he was following had murdered Mrs. Overton he may tell us who the murderer is."

"Course he will," snapped Sawtell. "I'll locate him pronto."

"If you do locate him, he won't tell you," Bony quietly stated.

"Won't tell! Coo! He'll tell, all right."

"Have you ever been able to make a blackfellow talk when

he will not? No, Sawtell, you won't make him talk. I made the mistake of not keeping my eye on him, but we were all too busy last night. Locate him if you can, but don't let him suspect that we know of his trickery."

"Why not? What's his little game?" asked Walters.

"If he knows who murdered Mrs. Overton, his little game is blackmail. To blackmail, he must contact the murderer. He, therefore, could lead us to the murderer, provided we were sufficiently expert in shadowing him. It will be a task for me. However, I fear much for Abie."

"You're right, Bony. Abie would be a mouse trying to blackmail a cat." Walters chewed his upper lip. "Well, what next?"

"Relax till the reinforcements arrive. You two get on with your routine jobs. I'll look around for Abie." Bony smiled, and they wondered at his calm demeanour. "When you go out, be sure you haven't a drawing pin stuck to one of your shoes."

Bony left. Walters scratched his chin. Sawtell said:

"What's he mean by that crack?"

"That I am the murderer," replied Walters. "Told me I wore down my shoes same way as the murderer does, that I make the same stride as the murderer does, that I am the murderer's weight. Nice chap, isn't he?"

"Are you the murderer?" asked the sergeant.

"Are you?" shouted the inspector.

Sawtell burst into laughter. Walters grinned. The tension vanished.

Bony visited the stores, at which he purchased drawing pins and gained the information that the Government Offices, the Council Office, the State School, and the college did not purchase their drawing pins at the stores. The drawing pin attached to the murderer's shoe was useless as a lead, but as one of many pieces with which to identify the murderer it did have value.

Any man in Broome being sufficiently astute to wear rubber gloves, and to clean door handles so that the imprint of the rubber would not be recorded, would be wide awake to the ability of the native trackers and would almost certainly use a pair of discarded shoes in which to commit his crimes. It was most improbable that he would wear the shoes save when on murder bent. As this expert on tracks was aware, no two men walk exactly alike, and the tracks of the murderer, seen in Mrs. Overton's house and on her garden paths, rendered to Bony distinguishing peculiarities which would be registered by the ground from any other shoes he wore.

But, like the drawing pin, footprints could not be regarded as conclusive evidence, but as supporting evidence of the contiguity of the murderer with his victim. Bony had not told Inspector Walters that the murderer placed the same pressure on his toes as upon his heels, whilst the inspector dug his heels into cement, such being the emphasis with which he placed his heels.

Bony was "hoorayed" by Keith Walters racing home on his bicycle for lunch, and the boy was asked to stop. Keith circled and drew alongside.

"Have you seen Abie today?" Bony asked.

"No. What's he done, Mr. Knapp?"

"Absent from duty. D'you know of any blacks camped near the town?"

Keith shook his head and said the nearest camp was on the Cuvier Creek half a mile down from Dampier's Hotel.

"Have you ever visited the blacks' camp out there?"

"Rather. They put on a corroboree a couple of months ago. We watched 'em throwing spears and boomerangs and things."

"Did you, indeed. That must have been interesting. How did you go?"

"In cars. All the school couldn't go, you know, so we cast lots. I was lucky. The masters cast lots too."

"And who were the lucky masters, d'you remember?"

"Mr. Percival, and old Stinks, and Tubby Wilson. The head arrived after we did. Mrs. Sayers brought him, Old Briggs driving. She shouted tea for all of us. Her car was loaded with eats." The boy's face became swiftly serious. "I forgot about Mrs. Overton. Mrs. Sayers brought her too."

"Did you like Mrs. Overton?"

"Oh yes. All the fellows liked her. She was a rattlin' good sport. One of the prefects was caught out crying about her being killed like that, but no one chiacked him for it. We all felt like it, you see."

"Yes, I suppose you did. Well, you had better get along home for lunch. I'll not be long after you."

At the Police Station office the Derby constable was presented to Bony. He was dapper in physique but a hundred per cent in mental alertness. Sawtell was taking him home for lunch, and Mrs. Sawtell was putting him up. He would report to Bony at seven.

The children having left the luncheon table, Bony asked if there had arrived any communication from Darwin concerning Arthur Flinn. Walters said that Darwin knew nothing to Flinn's discredit and that for several years he had been the buying agent for a large jewellery firm in New York.

"Don't get us anywhere with Flinn," concluded the inspector.

Following lunch, Bony borrowed Mrs. Walters' alarm clock and permitted himself one hour of sleep. Meanwhile, Walters had telephoned Dampier's Hotel to ascertain if Abie had been seen out there. No one at the hotel had seen Abie, and the lubras working there had not seen him at the camp. Keith received orders to prospect for the tracker on his bike when he left school for the day.

Awakened by the clock at two, Bony spent an hour doing nothing bar meditate and chain-smoke. He had afternoon tea with Mrs. Walters at three o'clock, and at three-thirty was sauntering into Chinatown. And shortly afterwards he was met by Johnno.

"Oh, Mr. Knapp! I look out for you. I try see you arrive. You arrive, eh?"

"I have arrived," agreed Bony, unable to withstand the smiling face of the sunny Javanese.

"You like go fish, eh?" Johnno went on, shoulders and arms expressing recognition of a wish which must be granted. "I

144

take you see my friend. He has motorboat. Sometimes motor-boat he go ahead when my friend say go astern, and he go astern when my friend he says go ahead. No matter. We arrive, we put out the lines." Johnno's hand and arms illustrated putting out the lines as though they were employed heaving a drunk out of a music hall. "No fish, no matter. We sleep, we eat, we drink. You come now see my friend?"

"Yes, Johnno, why not?"

They walked together along the ill-kept sidewalk fronting the inhabited iron shacks with their leaning veranda posts and rotted floor boards.

"You live always in Broome?" Johnno asked.

"No, Johnno. I must soon leave and go back to work. But I shall always remember you and our drive with Mr. Dickenson to Dampier's Hotel."

"Ah! We go one night before you leave. We have night out, eh?"

"I will think that over, Johnno," Bony said, the twinkle in his eyes. "We might make a party of it."

Johnno was immensely pleased. He conducted Bony past the store and toward a large shed where the street ended above the slope to the beach. They passed between the shed and a huge stack of empty oil drums, and in this narrow sandy lane-way Bony saw the tracks of a man who wore a size-eight shoe and who pressed his feet evenly on the ground. The tracks stopped at the bottom of four steps leading to a loading stage at the wide doors of the shed.

As they mounted the steps, Bony heard from within the shed a sound like flakes of slate falling upon a marble slab. The smell of ozone was strong, and of tar, and when he entered the shed he saw against the far side a small mountain of pearl shell. At the foot of the mountain squatted two of Johnno's countrymen. They were sorting the pearl shells into large and shallow floor bins, and the light from the opened doors formed bars of pearl as the shell was tossed through the air into one or other of the several bins.

A man was packing shell into a crate. There was another

man, his back to Bony, who was kneeling beside the bin containing the largest size shell, and Bony watched him select a shell, hold it to catch the light, and then press its cool, silken surface to his cheek.

Johnno spoke in his own language to the shell packer, and the kneeling man turned, the shell still pressed to his cheek. His dark eyes flared with resentment on seeing Bony, and tossing the shell back upon the heap, he hastily rose to his feet, spoke sharply to the packer, and strode from the shed.

Mr. Arthur Flinn surely loved the touch of pearl . . . and silk?

The man packing the shell was a Chinese in middle age. His fingers were long and tapering, and as each piece was placed in the stout wooden crate the fingers seemed to croon their farewell. To one side was a stack of crates stencilled with initials and the words "NEW YORK," and in a corner were long sacks of shell as brought ashore from the luggers.

"Here my friend," proudly announced Johnno. "He take us fishing. He has nice motorboat."

"May go out on Saturday," the packer said without accent. "You'll be welcome."

"I shall be glad to go out if I can manage it. Thank you. What's your name?"

"Bill Lung. What's yours?"

"Alfred Knapp," replied Bony. "Merely visiting, you know. Interesting place, Broome. Lot of shell here?"

"Little to what it was before the war. Only a few luggers working these days."

The fingers had not ceased their employment, lifting the shell from the nearby floor bin and expertly placing it in the crate. Now and then a shell would be discarded, being tossed into one or other of the remaining bins.

Johnno explained that Bill Lung was a real Australian, having been born in Broome and having all his life worked in a packing shed. Bill Lung's expression remained bland throughout until Johnno mentioned an Australian wife and eight children. Then the large face expanded roundly into a happy smile.

The Javanese was a born exhibitor. Having exhibited Bill Lung, and doing his best with Bony, he exhibited the contents of the shed, explaining the various grades into which the men at the heap of shell sorted it. The bin marked "Extra Heavy" was Johnno's showpiece. Before this bin had knelt Arthur Flinn, and now Bony knelt and picked up specimen shells measuring from six to seven inches across and gleaming with an opalescent lustre shading to pale gold along the edges. As Flinn had done, Bony pressed a plate of pearl to his cheek and, feeling its cool, silky caress, fancied he could hear the sighing wind making love to the tropic seas. Bill Lung's fingers momentarily stopped work, and into the narrow eyes crept a furtive smile of sympathetic understanding.

Johnno sprang up and regarded his wristlet watch with dramatic dismay.

"I go!" he exclaimed. "I have to arrive and take lady to toptown store. I see you sometime, eh? P'haps Saturday. You tell Bill any time you go fishing. We have good time. Now I go to arrive."

He hurried away, and the Chinese selected a shell and presented it to Bony.

"Take it home, and when trouble comes to you, look at it and touch it and let it tell you its secrets."

"What do these shells tell you, Bill Lung?"

"Of things which are beyond dreams."

"Things which send some men mad."

"There's always the weaklings, Mr. Knapp . . . men who smoke too much, or eat too much, or dream too much. My illustrious father used to say that to play with a snake is foolishness, and to run from it is cowardice. It is wisdom to kill the snake and wear its skin as your girdle."

"Your father was a wise man," Bony said. "Well, I'll get along. If you have room for me in your boat, I'll try to make the trip. And thank you. Tell me, before I go, which would you choose, a pearl or a diamond?"

"I'd choose the pearl."

"Why?"

"For what it tells me through my fingers. A pearl is alive; a diamond is dead and can't speak. My father used to say: 'Select for a bride the woman who prefers pearls to diamonds. The woman who loves pearls will bear you many children.'"

148

Bony smiled down at the packer.

"I bet your bride preferred pearls," he said. "Mine did."

Leaving the shed, he sauntered along the coast road, passing the Seahorse Hotel, and, when a hundred yards beyond it, he left the road and climbed the coast sand dunes. On the summit, he sat gazing out over Roebuck Bay with its fringe of green mangroves. The tide was high, and the near Indian Ocean was placid and delphinium blue. The long white jetty seemed to be straining to reach the pavement of gold laid down by the westering sun.

A lugger was anchored at the mouth of the creek, and the high voices of the men aboard her reached Bony, bringing a nostalgia for the open sea and the great game fish inhabiting it. Far out another lugger was headed for the bay, a stubby black pencil on a silver-grey slate.

That Chinese shell packer was not an oddity in Australia. Bony had met many like him, men born in Australia of Chinese parents and educated in Australian schools. They spoke English fluently and the language of their parents indifferently, and they invariably appended with great success the old civilisation to the new. Bill Lung was an epicure of the senses rather than a sensualist.

That he loved the feel of pearl shell was unashamedly revealed by those crooning fingers. Bony wondered what had been in the mind of the Chinese as he watched Flinn handle and caress the shells of pearl. Mr. Arthur Flinn was certainly a large piece of the material being gathered by Bony. With but little more in his possession, Bony would see his picture of the murderer.

Without standing, he turned himself about and was presented with a picture of the town. The first impression was an extensive jumble of iron roofs laid flat on a floor of tree foliage. Then the eye discerned the wide roadways crisscrossing the area within the curve of Dampier Creek. Beyond the creek to the southward, the land was grey green and featureless as far as the distant fringe of paperbark scrub. Beyond the town to the northeast lay the open spaces of the airport, with its buildings and radio mast, and toward the ocean the white-painted Mission buildings and the college, occupying the highest point of Broome.

Like the placid ocean, Broome appeared languorous. Down in the road, or street, skirting the protective sand dune, were but two men and three children. There were several people on the veranda of the Seahorse Hotel, and two cars were parked without. In the yard of the hotel, clothes hung motionless on a line. Bony's gaze passed over the town, noting clothes drying at four places, and he was reminded of the coming night and the responsibilities it would bring.

Slithering down the slope of the dune, Bony emptied his shoes of sand and walked briskly that he would not delay the evening meal. When approaching the Police Station, Keith came to meet him.

"Can't find Abie," the boy said. "I've been scouting around for him, too."

"He might have gone bush," surmised Bony. "Black trackers often do, you know. I wouldn't be surprised, though, if he turned up in time to draw his dinner at the kitchen."

"That's likely, Mr. Knapp. The blacks always seem to be hanging around at mealtimes. I asked Sister King if she had seen Abie, and she said perhaps he's cleared off to a quiet camp to have a good go at the petrol."

"Oh! Who is Sister King?"

"Sister King's up at the Mission. The blacks go there, you know, for clothes and things. A lot of the black kids live there. The Sisters make 'em go to their school."

"That's very good of the Sisters, Keith. Without education no one goes far in this world. Did Sister King say when she last saw Abie?"

"Yes, she did, Mr. Knapp. She said he was there yesterday just before dark. He wanted a pair of socks. He couldn't have wanted 'em for himself, because I know he never wears any socks. D'you know what I think?"

"What do you think?"

"I think," the boy ran on with assurance in his voice, "I

think Abie wanted the socks to trade for some petrol. Anyway, he'll turn up again, and he'll be sick enough when he does. He did it a long time ago. Was away for a week, and Constable Pedersen trounced him in the stables."

"Thoroughly?" Bony asked, and Keith grinned and said that the "trouncing" had "fixed" Abie till that day he had been found behind the gum tree in the compound.

After dinner Bony and Inspector Walters retired to the office, where the former opened his mail, comprising several official communications from Perth and one from Brisbane.

"The only fingerprints raised on those torn garments I sent down to Perth were those of Mrs. Overton," Bony commented.

"I didn't hope for much, did you?"

Bony regarded Walters pensively.

"No, I did not. However, two pieces of torn silk bore the imprints of a man's teeth, both upper and lower teeth."

"The fellow must be an animal," Walters said. "Fits in with what Dickenson said about the man he saw champing his teeth. Where does it get us?"

"Of itself, nowhere. I want only one, or perhaps two pieces to complete my picture puzzle. I want time, Walters, to find those vitally necessary pieces. Once I complete my picture, then we can move to locate the three stolen nightgowns."

"You think he's kept them?"

"I'm sure he has. He would keep something to gloat over. I believe he stole them for the purpose of retaining proof that he had conquered a devil which threatened to destroy him."

"It all seems pretty deep to me," Walters stated. "He must kill for the lust of it."

"No, he had his reasons for destroying these women," Bony said. "I know why he killed Mrs. Cotton, and why he killed Mrs. Eltham. I am not sure why he killed Mrs. Overton, but if he makes an attempt to kill Mrs. Sayers, I shall be sure why he killed Mrs. Overton and why he attempted to kill Mrs. Sayers. And when I know that, my picture will be complete and I shall see him."

Walters regarded Bony intently.

"You really think he will make an attempt to strangle Mrs. Sayers?" he asked.

"I am hoping he will."

"You said that Mrs. Sayers and Briggs have agreed to take every precaution," stated Walters.

"Yes. You may be easy in your mind regarding Mrs. Sayers. I will look after her. But we must not relax our efforts in other directions. I see Sawtell, with Clifford and Bolton, coming in. I'll lecture them on the necessity of being cautious. Does Bolton, the Derby man, know Broome?"

"He was stationed here for six years."

"That's good."

Walters admitted the three men, and Bony gave his lecture on when to be cautious, which was now, and why. Clifford was to watch all through the night the house occupied by Mrs. Abercrombie and her companion, and Bolton was to watch over Mrs. Clayton and her daughter. Under no circumstances save the gravest were they to disclose to anyone police interest in these houses.

"To sum up," Bony said in conclusion, "if you see anyone acting suspiciously, or even committing a minor crime, you are not to take action. By all means try to identify the person so acting, but not at the risk of yourselves being discovered. Should you see anyone attempting to break into the house you are protecting, let him get well and truly inside before you arrest him."

Walters said:

"I've left a couple of torches in the kitchen, and the wife will have a packet of sandwiches for you. You can go off duty at daybreak, and report back tomorrow evening."

When they had left, Sawtell asked if anything was known of Abie, and Bony passed on the information given by Keith, adding:

"I'll put Old Dickenson on to hunting for Abie. You haven't lost any petrol?"

"No. I checked up on it."

"Ah well! Perhaps the cat found no humour in being black-mailed by the mouse."

The evening was advanced when Bony set out to locate Mr. Dickenson. It was almost dark when he discovered him lying full length on a public bench. The old man appeared to be drunk. Bony leaned over him and spoke. Then he nudged him. Bony sighed, and was charitable. Mr. Earle Dickenson was not a broken reed but rather one badly bent.

Relieving the "body" of the Webley pistol, Bony walked on.

Chapter Twenty: POOR LITTLE MOUSE!

Inspector Walters marched into Bony's "office" and sat down in the visitor's chair. Bony completed the sentence he was writing into his casebook, set down the pen, and reached for tobacco and papers.

"A road worker has found Abie," Walters announced. "The body's lying half inside a road drain. The black was at his old trick of inhaling petrol fumes, and this time he passed out."

"I did think he might end up like that," murmured Bony.

"Might! Petrol's surer than booze. I caught Abie at it twice, and Pedersen found him that bad that if he'd struck a match the feller would have exploded. Should be made a flogging matter for a native to be found drunk on booze or anything else. The old days and the old ways were good. I'd flog more and imprison less."

"The aborigines would prefer that way."

Walters snorted. "I'm sure they would. Like the birds, they can't bear loss of freedom, but a taste of jail doesn't last as long as a flogging. It's a damn nuisance. The other tracker's gone on walk-about, and I don't know yet when to expect Pedersen back with his boy. I'll have to run out to the body with the doctor. Care to come?"

Bony nodded and they went out to the open garage in the compound. Walters took his own car, and Bony sat in the rear seat as the doctor would want to hear the details on the way. They had to drive to the hospital, where Dr. Mitchell was making his morning round, and they had to wait twenty minutes. The interval stressed Walters' intolerance of procrastination and Bony's unruffled patience.

"Another body, eh?" exclaimed the medico, sliding in beside the inspector. "Good morning, Bony! Altogether too many unauthorised corpses in Broome lately. This blackfeller was addicted to petrol inhalation, wasn't he?"

The inspector said Abie was a confirmed addict and asked the doctor what kind of a kick petrol gave, as it might be cheaper than beer to a man sacked from the Police Force. The doctor replied that his knowledge of the subject was exceedingly slight and that he didn't intend to try it on himself to extend that knowledge.

Walters drove northward to take the right-hand road to the airport. The macadamised road was black, and here and there white-painted posts marked the culverts. A man was standing at one of the culverts a hundred yards beyond the entrance to the airport, and here Walters stopped his car. The roadman pointed down to the drain.

"He's down there, Inspector," he said. "I wouldn't have seen him only I was working just here."

The party stood at the edge of the culvert. The stormwater drain where it passed under the road was four feet deep and a yard wide, and all the upper part of the body could be seen, the legs being inside the culvert. Either side the road grew thick coastal bush and wire grass, and the bed of the drain was dry and covered with grass too resilient to be broken down. As the road worker had pointed out, the body would not be noticed by a road traveller, for Abie was dressed in his tracker's uniform of khaki overcoat which merged into the colour of the drain.

"Have you been down there?" Bony asked, and the man shook his head.

The body was lying on its back, the face masked by a blue-spotted brown neckcloth. Abie's hat was under the head as a pillow, and near the knees was a beer bottle. The position of the corpse was composed as though Abie had made himself quite comfortable along the bed of the drain.

Dr. Mitchell stepped down from the culvert and sniffed at the brightly coloured cloth.

"Petrol, all right," he said. Picking up the bottle, he turned

155

it upside down. It was empty. He sniffed at it and again said: "Petrol, all right."

On lifting the cloth, they saw that Abie's face was composed. Even the jaw had not "dropped," for the buttoned collar of the military tunic had kept it up after death had taken place.

Dr. Mitchell clambered out of the drain and dusted his knees.

"I'm satisfied if you are," he said to Walters.

The inspector glanced at Bony, who imperceptibly nodded.

"Right-oh! We'll get back," Walters briskly decided. "You come along to the station, Tom, and we'll have you make a formal declaration. Can we have the body buried this afternoon, Doctor?"

"Oh yes."

Bony refrained from asking for an estimate of the time Abie had been dead, and on Walters saying he would send the undertaker out immediately, Bony offered to await his arrival. Walters nodded and slid in behind the wheel, the others also entering the car. It was driven to the end of the bitumen roadway to turn the vehicle, and as it was driven back past Bony, Walters noted that he was making a cigarette. He wondered, but said nothing.

The car having disappeared, Bony stepped down into the drain and picked up the bottle by inserting his little finger into the mouth. The surface was clean enough, seeming to prove that it had rested in one of the deep pockets of Abie's overcoat. Bony looked for the cork and failed to find it. He lifted the cloth from the dead face and thoughtfully studied the position of the eyelids. He unhooked the collar of the tunic and examined the neck, deciding that Abie had not been strangled. He looked for and found the aborigine's dilly bag, without which no blackfellow feels decently clothed. It was made of kangaroo hide softened with grease and was suspended from the neck by human hair. It contained four magic healing stones, the beak of a small bird, a letter stick, and a plug of chewing tobacco.

The pockets of the tunic contained nothing, but the over-coat produced a pair of socks, clean and darned, and more chewing tobacco.

Bony returned the aborigine's treasures to the dilly bag and the socks and tobacco to the overcoat pocket. He spent more than ten minutes in a fruitless search for the bottle cork before leaving the drain for the road. Eventually he found the cork.

The picture presented was as follows. Abie, in possession of a bottle containing petrol, corked and carried in a pocket of the overcoat, had chosen the bed of a storm-water drain in which to indulge his singular passion. He chose the drain because of its privacy and the softness of the bed provided by the thick grass. The preparations for the debauch were simple. He made himself comfortable, and then uncorked the bottle. He had, apparently, poured the entire contents of the bottle onto the cloth, and then had no need to recork the bottle.

The bottle was left by his side, but the cork was neither in the drain nor on one of the banks. It was lying on the far side of the road, where it was impossible for Abie to toss it from his position in the drain. He could have tossed it where Bony found it by standing up, but it was illogical to assume that he had done this, as he would be thinking only of placing the saturated cloth over his face.

Again apparently, the dead man had chosen the drain primarily for its privacy. Then why had he not crawled into the culvert beneath the road? The culvert was large and airy and dust dry.

Again Bony went down into the drain, this time to examine the ground on which the dead man's military boots rested. Inside the culvert there was no grass. The dry sand loam was scored by the heels of the boots when Abie had pushed his feet into the culvert . . . or when they had been pushed in after he died. He could have entered the culvert quite easily, but his dead body could not be pushed in and then carefully arranged with the petrol-soaked cloth over the face . . . unless it was in a state of rigor mortis.

The position of the cork was decidedly significant. The bottle itself gave conclusive evidence. Having carried it to the Police Station with a finger into its mouth, Bony tested it for fingerprints. There were the fingerprints of Dr. Mitchell's left hand, and Bony had noted that the doctor had picked up the bottle with his left hand. There were no other fingerprints—not even those of the dead man.

The evidence was such that normally a post-mortem would be inevitable. Bony was confident that a post-mortem would disclose that Abie had not died from petroleum poisoning. He was sure that the tracker had been a mouse that had attempted to blackmail a cat. A post-mortem would mean an inquest, and an inquest on Abie would certainly reveal to his murderer that the police in Broome were not as stupid as he was doubtless thinking. The result would be caution, and from Bony's point of view he had been cautious long enough.

Inspector Walters was late for lunch. He arrived after the children had returned to school, explaining to Bony that he had been completing arrangements for the disposal of Abie's body.

"The doctor gave his certificate?" mildly enquired Bony.

"Oh yes. Case quite clear. The coroner agrees that an inquest is not necessary. Abie was bound to do it sooner or later."

"Have you known of a similar case of death through petrol inhalation among the aborigines?"

"No. Plenty of instances of blacks stealing petrol for the purpose of making themselves drunk . . . if the effect can be classed as drunkenness. The practise was unknown before the war."

"And the burial will take place this afternoon?"

"Yes. The Reverend Kendrake has agreed to read over him at four. I contacted Black Mark to send word to the blacks' camp. They'll all come in somehow or other. There won't be any corroboree at the cemetery, because to them Abie was a proper policeman and must be buried white-feller fashion."

Bony stood up, smiling whimsically.

"I may attend the funeral. I like funerals. Could you borrow from the postmaster the Meteorological Reports covering the last three years?"

Walters replied that he would and refrained from pressing for a reason. Bony went to his "office," and he had barely begun work on his notes when Mrs. Walters came to him with an unposted letter.

"A small Javanese boy brought it to the kitchen door."

Bony thanked her. The envelope was addressed to Mr. Knapp, Police Station, in a style of handwriting often termed copperplate. It was so skilfully done that Bony cut the envelope with a knife that he might preserve it. Within was a letter written in the same manner.

"Dear Mr. Knapp," Bony read. "Circumstances have provided me with information which I am hopeful will erase from your mind my default of yesterday evening. You will find me contrite but unbowed on the public bench outside the Post Office. Earle Dickenson."

Three minutes later Bony was sitting down beside Mr. Dickenson and interrupting the old man's apology by saying:

"In military, and police, parlance, you were off duty, so there was no harm done. I understand how strong an enemy can be. I removed the Webley from your pocket in case someone else did."

"Yes, I was off duty. I did intend waiting for you to transmit further orders, but . . . Abie lasted longer than I expected."

"Ah! You heard about that?"

"News passes quickly in Broome." Mr. Dickenson sighed. "I feel sorrow for Abie, and for Tojo and Hitler and all those others who drank the wine of power. I understand that he died of petrol fumes. Is that so?"

Bony sketched the scene at the storm-water drain that morning.

"Is it your opinion that accidentally he administered to himself too much petrol?"

"Why do you ask that?" countered Bony.

"Because I had the thought that it wasn't petrol that killed

159

him. And also because the blacks are today so wise as to the uses and dangers of petrol that Abie would not have made a mistake which could be credited only to a novice. When speaking of him the other day, you mentioned the possibility that he may have been trailing someone when scouting around the town in the small hours. I think now it's quite probable, because I'm sure he did not die of petrol fumes."

Bony waited, and the old man proceeded:

"When I woke on the bench last night it was very late and I was contrite. I knew you had visited me, because although the pistol was gone from my pocket my money was intact. I sat there for some time, and then felt the urge to take a long walk. I passed through Chinatown and took the track up the creek and then followed a path across the marsh which would take me to the airport entrance, my intention being to return to the town that way.

"On nearing the ground rise to the road where there is light scrub, I heard someone talking, and then as I drew nearer, I decided it was someone talking to himself. I found Abie under a tree. I asked him what he was doing there. He was drunk. He struggled to his knees and mumbled something, and he offered me a bottle.

"Another time, perhaps, I may have accepted his hospitality. I declined, and he seemed to insist. It was quite dark, you know. I took the bottle and found that it contained whisky . . . about a quarter full. Abie then fell on his back, and I thought he was very drunk. As he was lying close to the tree, I propped the bottle against it and left him.

"During the remainder of my walk, I pondered on Abie and his whisky, and I reached the conclusion that someone at the airport had given the whisky to him, or that he had stolen it from the airport. Then, this morning, I hear that Abie was found in a drain with a petrol rag over his face.

"When I thought Abie collapsed under the influence of whisky, it might be that he collapsed under the influence of whisky plus the influence of poison. Abie wouldn't go all the way out to that tree with a bottle of whisky and another bottle containing petrol, to have a go at the petrol after drinking the whisky." Mr. Dickenson hesitated before adding: "Any more than I would take on the battery acid after a sip or two of whisky. And he wouldn't take petrol with him to get himself over the effects of a bender on whisky. The abos aren't as provident as all that."

During a full minute Bony made no further comment.

"Your deduction is sound. You said you thought you heard voices as you approached the tree from the marsh. If the poisoner was then with Abie, he would have heard your approach. He would then have heard what took place when you found Abie, and he would not have proceeded to stage the death-by-misadventure scene at the culvert, knowing that your testimony would nullify all his trouble. I think you were fortunate."

"How so?"

"That the poisoner was not with Abie when you arrived there. Had he been with Abie, and hidden in the darkness, he would not have staged the petrol-fumes act. However, be advised and don't sleep on public benches."

Chapter Twenty-one: SEVERAL FACETS

Bony arrived at the cemetery a few minutes before the cortege. The ancient motor hearse was driven by an elderly white man smoking a calabash pipe. Beside him sat a very fat Malay chewing tobacco. After the hearse came a senile car crammed with aborigines with two on either running board. Following the car were two vehicles which, imaginatively, could be designated as trucks. They were loaded with men, their women and children and dogs. The men were shouting from truck to truck, the women were wailing, the children were bored, and all the dogs were barking. Last to arrive, and only just in time to catch up, was Mr. Kendrake, the minister.

Bony followed the minister's car along the central roadway, on either side of which stood ornate monuments to Japanese divers who had perished on the shell beds and elaborate memorials to wealthy Chinese and Malayans.

The cortege halted in a far corner of the cemetery, and there Abie was laid to rest and the minister preached sternly on the evils of drink and petrol fumes. The women wailed throughout, and the dogs barked continuously, but the powerful voice of the minister cowed the men and the children to solemnity.

Standing on the outskirts of the crowd, Bony was sad: for this race was dying, and the remnant here clothed in rags and gaudy finery presented the dreadful tragedy of a once rigidly moral, supremely free people being devoured by an alien and stupid civilisation.

Two of the women captured Bony's attention. One was a wizened old creature who was weeping with complete abandon. She was wearing a military overcoat which swept the ground at her feet, and on her head was a kind of turban of faded blue. The other was the maid he had interviewed at Dampier's Hotel. She was dressed in a brown frock and wore nylon stockings. Irene smiled shyly at Bony, and when the service was over, he went to her.

"Hallo, Bon-ee! Thank you for the stockings. I'm . . ."

"Yes, I see you are wearing them. They look very nice, Irene. Who is the old woman crying so much?"

"She's Lilia, Abie's grandmother."

"Ah! I ought to have guessed. She's very old."

"She says she remembers when there weren't any white people in this country. She said she ought to have Abie's overcoat, so they gave it to her."

"She's looking this way. Call her over," requested Bony.

The girl beckoned and the ancient approached, looking like a candle snuffer with a turbaned monkey for its top.

"Where you bin gettum hat, Lilia?" Bony asked, and the old woman blinked back her tears and shook her head. Irene explained that Lilia couldn't understand English, and that to within a few years ago she had been a desert black. The girl spoke in a dialect strange to Bony.

"She says that Abie gave the hat to her a long time ago. She says he gave it to her last winter to keep her head warm."

"Ask her to let us see the hat," Bony murmured, and when Irene had made the request known, off came the turban and it was unrolled to be disclosed as a silk nightgown.

"Tell her it's very pretty," and whilst Irene was translating, Bony produced a stick of tobacco. The small eyes deep in their sockets brightened to black beads, and a skinny hand abruptly closed over the tobacco. The old woman glanced about to see if the gift had been observed, and in a flash the tobacco disappeared.

"Ask her if she knows who gave Abie the nightgown, Irene."

The old woman negatived this question, and Bony let her hobble away toward the trucks, and they watched her compete with the women and the children and dogs to gain a place.

"They're going now," Irene said, and Bony sensed that she, too, would have to compete for a seat. Smilingly, he let her go

163

and then with amusement watched her ordering a youth from the car that she might ride in it.

Pensively, Bony walked to the airport gateway. He thought it improbable that Abie had stolen the nightgowns belonging to the three murdered women. To accept that probability meant accepting the theory that Abie stole at the instigation of the murderer, which wasn't logical, for no white man would trust an aborigine to that extent. Abie could have taken it from discarded clothing sent to the Mission. Anyway, it was not nearly as important as Mr. Dickenson's adventure.

Bony located the tree beside the road, an odd broad-leafed mulga about which grew no herbage or grass. It was easy tracking and the story plain to read. A man wearing rubber-soled shoes had stepped off the road with Abie and had stood with him under the tree. Abie had sat or had fallen down, and the man had hurriedly walked away to the road. The man wearing the rubber-soled shoes had returned to the tree and, on again departing to the road, he had carried a heavy burden. The shoes were new and the wearer pressed hard on the inside edge of the heels.

He had also taken the whisky bottle!

Bony found Mr. Dickenson on the bench outside the Sea-horse Hotel. It was nearing six o'clock and the place was packed. With his back to the hotel, he said softly:

"Stand up and ask me to have a drink."

Mr. Dickenson obliged, and Bony markedly hesitated to accept the suggestion before accompanying the old man into the bar. They found a reasonably quiet corner, and Bony edged his way through the press to the counter and bought the drinks. Everyone seemed too busy to notice them.

"I visited that tree," Bony said. "Your inferences, I think, are correct. In view of the possibility that you were seen with Abie, keep on your toes."

"To be forewarned is . . ."

"Is not to be immune from attack. Have you seen Flinn about?"

"I haven't seen him all day. Can we have another drink?"

164

"One more. You get them."

Mr. Dickenson had to fight his way through the crush to reach the counter.

"Would you grant me a favour?" Bony asked when the old man emerged without spilling the liquor. "I want you to pick up Flinn and keep with him until he goes to his room to sleep. What d'you think of a man who likes the touch of pearl against his face?"

Mr. Dickenson pondered, rubbing his long nose with his free hand.

"Pearl shell and pearls have a strong pull over some men. Naked gold has a similar influence over other men. I once knew a man who traded in furs. He was fascinated by fur. He liked to feel the touch of fur. He liked cats. He died of fatty degeneration of the heart. Ate and drank too much."

Leaving the bar, they sat on the low veranda, and Bony related what he had seen in the shell-packing shed, the while Mr. Dickenson gazed seaward at the clouds lying along the northwest horizon.

"Going to be a dark night," predicted the old man. "I told you before, if I remember rightly, that Flinn is a flash. You know more than I do. My reading of Flinn is that he might murder if he was threatened by something big. Abie could have been blackmailing Flinn, but I don't see how those three women could have threatened him or could have been a threat to him."

"They were a decided threat to the man who killed them," Bony said quietly.

"Oh!" Mr. Dickenson regarded Bony thoughtfully. "Then Flinn is a probability."

"Which is why I want you to keep both eyes on him, and at the same time look out for yourself. Is there a lock to your room?"

"Both a lock and a bolt."

"Then use both. What do those clouds mean? Rain? Wind?"

"I think neither. The glass is too high and the time of year against rain. The night will be dark and likely enough it will be a damp day tomorrow."

"Meaning?"

"A damp sea wind to annoy the Chinese laundryman."

"Well, I shall be late for dinner. Look after yourself. Be outside the Post Office at six in the morning. You'll not fail?"

"I shall be on duty," Mr. Dickenson pointed out stiffly.

"Yes, of course. Remember, keep looking over your shoulder."

Mr. Dickenson smiled, nodded, and departed for the hotel diningroom. Bony went back to the Police Station to call Mrs. Sayers. She had intended to go to a card party, but that could go to the devil as she would much prefer to entertain Mr. Knapp. At eight Bony presented himself.

"A very good evening, Mr. Knapp. So glad you've come."

"It's generous of you to choose my company against the lure of the card table," he murmured. Mrs. Sayers led the way to the lounge. She wore a white woollen sweater, white shorts, and white toeless sandals. Her legs were untanned, her eyes were bright, and her hair gleamed like old copper. Bony did not betray his astonishment at such literal interpretation of informal evening wear.

Nonchalantly he said:

"I hope you and Briggs have been carrying out the arrangements we agreed on."

"Briggs has been more determined about it than I have. I don't believe even now that I shall be attacked. There's no reason for it, but then . . . you have been anxious, I know." Mrs. Sayers giggled and called loudly for Briggs.

Briggs appeared instantly, standing just within the doorway of the lounge and mechanically chewing. Mrs. Sayers stubbed her cigarette and moved to the centre of the room.

"Briggs," she cried, "come and strangle me."

The chewing was switched off, and Briggs said:

"No fear, Mavis. I've had it."

"Do as you're told, Briggs. At once."

She-who-must-be-obeyed stood passively with her hands on

166

her wide hips. Briggs switched on the chewing and advanced. His lips parted and the chewing teeth clicked. His eyes reminded Bony of Abie's grandmother. He wavered, feinted, lunged. Up came Mrs. Sayers' arms. Under them went Briggs' crablike hands, and his body flashed slightly to one side. He managed to place his hands about her throat, and Mrs. Sayers promptly sank upon her knees and then catapulted herself forward. Briggs went backward and his hands flew wide, and then he was on his back and Mrs. Sayers' knees were pressing hard into his stomach and her hands were about his throat.

"Bravo!" exclaimed Bony.

Mrs. Sayers laughingly rose from Briggs and pulled him to his feet. He forgot to switch on the chewing and said:

"Easy enough when ya have warning. Another tale when there's no warning. Any'ow, you haven't forgot much."

"I've forgotten nothing, Briggs. No man is going to strangle me."

Then her left wrist was caught in a wheel-puller and her arm was braced up her back. A knee was forced into the small of her back, and a hand covered her throat and her head was brought against a hard shoulder. She sagged her knees, but the hand about her throat remained, pressing it and clamping her head against Bony's shoulder. Briggs said three times: "Bravo!"

Mrs. Sayers was panting slightly when released and gallantly raised to her feet. There was no mockery in her eyes.

"As Briggs said, the tale is different when there's no warning," Bony murmured. "Forgive me for that small demonstration. Under all the circumstances, I felt it was warranted."

"I been telling her——" Briggs cut in and was then cut out.

"Briggs, fetch some soda water. I want a drink." Mrs. Sayers turned to Bony, and now she was laughing. "You're a remarkable man, Mr. Knapp. I never thought it was in you. I remember that you like the flavour of whisky in soda water."

"When we disclose who killed Mrs. Overton and those other women, you will say you never thought it was in him," Bony insisted. "If he should attack you, you will not have any warning. I do hope you'll continue to co-operate with me."

"Of course I will." Mrs. Sayers took the soda from Briggs, and Briggs lined up with them at the sideboard. About to snub him, she changed her mind and gave him a drink.

"The bell working all right?" Bony asked.

Briggs nodded and Mrs. Sayers said they tested it each evening.

He was dismissed then, and Bony accepted a chair opposite his hostess.

"I would like to ask you an impertinent question, Mrs. Sayers. Why did you quarrel with Mr. Percival?"

"You heard about that? Really I oughtn't to have flared up like I did, Mr. Knapp. He came here one night complaining that Mr. Rose as headmaster was becoming far too easygoing with the boys and they were taking advantage of it. I said it had nothing to do with me, and he came back by saying I was the member of the Board of Control who had the most influence, and he wanted me to use it against Mr. Rose. Then he said he wouldn't have minded being stood down if Mr. Rose had turned out to be fitted for the headmastership. The discussion became heated when he blamed me for the Board's decision to appoint Mr. Rose in his stead, and I ordered him out of the house. Afterwards I told him I was sorry, and we were friends again."

"Has he visited you often?"

"Yes, been here lots of times."

"How many people, d'you think, would know the plan of this house?" asked Bony.

"Everyone in Broome, I should think. I don't mind 'em wandering around at my parties."

"Dear me! And I am supposed to be infallible. Would you have your domestic do the washing tomorrow?"

"I would, but there isn't any. She washed on Monday."

"You would be most helpful if you did have your personal washing left out on the line tomorrow night."

Mrs. Sayers' wide mouth formed an O.

"All right," she assented. Then she giggled and cried: "I think you're just the loveliest man!"

Chapter Twenty-two: THE FISHERMAN

The next day being Saturday, Bony went fishing in the afternoon with Bill Lung and Johnno. Sawtell, who happened to be in Chinatown, saw the three men in the boat heading down the creek for the open sea, and he snorted with astonishment.

The boat could not be termed a motor cruiser and there was nothing of comfort in it and little of cleanliness. Pieces of bait were still about from a previous trip, and the fish Johnno was cutting into bait was far from fresh. He sang as he worked, and the Chinese owner stood with the tiller between his legs and steered. Despite the smell of petrol he lit a cheroot from a match seeming to have a flame a yard high.

Out in the broad Roebuck Bay there was little wind. Through the holes in the canopy of mottled grey cloud the sunlight fell in bright bars of brass to rest upon the world. The water of the comparatively shallow bay was clear light green, and so, too, was the gull which flew over the motorboat. Bony had never before seen a green sea gull. The wings and breast were diaphanously emitting the most wondrous tint.

Conversation being difficult because of the engine noise, Bony was content to loll on the stern thwart and appreciate the surroundings. Broome hidden, save for a few buildings, behind the salmon-pink dunes, would entice the seafarer to think it a metropolis. The long white jetty and the buildings at its base appeared to have no purpose, and farther to the north the large sharp-angled Cave Hill College threatened the sprawling Mission.

Bony felt inexpressibly sleepy. For a week his sleep had been taken in minim doses, and now the sea air made a definite attack on his eyelids. Johnno saw him rubbing his eyes, and laughed. Bill Lung was looking for his seamarks and yet left the tiller to fetch a pair of tinted glasses from the toolbox.

169

The engine being stopped and the anchor tossed outboard, the ensuing silence lingered beyond Johnno's chatter and Bill Lung's soft drawling voice. Two gulls came winging above them, and Bony removed the glasses. The sun was now shining on this deep water, and the gulls overhead were translucently blue.

"I've fished often enough in the Pacific, but I've never seen green and blue gulls until today," remarked Bony. "They must reflect the colour of the sea."

"That's so," agreed Bill Lung. "I've never noticed it before. Be good for trade if some of the pearl shells was coloured like that!"

They fished for an hour and caught nothing. Then Bony's line was taken away despite all his efforts. He had fastened the end of the strong hand line round the thwart, and the line became taut and then snapped asunder.

"That feller too big, eh?" laughed Johnno. "He's a sting ray, perhaps, or a shark. Good-bye, line and hooks. Good-bye, everything."

At the end of a further hour, during which Johnno landed a small flathead and nearly went overboard in his excitement, Bony knew he would have to sleep. There were many questions he had wanted to put to Bill Lung, but these would have to wait. Sleep he must. He slid off the thwart for the bottom of the boat and slept.

The renewed uproar of the engine awoke him. He felt refreshed and surprised by the setting sun spraying the sea with crimson lacquer. The cloud canopy was now salmon pink and the dunes of Broome were white. Bill Lung pointed upward at the flying gulls. They were crimson.

On the way home, Johnno sat up in the bow and sang, and Bony sat with the Chinese at the tiller.

"Thanks for the trip," he said. "I'll remember it, and the gulls."

"Like Broome?"

"Very much. Should be all right now the strangler has been caught."

170

"Think he has?" shrewdly parried Lung.

"Don't you?"

"Perhaps. Perhaps not. Remember the ripped nightdresses left beside the bodies. Don't tally with a young man."

"Then what kind of a man would he be?" asked Bony.

Lung continued to gaze toward the mouth of Dampier's Creek, now opening to them amid the mangroves.

"Well?"

"I've often tried to imagine killing someone," he said. "And I haven't succeeded. I can't even imagine the frame of mind I'd have to be in to kill a man, let alone a woman. The killer here, I'd say, would be about as old as you and me. As my father would say: 'The wise man feasts in the morning, for the night will bring gall to his palate.' "

The sun had set when they stepped ashore. Johnno hurried away to his lodgings to eat preparatory to the night's work with his taxi, and Bony sought Mr. Dickenson. Having found him with the aid of two coloured children, he gave his orders for the night and walked briskly to the Police Station.

"I do really regret being late," he told Mrs. Walters. "Normally I'd have no excuses."

"Don't worry about it," she said. "We've just finished washing the dishes. I'm breaking Harry in good and proper."

"You've set a terrible example," complained the inspector. "And then you leave me to it and go fishing. Catch anything?"

"No, but I'm going out fishing again tonight."

"Must be nice to be in a Criminal Investigation Branch."

"There are advantages," admitted Bony, and sped away to shower and change. When he sat down to dinner, Walters sat by the window.

"Any alteration of duty for Clifford and Bolton?" asked the inspector.

"No."

"Sawtell reports that it looks as though Mrs. Sayers' washing will be left out all night." He thought he was imparting an item of news missed by this detective who wasted time on a fishing trip.

171

"Mrs. Sayers is splendidly co-operative," averred Bony. "I have but to suggest anything to her. I shall be on hand."

"You working to a plan?" Walters asked, and Bony admitted to it. Mrs. Walters sat at the table with him, and noting the faint evidence of strain under his eyes, she said:

"Why not a night in bed? Harry or Sergeant Sawtell could watch that line."

He smiled at her provokingly.

"I had three hours' sleep this afternoon," he said. "I went fishing that I should sleep, and now I'm very much awake and ready to fish all night."

"Better have someone with you, in case you get a bite too heavy to land," urged Walters.

"Oh, I won't land him tonight. I want only to feel him nibbling. Once I know he's nibbling, I'll prepare a bait with a dozen hooks buried in it. That will be a bait he'll take, and he won't get away."

"Do you know who he is, Bony?"

"Now, Mrs. Walters, what d'you expect me to answer to that? If he nibbles at the line tonight, I'll know who he is, although it will be so dark that I'll see only the blurred shape of him. As I told you, he has been drawing a sketch of himself, and if he steals a garment from Mrs. Sayers' line tonight he will have added the final and vital feature of identity."

The children came in from the compound to work at home lessons and Walters departed for the office. He was faintly irritated by Bony's evasiveness; at one moment feeling high confidence in him and in the next assailed by doubts and the gnawing fear that a fourth widow would be strangled.

When Bony closed the kitchen door and stepped down to the compound the night was dark and fragrant with the scent of ozone, eucalyptus, and roses. The clouds were thinning, and two widely separated stars were tired and pale.

Ten minutes later Bony joined Mr. Dickenson, who was seated with his back to the wide trunk of one of Mrs. Sayers' two palm trees. The old man was correctly sober and very much awake.

"All quiet," he said softly.

Having settled beside Mr. Dickenson, Bony surveyed his skylines. He could see the outline of the house, and the outlines of Briggs' cottage and the garage. He could also see the futuristic pattern made by the garments on the line. There was a light on the front veranda, and another in the lounge, and because it was a quarter to ten, Bony knew that Briggs would now be returning from the hotel and that Mrs. Sayers would be seated in her lounge and facing the door.

The proof he had provided that she could, without warning, be strangled had impressed Mrs. Sayers. She had accepted Bony's orders covering this night as willingly as her henchman had done.

Old Dickenson had gained his position under the palm tree before Briggs left, and he was able to watch the rear door. He had reported that he had seen nothing moving excepting Briggs. There was a dog chained to its kennel at the rear of the garage, and Briggs had fed the animal before leaving for the hotel. Its value as a watchdog was established when it voiced no protest at the arrival first of Mr. Dickenson and then of Bony.

Punctually at ten Briggs could be heard coming in from the front gate. Skirting the house, he entered by the rear door. A few moments later he closed the storm shutters and fastened several windows, and twenty minutes after he left by the rear door. The watchers heard the key being turned in the lock and withdrawn. Then the veranda light was put out and that in the lounge. Mrs. Sayers' bedroom was on the far side of the house, and Bony was confident that she would obey orders and lock her bedroom door despite Briggs' search of the entire house.

Satisfied that all these precautions had been taken, Bony settled to wait for the fish. He had sat here through several nights, accepting the additional precaution against an attack on Mrs. Sayers with patience, and patiently awaiting this particular night when there was reason for clothes to be left on the line.

173

The hours passed. At eleven the Seahorse Hotel closed, and thereafter the raised voices in that direction weakened into the silence. Now and then a dog barked, but never did Mrs. Sayers' dog so much as yelp in a dream. A night bird flew into the palm tree and for a little while preened its feathers. The sound of it could be heard by the two men. From the direction of the airport the noise of a car leaving town continued to dwindle for a long time before it was submerged.

Unfortunate Abie. And fortunate Mr. Dickenson. The murderer had struck at Abie swiftly and surely when the tracker had attempted blackmail. There was no doubt in Bony's mind of blackmail. The price of silence—at least a half bottle of whisky—had been paid. The price had been paid under that tree opposite the entrance to the airport. Having paid the price, the murderer withdrew that he would not by chance be discovered with a dying aborigine. Subsequently, having given the poison in the whisky time to do its work, he went back to move the body to the culvert and there had arranged the body and the petrol-soaked cloth over the face. Clever? No . . . stupid. He had repeated mistakes . . . the old mistakes. When wearing rubber gloves, he had wiped clean door handles, and he must wipe clean the petrol bottle before leaving it at Abie's side. And the cork . . . it might never be known why he tossed it so far away.

Yes, fortunate Mr. Dickenson. He had, indeed, been fortunate when finding Abie during the period the murderer was absent, for had he seen the murderer with Abie, his life would have been cut off abruptly. There were other aspects . . .

The night bird flew out of the tree and vented its long wailing cry. The sound roused Bony from meditation, and thirty seconds afterward a cold finger touched the nape of his neck and moved rapidly upward into his scalp. Again that extra sense inherited from his maternal ancestors gave its warning, and he reached out and pressed lightly on Mr. Dickenson's arm.

The void below the skylines remained featureless. No dog barked. No motor hummed. The silence was profound as Bony waited for the warning to materialise. Presently it did in the sound as of paper being rubbed lightly on paper.

This sound ceased. Taut nerves were struck a blow by the shrill crowing of a rooster in the neighbouring garden. The crowing died in a gurgle, as though the bird realised its silly miscalculation of the dawn. Again the sound of paper rubbing on paper . . . this time louder. Someone was walking on the lawn, sliding his feet forward as though to prevent tripping over one of Mrs. Sayers' croquet hoops.

Then Bony saw the figure silhouetted against the featureless backdrop of the cloud-covered sky. It was growing slowly larger. It was coming to the palm tree. It vanished when it entered the black void beneath the branches of the tree just beyond Mr. Dickenson. It would be damn tragic luck if the intruder fell over Mr. Dickenson's legs.

Bony accepted a big risk of being discovered. He found Mr. Dickenson's knee, placed his hand under it and the other about the ankle, and lifted the leg until the knee almost touched the old man's chest. Mr. Dickenson, realising what was meant, soundlessly lifted the other leg. Bony followed suit.

Nothing emerged from the limitless silence. Precisely where the unknown man was standing could not possibly be determined. That he remained within the blackness beneath the wide-spreading fronds of the palm tree was certain. Even had Bony not seen him enter that darkness, the icy finger continuing to run up and down the nape of his neck was sufficient acknowledgement of the menace. Softly, and yet dreadfully distinct, there came to Bony and Mr. Dickenson the sound of tapping teeth.

The temptation to spring forward and blindly seek to reach and arrest this teeth-clicking man Mr. Dickenson had both seen and heard leaving the house of murdered Mrs. Eltham had sternly to be resisted by the taut Bonaparte. What the old man was thinking and feeling Bony could imagine, and during these moments of suspense he felt admiration for the self-command of Mr. Dickenson. Not a tremor evinced itself in the arm Bony lightly was grasping.

175

Although the man could not be seen, he could continue to be heard. Bony could "feel" him standing within a foot or two of his companion's bunched legs. He was probably waiting to be sure of his next move, assessing the odds in his favour. He was like the swordfish leisurely following the bait fish trolled behind the angler's launch, "eyeing" it, "smelling" it, waiting to be sure before striking. The greatest fish Bony had ever raised was now following the bait on that clothesline, not the clean, fighting swordfish but the stalking mako shark, the shark that can hate and will endeavour to leap into the boat to get at the angler.

The teeth-clicking stopped. The next minute was as an hour, Bony motionless in the stern of his launch and waiting, waiting for the shark to make up its mind to strike at the bait.

Abruptly the arc of lesser darkness toward the clothesline was blotted out, and then it returned to frame the shapeless mass of the unknown as he left the darkness beneath the tree and went forward slithering his feet over the grass. The fish was coming after the bait. In two seconds, one second, it would push its fearful snout out of the ocean to seize it.

Bony went forward to lie prostrate and seek the skyline above the hanging clothes. He saw the clothes against the sky jerk and struggle as though alive. He saw the shapeless mass of the "shark" at the bait, witnessed the "shark" slip down into the sea of darkness toward the house.

Bony turned, sought for and found the Vandyke beard, and drew Mr. Dickenson's head forward to him.

"Don't move away," he breathed.

On hands and knees, he "ran" towards the house over the lawn. He heard the sound of paper rubbing on paper, and then soft footsteps on the driveway. The murderer was leaving by the front gate, and the triumphant Bony wanted to shout his name.

Chapter Twenty-three: BAITING THE HOOK

In accordance with wishes expressed in Bony's note discovered on the kitchen table the following morning, Inspector Walters roused Bony at eleven with a cup of tea and a biscuit.

"Ah . . . good morning," Bony greeted him. "Sawtell here?"

"Yes. Did the fish nibble?" asked Walters with ill-restrained eagerness.

"He did. Fetch Sawtell and we'll discuss it."

When the sergeant saw Bony's striking silk pyjamas, his eyes widened but he made no reference to them. Invariably conservative in clothes, Bony was excused by the discerning Sawtell now seated at the foot of the bed as the inspector occupied the only chair. Damn it! A man was entitled to have one outlet for a love of colours.

"How did the fishing go?" he asked, and being Sunday morning, he lit one of his favourite cigars.

"The fish nibbled. He detached Mrs. Sayers' silk nightgown from her clothesline. Same man Dickenson saw leaving Mrs. Eltham's house. Clicked his teeth as though extremely cold."

"Who is he?" asked Walters.

"It was too dark to identify him."

"Did you trail him?" persisted the inspector.

"As far as to be sure he made no attempt to enter the house. The risk of arousing his suspicions was too acute. He'll come again, and he won't throw up the hook we'll bait for him."

Walters was grim.

"Why fish for him again?" he objected. "You said that if he attempted to strangle Mrs. Sayers, you would know who he is. If you know him, let's go after him. Possession of those four nightgowns will be evidence enough for the Crown Prosecutor."

177

"I agree with you . . . if we found those four nightgowns in his possession. But we cannot be sure they are in his possession. When he stole that nightgown last night, he completed his sketch of himself." Bony lit an alleged cigarette, and the two men impatiently waited for him to continue. "I can now see him, but if he has destroyed those nightgowns, the remaining evidence I hold would not be sufficient. And further, there would be a row if we acted now on a search warrant and did not find those garments in his possession. I have sufficient evidence to convince you, to convince the Crown Prosecutor himself, but not sufficient clear-cut proof to induce the Crown Prosecutor to take action. We are left with no alternative but to catch the murderer in the very act."

"Who is he?" bluntly asked Sawtell.

Seeing the slow smile on Bony's face, both men knew they were butting their heads against a brick wall. Bony pressed on, an edge to his voice:

"He murdered Mrs. Cotton presumably because she sold liquor. He murdered Mrs. Eltham presumably because she sold her affections. On the face of it, he murdered Mrs. Overton presumably because she gave herself to good works. Doesn't make sense, does it? When you detect why he attempts to murder Mrs. Sayers you will have in the motives behind the attacks on the four women the inner motive: for actually there is only one motive, and it presents a clear picture of the man."

"Wouldn't that evidence of motive be good enough for the Crown Prosecutor, even though the stolen nightgowns weren't found in his possession?" argued Sawtell.

"Not good enough for the Crown Prosecutor to advise action on a capital indictment. Assuming I had apprehended this fellow after he had removed the garment from the line, with what could he be charged? With the theft of a garment, to wit, a woman's nightgown. Admittedly, we could have applied for a warrant to search his house. If we did not find those other three nightgowns in his house, he, being a first offender and neither an Asian nor a poor white, would certainly be discharged on a bond of good behaviour. I'm not

178

going to gamble on the chance that he has retained the four nightgowns."

"Catching him in the act would certainly clinch the job," admitted Walters. "How d'you propose to do that?"

"I shall be right inside the room where he attacks Mrs. Sayers."

"In her bedroom?"

"In her bedroom."

"Jumping cats!" purred Sawtell. "She stand for that?"

"She will. I haven't asked her yet, but she will." Bony left the bed and from the wardrobe took a dressing gown. Sawtell audibly gasped when he saw it, a creation of pastel blue with yellow collar and cuffs and a large bright red pocket. The sergeant couldn't remove his gaze from it when it encased the striped yellow-and-green pyjamas. Bony snatched up a towel, saying: "The slightest incautious move on our part will frighten off this mako shark from the hook I'll bait with Mrs. Sayers."

Walters stood up to regard Bony with cold pensiveness.

"Have you calculated the danger to Mrs. Sayers?" he asked.

"I've already worked out the finer points," Bony replied brightly. He turned to Sawtell: "In your private laboratory, have you a camera fitted with an automatic flashlight?"

The sergeant nodded. Then he burst into low laughter.

"You're not aiming to take a flashlight picture of the man strangling Mrs. Sayers, are you?"

"It is my intention to make the effort. In the compound I have observed a portable blacksmith's forge and anvil. D'you know anything of ironwork?"

"I can make horseshoes," admitted Sawtell.

"Good! Try your hand on making a collar for Mrs. Sayers. Fashion it with sheet-roofing iron, and use Mrs. Walters as your model. See that the bottom edge is packed with material so that the collar will not cut the lady's neck, and that it fits well enough to prevent the man's hands from slipping in under it to reach the throat. If you make it slightly too large for Mrs. Walters, it will fit Mrs. Sayers."

The unease and doubt fled from Inspector Walters before the brilliance of this facet of Napoleon Bonaparte.

"Think you can do it, Sawtell?" he asked.

"Give it a try, anyway," replied the sergeant. "When do you want it, Bony?"

"I'd like to have it by four this afternoon. And remember that the children will be about. Don't let them see their mother as the model for an iron collar."

Sawtell, as Bony was aware, did not need the forge and anvil to make the collar. He shut himself into the trade shop and began work on a piece of galvanised sheet iron. At one o'clock he was due home for dinner, and on his return he brought a large brown-paper parcel which he opened on Bony's table. Within half an hour Bony had mastered the mechanism of the flashlight attachment to which the sergeant had added a long cord shutter release.

Meanwhile, Keith Walters had been despatched to Mrs. Sayers with a note and a cylindrical-shaped parcel. He had received clear instructions on the way he was to take to Mrs. Sayers', and the way he was to return. Bony questioned him on his return to be assured that the boy had carried out the instructions.

"You're a good scout, Keith," Bony complimented him. "Now, don't be curious and ask questions. And don't talk about that little job."

The boy promised, and Bony spent two hours writing in his "office." He was called for afternoon tea at four o'clock by Mrs. Walters, whose eyes were bright with controlled excitement, and on being taken to the lounge, he found Walters and the sergeant already there. Displayed on a small table was the iron collar.

"Fit it on, Esther," requested Walters.

"It's a little too big for me, and so I'm sure it'll do," she said.

Sawtell had actually painted the thing with a fast-drying enamel, achieving a near flesh colour which was a credit to him. At the top and bottom edges he had drilled holes and

180

through them laced a thick strand from a dressing-gown girdle. He had fashioned the collar in two pieces, hinged at the back and fastened at the front with strong clips. Without much trouble, Mrs. Walters placed the collar about her neck and stood back for examination. She had to hold her chin high, but the chin maintained the collar down upon the collarbone.

"Excellent!" cried Bony. "Congratulations, my dear Sawtell. Why, even the most fastidious woman could not object to wearing the ornament. Permit me, Mrs. Walters."

Placing his hands about Mrs. Walters' protected neck, he was instantly satisfied that the iron collar was a hundred per cent efficient. Mrs. Walters was thrilled. Sawtell was proud of his work, and Walters was relieved of one of his gnawing worries. To him Bony proferred a foolscap-size envelope, saying:

"I have recorded in detail my fishing strategy. I would like you to study it with Sawtell, and adhere rigidly to the parts I have set out for you and Sawtell and the two constables. I do not expect the shark to take the bait tonight, but we must all be prepared and waiting. You will find how much I have stressed the vital necessity for caution that the shark will not become suspicious and sheer off."

"We'll be with you all the way," declared Walters.

A few minutes later Bony left the Police Station. He carried Sawtell's camera and iron collar parcelled in brown paper. Other oddments were stuffed into his pockets, spoiling the "set" of his pin-striped dark grey suit. He walked with the slow tread of the locals, and first passed through a section of Chinatown, where he met Mr. Dickenson and spent ten minutes instructing him. Eventually he approached Mrs. Sayers' house from a side street, keeping beneath the roadside trees until he reached her front gate. It was five o'clock when Mrs. Sayers welcomed him.

"It seems hours that I've been waiting for you," she said, her face slightly flushed beneath the make-up. "There was no need to send the domestic home early, as she always goes home at two on Sundays . . . and I'm just dying to know what's in that parcel young Keith Walters brought."

"You would never guess," he told her smilingly. "Or what's in this one. Now, with your permission, shall we have Briggs in? There are proposals to be accepted and things to do before nightfall."

"He may not be awake . . . He sat up all last night, and the night before." An expression strange to Bony lit the brown eyes. "You see, Briggs is devoted to me, and he's been a little bit difficult."

"Anxious, and inclined not to obey orders, eh?"

"That's it. This morning he rebelled when he heard about the nightie being stolen. Did you see him—the thief, I mean?"

"I saw him, but I could not identify him. If you don't mind, I'll rouse Briggs. He'll be less rebellious when he knows the details of a little plan I want to put into operation." Bony smiled again. "I am taking it for granted that you will not rebel."

"Only if you leave me out of it."

"My dear Mrs. Sayers, you are the keystone of the arch, the kernel of the nut, the very sun of the universe, the irresistible lure. Without you I am lost. Ah! This might be Briggs."

Footsteps in the passage beyond the lounge door. Then Briggs stood in the entrance, the chewing switched on. The small black eyes were not friendly.

"Briggs, come in," commanded Mrs. Sayers. "Mr. Knapp wants to talk to us."

Bony unwrapped his parcel, the woman and her manservant-friend standing with him. Neither spoke when the camera was disclosed, and Briggs remained silent when Bony removed the wrapping about the iron collar.

"Whatever is that?" asked Mrs. Sayers, and Bony turned to her, the collar held forward.

"I am going to call it 'Lady-May-Venture,'" he replied. "Sawtell and I plan to mass-produce. It'll be all the rage. Bound to be. Permit me."

Bony swung the collar open like a bracelet and gently "wrapped" it about Mrs. Sayers' neck, fastening it.

182

"Chin up, please. Ah! An excellent fit." Bony stepped back, and Mrs. Sayers worked her chin up and down. "Briggs, try to strangle Mrs. Sayers."

Briggs, who had stopped chewing, said:

"Stone the crows!"

Mrs. Sayers giggled. Briggs clamped his hands about her neck and squeezed. Briggs exerted himself. Mrs. Sayers giggled again. Then swiftly she was serious, and when Briggs drew back, she said:

"Are you sure I'll be attacked?"

"Yes," answered Bony. "Now let me show you how to remove that thing, and then we'll talk. Satisfied, Briggs?"

"Yes, up to a point."

"What I am going to propose," Bony prefaced his explanation, "is nothing less than arresting the killer of these Broome women in the act of attempting to kill you, Mrs. Sayers. He is both ruthless and cunning, and he's the type having the instincts of the brute and the brain of the human thinker. This one has succeeded so well that we haven't sufficient evidence to ask for a warrant to search his home.

"Having stolen your nightgown, he has begun the plan which he has successfully executed thrice. If he meets with opposition anywhere along the line of this fourth progress of his plan, he will retire until he feels sure he can strike down another victim. He may wait a month, six months, a year, and for obvious reasons we can neither give up hunting for him nor permit him to formulate an entirely different plan.

"Having stolen your nightgown, it will be his intention to gain entrance to this house for the purpose of destroying you. I want him to make the attempt. I want him to enter this house, to find you in your room, to attempt to kill you. I want to take a picture of him in the very act. I want to be with you, even in your room, waiting for him.

"Without that collar, I wouldn't think to expose you to such terrible risk. Wearing it, you will not be exposed to physical risk but you will require courage and the ability to withstand great nervous tension. There are two reasons for believing he won't harm you. One, that you will be waiting for him, as you waited for Briggs, and two, I shall be with you."

"Why, Mr. Knapp, I wouldn't have believed that Broome could stage such an adventure."

"We may have to wait all night in the dark for two or three, or even five, nights."

"In my bedroom?"

"In your bedroom. You will be lying on your bed, and I shall be seated on a chair in a corner of the room. I do hope you will not be acutely embarrassed."

"I bet not as much as you," Mrs. Sayers said with conviction. She broke into low laughter. "Oh, what a man! You tell me I'm to go to bed and that you'll sit by my bed all night, and then you express very politely the hope that I shall not be embarrassed. And what makes it so funny is that you're quite sincere about it."

"Sincerity, Mrs. Sayers, is one of my virtues," he said stiffly.

"I believe that," she hastened to assure him. "It's just the situation that's so funny when I think of what the social lights of this town will think when they hear about it. Where will Briggs be waiting?"

"In his room," replied Bony. "I cannot stress too much the importance of both Briggs and you continuing your normal routine. On one point only do I ask for sacrifice, and that is you will neither entertain at night nor accept invitations to spend the evenings away from home. I would like to stay here, to sleep in a spare room during the day, concealed from your domestic. No one must even suspect I'm in the house, and no one must think either of you is alarmed or suspects trouble. That is my plan."

Mrs. Sayers, who had again become grave, looked at Briggs. Briggs, who had forgotten to switch on his chewing, nodded his head slowly and with deliberation.

"Seems all correct at first look," he conceded. "Goes a bit deeper, I suppose?"

"Yes, there are further details, Briggs. What d'you think about it, Mrs. Sayers?"

184

"I like it, Mr. Knapp. The more I remember Mabel Overton, the better I like it. It's a perfect plan, and I'm already worked up to get my hands on that strangling beast. I'll give him what he's been begging for."

Bony smiled bleakly.

"Accept my grateful thanks," he said. "How long have you been closing the storm shutters at night?"

"Ever since the Eltham woman was murdered," answered Briggs.

"When the shutters are fastened, is it possible to see into the house?"

"Don't know. Might be at the sides."

"Can anyone see down through the ventilators along the top of the shutters?"

"No. I'm sure about that."

"Well, then, after dark tonight, ascertain if it's possible to see into the house from outside. And at the same time test the blinds or curtains of the remaining rooms. There's a job I want you to do now. It's probable that the murderer will have seen the alarm-bell wire passing from the house to your room, and will cut it. Without taking down the wire, do you think you could rearrange the alarm system?"

"So that if he cuts the present wire it won't make no difference, yes."

"I brought wire in case you haven't any. You were at sea for several years, were you not?"

"For about twelve years."

"Do you know anything about firing rockets?"

"All there is. Why?"

"That other parcel contains six rockets. They are an important part of our plan. Now you get along with that wiring. Take it underground so that it cannot be cut outside the house. As I said, leave the present wiring crossing the yard. He's almost certain to cut that, as well as the telephone wires. Meanwhile, Mrs. Sayers, I would like to ramble about your house."

Mrs. Sayers' house was one of the largest in Broome, having five bedrooms in addition to the usual living rooms. Like that occupied by the late Mrs. Overton, her house faced the west. The front door gave access to the exceptionally deep veranda which was wholly protected by storm shutters. A second door gave entry to the house, the dividing passage running straight to the kitchen at the rear.

The room across the passage from the lounge was Mrs. Sayers' bedroom. It was large, and the french windows opened to the veranda. There was a tallboy in the corner almost opposite the door, and Bony had placed a chair between the tallboy and the windows, so that by gently moving the edge of the curtain he could see anyone standing at the electric meter and light switch. Having focused the lens to cover the room between the bed and door, he had screwed the camera to the tallboy and had brought the wiring from the alarm bell in Briggs' room to a press button attached to the edge of the chair.

The first night the shark did not rise to the bait fish as represented by Mrs. Sayers, who lay on her bed, a satin nightgown over shorts and blousette, and the iron collar about her neck. She suffered no inconvenience from Sawtell's invention, and from 2 A.M. she slept until Briggs woke her with morning tea. Bony was then sleeping in the next bedroom, to which he had retired shortly after daybreak.

The one difficulty to his presence in the house was the domestic. He could have left at dawn for his bed at the Police Station and returned to the house after dark, but the coming and going even at these hours might be noted by a man who excelled in cautiousness.

It was a few minutes after five in the afternoon when Bony

awoke, and it was not till seven twenty-five that Mrs. Sayers called him to a meal she had prepared. He insisted on washing the utensils whilst Mrs. Sayers cleared the table, and then he spent half an hour again going over the drill with her and Briggs, placing emphasis on the importance of the ban of silence imposed between them on the one hand and himself on the other. By neither word nor gesture were they to betray his presence. The same ban was imposed on Mr. Dickenson, who was living in Briggs' room.

When Briggs left for the hotel at nine o'clock, Mrs. Sayers, dressed again in shorts, occupied herself with a book in the lounge, and Bony sat on a chair just within the doorway of the room he had occupied all day. The back door was closed and the kitchen light switched off, as was Briggs' custom when departing. The veranda lights were on and the house door to the veranda was open, it being seldom closed.

Outside, it was quite dark. An easterly wind had sprung up at sunset, and it sibilantly rustled the branches of the twin palm trees and played on the taut telephone wires affixed to the house on the outside of Mrs. Sayers' bedroom. An excellent fishing night.

By Bony's luminous wrist watch it was nine-thirty when there was a ring at the veranda doorbell. A moment later Mrs. Sayers appeared in the passage to answer the summons. Then Bony heard the veranda door being opened and Mrs. Sayers speaking:

"Why, Mr. Willis! How nice of you to call. Do come in."

The man's voice Bony did not recognise, nor did he know him when he followed Mrs. Sayers into the lounge.

"I won't detain you long, Mrs. Sayers," he said. "I've called on behalf of several of our fellow townsmen who have come together to discuss a project which we think would succeed if you will consent to join us."

It was proposed to erect a building combining under the same roof a library, a museum, and a hall to be used for the exhibition of educational pictures and for lectures by prominent visitors. The money was to be raised by public subscription and controlled by a trust headed, it was hoped, by the philanthropic Mrs. Sayers.

Mrs. Sayers was offering encouragement to Mr. Willis when Bony felt a sudden alteration of air pressure. Another alteration occurred immediately afterwards, and there was no doubt that someone had opened and closed the kitchen door.

Knowing that to anyone in the kitchen he would be silhouetted against the indirect veranda lighting, Bony edged his face round the bedroom doorframe and viewed the passage with one eye. It could not be Briggs who had opened the kitchen door, for Briggs would have switched on the kitchen light.

The illumination from the veranda lights dwindled into a void halfway along the passage, and within the void was the entrance to the kitchen. It certainly hadn't been Briggs who had entered, and Mr. Dickenson had received clear instructions to lie snug until signalled into action by the bell under Briggs' pillow.

Mrs. Sayers was intimating to her visitor that she would consider his proposition, when Bony saw movement at the end of the passage. At first indefinite, it resolved into the figure of a man. He was coming from the kitchen, but before he could be identified, he stopped before the door of a bedroom which Bony was aware was unfurnished and went in.

There was no resultant light in the unoccupied room, and Bony could not be sure if the man had closed the door after him. He had made no sound when opening it.

As he had often watched the fin of a swordfish knifing the surface of the turbulent ocean to approach the trolled bait, so did he sit on the chair moved to permit him to watch that dark passage. This time he had seen no swordfish fin, clean of line and direct in progress. This fin was the fin of a shark, the fin of a mako shark . . . the biggest and most ferocious human shark ever to rise to Bony's trolled bait; and the hair at the nape of his neck became stiff, the point of an icicle moved up and down his spine, and every nerve tingled and whined with tautness like the telephone wires without.

188

Mrs. Sayers conducted her visitor to the door and bade him good night. If she noticed Bony, she said nothing as she passed back into the lounge, and Bony did not remove his gaze from that hypothetical shark's fin.

Eventually Briggs came in by the kitchen door, switched on the light and then the hot point to prepare coffee. The kitchen light completed the illumination of the passage, and Bony, watching Briggs approach, drew back a little. Briggs, who must have seen him, completely ignored him, and entered the lounge to receive final instructions.

"Anything you want, Mavis, 'fore I lock up?"

"Yes, Briggs. I would like a pot of coffee and some sandwiches brought to my room. I'm going to bed. I've a nasty headache."

"All right! You better take a couple of tablets. Got any?"

"No. Bring me a packet with the coffee."

The identical conversation had been conducted the previous evening, and with voices slightly raised, so that should Mr. Hyde be outside the lounge windows he would know Mrs. Sayers' immediate plans. Tonight, in the unoccupied room along the passage, he was doubtless holding the door ajar. Briggs was perfect; Mrs. Sayers was superb.

Briggs proceeded with his chores, closing the storm shutters and locking the veranda door. As on the previous evening, he did not shut the door to the house and he did not make an inspection of the rooms, and when he was passing the room where lurked the "mako shark" Bony slipped into the bedroom occupied by Mrs. Sayers.

Mrs. Sayers came in and switched on the light. Bony commanded silence with two fingers pressed to lips. He wrote a note, using the tallboy for a desk, and, when Briggs knocked, he gave her the note, which she saw was directed to Briggs.

Briggs was told to enter and appeared with a tray covered with a cloth. He openly winked at Bony, dextrously removed the cloth and spread it on the bedside table. Then, having set out the supper, he stood with the tray under an arm and asked if there was anything further required. Presenting him with the note in which Bony had announced the arrival of the murderer, Mrs. Sayers said:

"That will be all, Briggs. Don't forget to put out the kitchen light. You've often forgotten it, remember, and I won't have wastage."

The wrinkled face slightly expanded in a grin.

"What a nark you are, Mavis," he grumbled. "Here's me having to think of everything, and you go crook. All right! Now take them tablets and sleep deep. Good night!"

The door closed behind him. Mrs. Sayers poured coffee for two, and she and Bony sat on the edge of the bed and munched sandwiches. In a low whisper, Bony told of what he had seen.

"He won't come for an hour or two. He'll wait to be sure Briggs is asleep. Bear in mind all the points I've given you, and keep a hard rein on your nerves. And remember, I want to take a picture of him, so try to avoid coming between him and the camera."

Mrs. Sayers nodded. Her eyes were bright with excitement, and she gained Bony's complete admiration when he failed to see a sign of fear. In his chair in the far corner, he smoked a last cigarette and watched her gathering the supper things with hands perfectly steady. She placed them on the dressing table, and Bony removed one cup and saucer, which he put into a drawer.

Again in his chair, he laughed silently when Mrs. Sayers slipped on her satin nightgown and, with a flourish, completed her ensemble with the iron collar. She smiled at him, and he knew she wanted to giggle. Then the mood passed and she stretched and raised her arms and tensed her muscles. Her face was very square and her eyes were small and wicked. Above the footrail of the bed, she waved to him before pulling on the light cord.

In the dark, Bony settled himself for what he expected to be a prolonged vigil. He could hear Mrs. Sayers moving on the bed. Briggs was still in the kitchen and he was whistling as though to send them a message of good cheer. A minute passed, and then the sound of the kitchen door being shut and locked. Silence descended like a desperate hand on an alarm clock.

The stage was set and the actors waiting for the curtain to go up. The play would begin with the entry of the man Bony had already identified with his "bits and pieces." The remaining actors had been drilled in their parts and were now waiting to receive their call. It was a situation and a moment to thrill the heart of one who loved the dramatic denouement.

When Bony pressed the button at the edge of his chair and tugged the cord operating the camera shutter and the automatic flashlight, Briggs would rush for the kitchen door and, if unable to unlock it, smash it with a sledge hammer. He would then race along the passage and, should there be no light in Mrs. Sayers' room, he was to make for the master switch before joining forces with Bony. Meanwhile, Mr. Dickenson was to emerge from the hut with a bucket of sand into which were partially embedded three wide mouthed bottles. Into the bottles he was to place rockets, the wicks of which were moistened with kerosene. Having fired the rockets, he was to make for the front veranda door and switch on all the lights.

The rockets would be seen by the two constables guarding the homes of Mrs. Abercrombie and Mrs. Clayton. They would at once race for Mrs. Sayers' house. Inspector Walters and Sergeant Sawtell would be waiting in the jeep, and they should arrive within three minutes of the signal being sent up.

Guile and patience were the attributes essential to landing this monster, with emphasis on guile. Police posted round the house would, under these circumstances, be foolish. To get within range of a tiger you don't blow whistles, and to hook a mako shark you don't use a bent pin. And when you have the co-operation of a woman like Mrs. Sayers, you try to so arrange matters that you will have the most complete and the most conclusive evidence to accompany your assertion that an attempt to murder did take place. The Crown

191

Prosecutor's ruling is ever: "He who asserts must prove." Bony waited with cold patience to provide a classic example of assertion with proof.

With the eyes of his mind, Bony could see the man skulking in that other dark room. He was crouched on the floor, recalling those ecstatic moments when he had killed three times and waiting for the moment to come when he would again kill. He had been a young man blessed with a retentive memory and the laudable desire for knowledge, and the road of his progress had been marked with his triumphs. He had been spurred by ambition to reach the goal of social distinction and power, and nothing had been permitted to come between him and those prizes. Normal human desires had been placed on the altar of asceticism and with unbreakable will maintained upon that altar.

He had fought a good fight—so he had thought—rushing to the shower and his books when the battle went against him. He had exchanged the pleasures of early manhood for knowledge. Knowledge would bring power. With power he would have social position, and once that was gained, all that which he had suppressed within himself could be given freedom of expression.

But, having entered the kingdom of ambition, he discovered that his knowledge did not include even the elementary knowledge of women. The years of self-denial had loaded him with honours, they had raised him high to a position of power . . . and they had stripped him of his youth. Wine he had expected, and vinegar he had received, in the critical flash of a discerning eye, the titter of scorn within a whisper, the lift of a luscious mouth. Lovely women wanted nothing of his knowledge. They are themselves a science, and only the ardent student acquires the counterscience. He had found himself too old to begin the study.

The pride of the successful man was overwhelmed. What he had with conscious will kept submerged rose from the subconscious to attack with long-pent fury. He had become the centre of contending forces, finally to emerge fearing that for which he yearned and fearing he would lose all the fruits of his emulation.

This dual fear had become directed to certain women whose activities threatened his power and whose sex tormented him.

Chapter Twenty-five: THE ANGLER WINS

To sit comfortably for thirty minutes and meditate on pleasing subjects is, in these hectic years, an experience. To sit on a hard chair for three hours, with hearing strained to locate the approach of a multiple murderer, is perhaps one degree easier to bear than lying on a bed and imaginatively dying a hundred deaths by strangulation. Had Mrs. Sayers screamed: "I can't bear it!" Bony would have been neither surprised nor angered.

The cessation of a sound so prolonged as to become unnoticed was at first not registered by Bony, and it was several seconds before he realised that the wind in the taut telephone wires had stopped. There could be only the one explanation— the murderer had cut the wires.

Holding the edge of the window curtain one inch from the frame, Bony kept watch on the veranda. He hoped that Mrs. Sayers had noted the cessation of wind playing on telephone wires, for then she would at least know that her ordeal was drawing to a climax.

A measureless period of emptiness was endured when imperceptibly the darkness of the veranda waned before the waxing of light. The light grew, but not sufficiently to illumine the furniture, and suddenly Bony saw its source, the round opaque disc of a flashlight masked by a cotton handkerchief.

The murderer was now facing the master light switch. He appeared to be standing there a long time, but actually was with infinite care raising the switch bar to prevent any metallic sound. A master in the art of noiseless movement, Bony felt admiration for the practitioner who equalled himself. The disc of light disappeared, and again imperceptibly the light waned. He was coming back into the passage.

Bony sat with one hand on the rod and the other about the

194

brake controlling the reel drum . . . one hand holding the camera release shutter and a finger of the other touching the smooth surface of the press button. When fishing, he sat with the base of the rod swivelled to the seat between his knees; now his knees gripped a sizable flashlight.

The murderer must now be outside the bedroom door. Bony could not hear him. Not a sound of him. Why the delay? There was no further precaution he need take. The telephone wires had been cut. The overhead wire to Briggs' alarm bell would have been cut, and the light power had been switched off. The victim was beyond communication with the outside world, as Mrs. Eltham had been and Mrs. Overton.

The door was being opened so silently and so slowly that there was no detectable difference in air pressure. Then as silently and slowly the door was closed.

Mrs. Sayers moved. She sighed. She breathed with soft rhythm.

Bony was wondering what was keeping the shark from taking the bait fish when he saw the brute's head rising above the surface. He was hearing the tapping of teeth, the sound he had heard once before.

The small disc of light appeared. It was directed to the floor. The diffused illuminant revealed the man standing with his back to the closed door. It revealed the footboard of the bed and the small table at the head of the bed whereon stood the useless telephone. The man who appeared to have the body of a giant advanced to the bed. Silence! And then the whispered command:

"Mrs. Sayers, I want you! Mrs. Sayers, I want you!"

Then Bony saw Mrs. Sayers sitting on the edge of the bed, and slowly she stood up.

"Oh, Mr. Rose, this is so sudden," she murmured.

The shark's jaw opened wide. The torch he carried he dropped as his hands darted towards his victim's throat.

Bony pressed his finger on the bell button and kept it there. He pulled on the camera shutter release. There was a flash of white light which lingered behind the eyes. A cry of astonishment. A woman's laughter which Bony remembered for many a year. A shout of fury.

Bony's torch beam revealed Mr. Rose. He was facing toward Bony, his back arched, his knees sagging, his mouth gaping, and his eyes white with agony. Mrs. Sayers was behind him. She was doing something to his left arm and something to his neck, as she shrieked:

"You dirty beast! You scum! I'll snap your neck like a carrot, you dirty, filthy, murderous swine."

A terrific blow was given to the back door. Bony laid his flashlight on the tallboy, directing its beam on the struggling Mr. Rose. He rushed forward, shouting:

"Don't injure him, Mrs. Sayers! Don't injure him!"

He swung a sock nicely filled with sand down hard on the head of Mr. Rose, and the abrupt weight sent Mrs. Sayers to the floor. There was a pounding of feet in the passage. The door was flung inward, and Briggs dived for the unconscious Mr. Rose, whom he thought was lying on Mrs. Sayers and strangling her.

"Let him be!" Bony shouted. "Let him be!"

"Let up, Briggs, you ruddy fool," screamed Mrs. Sayers. "Can't you see the scum's out of it? Pull him off me, d'you hear."

Bony rushed out to the master switch. On re-entering the passage, he collided with Mr. Dickenson, made no apology, and darted into the bedroom where he tugged the light cord.

Mr. Rose was now lying on his back on the floor. Briggs was bending forward, his hands working and extended towards the inert body. Mrs. Sayers was getting to her feet, and in a fit of wild hysteria. Bony dragged Briggs back and ordered him to attend to Mrs. Sayers. Briggs attended to her . . . slapping her face and shouting:

"Cut it out, Mavis. What's biting you?"

There came the roar of the police jeep. Mr. Dickenson, who had switched on the veranda lights, was in time to unlock the front door. And then Mrs. Sayers' bedroom was full of men.

Inspector Walters claimed that he was damned!

196

"What's the matter with him? Someone kill him?"

"I was persuaded to sandbag him," admitted Bony. "I had to be cruel to be kind."

"Why, it's a beaut!" shouted Sawtell. He rocked the developing dish, and Bony wanted to stop him so that he could appraise the value of the negative.

"It's got everything," chortled the sergeant as he transferred the plate from the developer to the fixing bath. "We'll have a proper look in a minute or two. How in hell did you pick on him?"

Bony did not answer the question. He was too absorbed by the promise of the picture he had taken to bother with explanations at this moment, and he waited with a mental breathlessness as he had so often done when the club secretary was weighing his marlin at the end of the jetty. Then Sawtell lifted the plate and held it before a white light.

Mr. Rose was turned three-quarter full to the camera. He had both hands about Mrs. Sayers' throat. The face was like that of a gargoyle but unmistakably his.

"Pretty, isn't he?" said Sawtell. "We could sell this picture to the newspapers for a million."

"I'd like a copy of it," murmured Bony. "It's unique. That woman! She behaved magnificently, although a little too roughly. I feared for Mr. Rose."

"Did you expect him to play up on amnesia?"

"Of course. His kind always do. Probably practised the surprised look before his mirror, just in case he was nabbed. This picture will rule out that defence when the case goes on trial. The politicians, though, will step in if we don't find those four nightgowns."

The police jeep and Inspector Walters' private car were loaded with men when they stopped before the main entrance of Cave Hill College. With them was Mrs. Sayers.

Mr. Percival met the party, astonishment plain on his florid face.

197

"I have here a warrant signed by Mr. Willis, Justice of the Peace, to conduct a search of the apartments occupied by Mr. Rose," Walters said in his official manner. "Mr. Rose was arrested early this morning and charged with wilful murder."

"Was charged . . . Mr. Rose was . . ." stuttered Mr. Percival.

"With murder, Mr. Percival," interrupted Mrs. Sayers. "You must manage the school until the Board meets. Meanwhile, take us to Mr. Rose's rooms."

Bony, Walters, and Sawtell, Mrs. Sayers and Briggs and Mr. Dickenson, the two constables and Mr. Willis passed up the wide stairs to the first floor. They entered the study, a handsome room overlooking the town. Books were ranged on shelves halfway up three of the walls. Behind the door stood two safes.

"Mr. Percival, these are Mr. Rose's keys," Bony said. "Kindly open the safes."

Without comment, Mr. Percival accepted the keys. The larger safe contained account books and chequebooks, an amount of cash, and several unpresented cheques. All were the property of the college. The smaller safe was opened, and Sawtell extracted the contents, comprising documents and bank passbooks. The silence in the headmaster's study was significant. Walters and the sergeant were grim.

"Where is the headmaster's bedroom?" quietly asked Bony.

"Beyond those curtains," replied Percival.

The party entered a room as large as the study and also overlooking the town. It was Sawtell who discovered the small safe in the corner behind the wardrobe. Mr. Percival was asked to open it. He was dazed by this extraordinary intrusion and the implications behind the search warrant. He tried four of the keys on the ring before succeeding in unlocking the safe, everyone present crowding behind him.

It was Sawtell who removed the contents, comprising a pair of binoculars, a pair of old shoes with a drawing pin still attached to the left sole and not used after Abie's attempted blackmail, and four silk nightgowns.

"That's the nightie he stole from my line," stated Mrs. Say-

198

ers a little shrilly. "And that one belonged to Mrs. Overton. I remember the time she bought it."

"Mr. Willis, kindly prepare declarations to be signed by every person in the room, setting out the contents of the safe as produced by Sergeant Sawtell in the presence of us all, and adding what Mrs. Sayers has said concerning two of the nightgowns. She will assist you to describe the nightgowns."

"We may return to the study?" asked the justice of the peace.

"Yes, of course."

Bony turned to the window. Before him was Broome. Aided by the binoculars found in the headmaster's private safe, he could clearly see the empty clotheslines behind the houses of the Widows of Broome.

Bony spent the entire afternoon compiling his report for the Criminal Investigation Branch, for Rose was to be taken to Perth by the two constables on the aircraft scheduled to leave at six that evening.

On returning from the airport, Inspector Walters found Bony already at dinner with his wife and two children. The relief from the strain under which he had been suffering was marked by unwonted joviality.

"It's me for a good long sleep tonight," he declared, and to Bony added: "And you're due for a good sleep too."

"We shall all sleep soundly tonight," Bony agreed. "By the way, I have taken the liberty of asking Mrs. Sayers and Briggs, Mr. Dickenson and Sawtell to be here at seven-thirty. I feel I owe it to them to give a short summary of my investigation. I presume you wish to be present."

"Of course I do."

"And you, Mrs. Walters, will be most welcome to join us. As you have cooked the dinner, your husband and I will do the washing up. It will be quite a little party with us all in the office."

"Blow the washing up!" snorted Walters.

"You will assist me in the washing up," Bony said with mock severity.

"Let the kids do it for once," argued the inspector.

Keith and Nanette looked uncomfortable and wordlessly appealed to Bony. Bony was firm.

"I am treating Keith and Nanette to the pictures to commemorate."

Inspector Walters and Inspector Bonaparte did accomplish the washing up of the dishes, and the children did eventually go off happily to the cinema, and Mrs. Walters did change her frock and join the party which gathered in the station office.

"I would like every one of you to accept my grateful thanks for your co-operation in the difficult investigation just concluded," Bony began. "From each I was given much, and together we have done excellent teamwork with which the great police organisations of the world's capitals would be well pleased.

"On this occasion I've been confronted by an adversary who was exceptionally intelligent, and, moreover, one who committed his crimes under the most favourable circumstances to himself. The murder of Mrs. Cotton provided no leads to her slayer and gave no indication of his motive. The murder of Mrs. Eltham was accompanied by similar negative results until I was informed that on the night after the homicide squad from Perth had left Broome a man was seen to leave her house in the early hours of the morning.

"What I discovered in Mrs. Eltham's wardrobe, and subsequently in Mrs. Cotton's wardrobe, was actually the first lead to the mind of the man who strangled these women. The second lead was the discovery that both the victims had previously lost a nightgown from their clothesline, and this second lead was closely allied with the first. Other than those two leads, I had nothing. I was shown the mentality of the murderer but gained nothing to assist in identifying him, other than the fact that he suffered from a peculiar skin disease named psoriasis.

"Most people, I think, are aware that police investigators very often know who has committed a crime and yet are unable to bring the criminal to trial through lack of sufficient evidence to place before a judge and jury. I had not sufficient evidence to suspect a particular person of these murders and, therefore, to my profound regret, was not in time to safeguard other possible victims.

"The murder of Mrs. Overton revealed that the murderer had adopted a plan of action which was fairly rigid, and this very plan indicated his type of mind and hinted, for that is the word, hinted at his background. His background was made a little more clear through his acts, which revealed several of his habits in normal life, such as his passion for tidiness.

"His knowledge of criminology was less than that of the average boy of sixteen. He wore rubber gloves to prevent leaving his fingerprints about the scene of his murders, and then illogically wiped clean the articles he did touch. It became obvious that the man who did that was, although intelligent, quite ignorant of crime detection, with which the general public is superficially familiar. I began to think the murderer was a man who had never wasted his time at the cinema and never read fiction less than a century old.

"That he stole women's silk nightgowns and destroyed women's silk underwear did not indicate the sex maniac but rather the introvert. His motive was certainly not material gain, and therein lay my greatest obstacle. I found clues which were extremely promising, but they turned out to be of value only as substantiative evidence. They did not lead to the murderer.

"The most promising of these clues was the shoe prints of the murderer in and about the house of Mrs. Overton. I have made a study of footprints, and am sure that the science of footprints could be far greater than the science of fingerprints. The shoe prints of the murderer assisted me further to build a picture of him, the picture of a man without a face. My picture grew to be that of a man weighing at least twelve stone, having a size-eight foot, burdened with an inferiority complex and enjoying good physical health."

Bony paused to light an alleged cigarette, and no one commented. Mrs. Sayers was looking at him as though he were a visitant from another world; Mr. Dickenson was steadily regarding his shabby boots; Inspector Walters was fiddling with a ruler. Briggs, of course, continued his chewing, and Sawtell and Mrs. Walters were tensed.

"Had I come across the man wearing the shoes in which he murdered Mrs. Overton," Bony proceeded, "I should have seen the face of the man of my picture. But before I could do that, poor misguided Abie must needs attempt to blackmail him. What I am going to say regarding Abie is off the record.

"Abie did not die of petrol poisoning but of another poison given him by the murderer he tried to blackmail. The fact that Abie was poisoned and not strangled took me another step toward the murderer. He poisoned Abie because he was a man, and an aborigine at that. He did not strangle Abie, because it would have dulled the memory of the ecstasy he experienced when strangling young and attractive women.

"Who of the men in Broome could this be? He was one having the attributes I have itemised and he suffered from psoriasis. I was left with three probables, and one of them I discarded when Bill Lung, the shell packer, quoted his father as saying: 'The wise man feasts in the morning before the night brings gall to his palate.' The discarded probable had certainly feasted in the morning, whilst the murderer had gall on his palate.

"When for the fourth time he stole a woman's nightgown, thus beginning for the fourth time a cycle of acts which with one exception had not varied, for me the two remaining probables were reduced to one certainty.

"He killed those three women and attempted to kill Mrs. Sayers because he hated them, and he destroyed the silk underwear because he hated something in himself. Psychologically it is too involved to present to a jury, which is why I took a picture of him attempting to strangle Mrs. Sayers, so that material proof against him would be strengthened.

"Hatred is often inspired by fear. This murderer was governed by fear . . . fear that what he had built would be destroyed. He had raised himself to a position of power, power over other minds, power to be increased by and through affec-

202

tion in those minds. He wanted to maintain that affection, because he had left it too late to gain the affection of even one woman. He wanted the affection of the boys whom he controlled, and these four women of Broome, with perhaps others, threatened his power to dominate affection.

"He murdered the attractive Mrs. Cotton because to him she was not fitted to be the mother of one of his boys. She sold liquor over the bar to leering, roystering men. She encouraged men and thus she was a menace to her son, and, through him, to other of his boys.

"He murdered the attractive Mrs. Eltham because of the easy bestowal of her favours. Her reputation was well known in the town and, he was sure, would be known to his older boys. What he had denied in himself was monstrous when he imagined it stirring in those boys.

"Now why should he have murdered the attractive Mrs. Overton? I'll return to Mrs. Overton after I've told you why he attempted to murder Mrs. Sayers. He tried to murder the attractive Mrs. Sayers because she was a dominant influence in the school. She was the most influential member of the Board of Control, and on occasions he had felt himself humiliated by her, and he the headmaster. She was held in great esteem by the boys, for on many occasions she had provided real schoolboy feasts.

"And so when he stole the nightgown belonging to Mrs. Sayers, and thus gave warning that she was to be his next victim, I knew who of the two probables was the murderer, and I knew why Mrs. Overton was murdered. The attractive Mrs. Overton was a great favourite with the college boys, and on the day she was buried at least one of the older boys openly wept. The murderer was he who was frantic for the affection of the boys. My discarded probable, whom we will call Happy, never cared a hoot for their affection. Ah, the car is coming."

Smiling, Bony rose to his feet. Mrs. Sayers crossed to him and took his hands. She wanted to speak, but could only look at him. Mr. Dickenson regarded Sawtell and smiled, and the sergeant nodded agreement with what he saw in the old man's expression.

From without came the noise of skidding tires and then a sudden stoppage of a roaring car engine.

"Mr. Dickenson and I promised ourselves an evening at Dampier's Hotel when the investigation was finished," Bony said. "Therefore, please excuse our hurried departure. Thank you for listening to me, and again for your unswerving co-operation."

"So you're going out to Dampier's Hotel, eh!" Walters said. "Well, I'm going out with you."

"Me too," added Sawtell.

"Hold everything!" cried Mrs. Sayers. "What a nice little party . . . to be left out of. Briggs, we shall also try the gin at Dampier's Hotel. Come on, Esther! Don't you be left out."

"I'm not going to be left out, Mavis," determinedly announced Mrs. Walters.

Johnno came bounding into the office.

"I arrive!" he said gravely, impressed by the gathering.

"Come along!" gurgled Mrs. Sayers. "We'll all pile into Johnno's car."

They trooped outside. The resplendent new edition of an automobile was ignored. Johnno held doors open and bowed them into his taxi. Mrs. Walters was obliged to sit on Sawtell's knees, and Mrs. Sayers giggled as she settled herself on the knees of Inspector Walters. Johnno forced his way in behind the steering wheel, and Mr. Dickenson said:

"Johnno, drive like hell."

The loaded car shot forward and proceeded to gather speed.

"I drive . . . like hell," shouted Johnno. "We arrive. We always arrive."